Advance praise for *Gee, That Was Fun*

"With uncanny wit and a pointillist painter's eye for detail, *Gee That Was Fun* eschews the grand episodes on which historical fiction so often relies, reminding us that the fabric of our lives and the trajectory of our country, for good or ill, are composed of the smaller moments: the daily decisions made and not made, the tiny revelations, the ordinary failures and triumphs. A fascinating and endlessly readable novel in vignettes."

—C. Matthew Smith, author of *Twentymile*

"You'll read Robert Fromberg's *Gee, That Was Fun* with a continuously mounting delight at what he is pulling off. Are these people and events real or fictional? You soon won't care, because you're in Fromberg's world now, a specific week in 1983, where you'll find the profound amid the quotidian, as long as you know exactly where to look. Just don't have the patty melt."

—Justin Bryant, author of *Thunder from a Clear Blue Sky*

"Robert Fromberg's *Gee, That Was Fun* is a series of sly vignettes that nonetheless demonstrate connection between disparate events and ourselves over a series of days. Moments that would otherwise be mundane become significant through the retelling. Fromberg's wit weaves the events with gentle rebuke and quiet dignity, but nevertheless delivers a sharp and incisive look at a time before the world as we know it irrevocably changes. It is a critical read delivered with such crooked charm one cannot help but be seduced."

—Cathleen Allyn Conway, author of *Bloofer* and *Nocturnes*

"This moving experimental novel focuses on events over a week in 1983—a botulism outbreak in Peoria, Illinois; ideological activities of President Ronald Reagan, other elected officials, and right-to-life groups, and machinations by Senator Jesse Helms to stop MLK Day from becoming a public holiday; and New York City, which begins with an air conditioner falling on a woman's head. Together they explore the randomness of events and their impact on our lives, whether wrought through accident, happenstance, or the misguided actions of people we don't even know. As in life, the victims of these events obtain no satisfaction or reparation and leave us shaking our fists at God with one question: Why? Robert Fromberg has written a unique and deeply meaningful work of fiction that scrutinizes the random punishments meted out by the universe."

—Christian Livermore, author of *The Very Special Dead*

Gee, That Was Fun

7 Days of Mayhem, 1983

GEE, THAT WAS FUN

7 DAYS OF MAYHEM, 1983

ROBERT FROMBERG

Trunk of My Car

Gee, That Was Fun: 7 Days of Mayhem, 1983

This work of historical fiction is a dramatization of certain facts and events. Some of the names have been changed and some of the events, characters, and characterizations have been fictionalized, modified, or composited for dramatic purposes. All characters' thoughts depicted in the work are products of the author's imagination.

Cover design and illustration by Claire Stamler-Goody
Interior design and layout by Todd Douglas, Bold Yellow

ISBN: 979-8-89424-000-8

A portion of this book was published in *The Gorko Gazette*

Published by
Trunk of My Car
Kailua, HI
trunkofmycar.org

For David and Deirdre

The gods
devised and measured out this devastation,
to make a song for those in times to come.

—Homer, *The Odyssey,* translated by Emily Wilson

Table of Contents

Friday, October 14, 1983

New York City

1. An air conditioner falls on Elisabeth Beaugrand's head.

At 8:04 a.m. on Friday, October 14, 1983, in the New York City neighborhood called Lenox Hill, Elisabeth Beaugrand stepped off a northbound First Avenue bus on the corner of 61st Street. The day before had been cloudy, but today the sun gave a dramatic look to the otherwise ordinary apartment buildings crammed side-by-side around her, and the temperature was a perfect-for-fall sixty degrees, although Elisabeth had dressed for yesterday's chillier weather and was warm in her cloth coat.

Elisabeth was sorry she would have to spend most of the day indoors at the flower shop, but at least she would be able to witness the outdoors through the shop's large front window. And before that, she would have the short walk between the bus stop and the shop, which was on 62nd Street just west of First Avenue.

From habit more than reason, Elisabeth walked north on the east side of First Avenue rather than crossing and walking on the west side of the street with the intention of crossing at 62nd Street. A dozen steps brought her to the middle of the block, where she approached an undistinguished four-story stucco apartment building at 1118 First Avenue.

The building's ground floor housed a comedy club called Dangerfield's, named after the famous comedian Rodney Dangerfield, whose famous bit involved him getting "no respect."

Elisabeth's path took her beneath the club's canvas canopy. Before she emerged on the other side, an air conditioner fell from a fourth-floor window, tore through the awning, and struck her on the back of the head.

New York Presbyterian Hospital was five blocks from the site of the accident. However, the paramedics chose to take Elisabeth to Bellevue Hospital, perhaps because it was closer to Elisabeth's home a mile and a half south on 330 East 33rd Street. At Bellevue, a spokesperson named Tony Knopp pronounced Elisabeth in stable condition, but cautioned, "It will be at least twenty-four hours to three days before we can determine the extent of spinal cord injuries, if any."

Under the Dangerfield's canopy, on the sidewalk near the fallen window air-conditioning unit, a passerby, Thomas Shaw, once an English major at New York University and now a proofreader for textbooks at McGraw Hill, where he would have been now but for the beautiful day leading him to call in sick, noticed two hardcover books. One was William Blake's *Complete Writings with Variant Readings* published by Oxford University Press and the other was *The Complete Poetical Works of Wordsworth,* a Cambridge Edition published by Houghton Mifflin. Thomas did not, however, notice that the two books were similar in physical depth, that this depth would fill the space from window ledge to the bottom of an air conditioner, and that the covers of the books were a bit soggy, rounded with age and ill use.

2. A co-op tries to evict an AIDS clinic.

At 10:15 a.m. on Friday, October 14, 1983, in Room 242 of the New York State Supreme Court on 60 Centre Street in Lower Manhattan,

Acting Justice Ira Gammerman issued an injunction against the tenant owners of a recently converted co-op building at 49 West 12th Street in the heart of Greenwich Village. One of the owners' first acts was attempting to evict Joseph A. Sonnabend from his office in the building, where he treated patients with AIDS. Sonnabend contended that the eviction was a violation of New York State's human rights laws, and Acting Justice Gammerman agreed that Dr. Sonnabend's evidence was strong enough to warrant the temporary injunction.

When he returned home, Dr. Sonnabend found in his mail a copy of the journal *Clinical Research,* volume 31, number 4, containing his article "Confidentiality, Informed Consent and Untoward Social Consequences in Research on a 'New Killer Disease' (AIDS)," incorporating research that had led Dr. Sonnabend to co-found the AIDS Medical Foundation.

After returning home from the hearing in Room 242, Dr. Sonnabend, called Joe by friends and colleagues, worked on a piano composition that he had tentatively titled "April," an upbeat, atonal piece in 6/8 time.

3. Governor Mario Cuomo cancels a trip but declines to say why. At 11:00 p.m. on Friday, October 14, 1983, speaking from his office on Third Avenue and 38th Street in Manhattan, New York Governor told reporters that he was canceling next week's scheduled two-day trip to Quebec.

Governor Cuomo said, "It is a personal reason. You can ask thirty-seven ways and I won't tell you anything else. It doesn't have anything to do with government. It doesn't have anything to do with the public. It is not embarrassing at all. Everybody has personal reasons."

4. The first inclusive language lectionary is released.

At 12:00 p.m. on Friday, October 14, 1983, the New York City-based National Council of the Churches of Christ in the United States of America released a book titled *An Inclusive Language Lectionary: Readings for Year A, Volume 1,* the result of three years of work by the Council's Inclusive Language Lectionary Committee.

The book's introduction said, "Scripture is written in patriarchal language, but God is not a patriarch. According to scripture, 'There is neither male nor female, for you are all one in Christ Jesus' (Gal. 3:28)."

Burton H. Throckmorton, Jr., a member of the Inclusive Language Lectionary Committee, said, "If the Word of God is not hearable by those who do not understand themselves to be addressed by the biblical language through which that Word is communicated, does it follow that the Word of God cannot any longer be heard by women who feel excluded by patriarchal language, or by men who feel themselves excluded by language that does not include women on an equal basis with them? Is the patriarchalism of the biblical languages, and of biblical faith as originally formulated, inherent in that faith? That is the fundamental question with which the church must wrestle in our day."

Later that day, Bruce M. Metzger, a biblical scholar, said in an address delivered at Princeton Theological Seminary in New Jersey, "It is not too much to say that some of the changes introduced in this lectionary are downright silly."

5. Mayor Ed Koch eats buttered crackers.

At 1:15 p.m. on Friday, October 14, 1983, at a press conference held in New York City Hall in Lower Manhattan, Mayor Ed Koch announced the launch of a federal surplus food distribution program to help combat hunger among city residents. At that time, the city commenced to distribute three hundred forty-five thousand pounds of surplus butter to the city's hungry.

At the press conference, Mayor Koch posed for photographs while eating buttered crackers, his eyes directed toward the right and above the heads of the crowd, as though toward a spot in another borough, perhaps another city, and another time.

6. George Ortiz asks Gloria Roman on a date.

At 6:40 p.m. on Friday, October 14, 1983, at a delicatessen on the corner of Wyckoff Street and Atlantic Avenue in the Prospect Heights neighborhood of Brooklyn, New York, George Ortiz, a 50-year-old auto mechanic stopping for a quart of milk on his way home from work, ran into his neighbor Gloria Roman, a 47-year-old cashier, who was also on her way home from work, stopping for chips that she intended to eat in front of the television that night watching the show *Dallas.* George and Gloria, both divorced, had known each other for years and occasionally had dinner or a drink together. Greeting Gloria at the cash register, George asked whether she would like to go out dancing that night.

"Friday night," he said, in a tone of slight sarcasm that acknowledged Friday night was something two people their age perhaps shouldn't find so special anymore.

"No thanks," said Gloria. "I'd rather just stay home tonight." She was glad that she could say that to George, knowing that he knew that there was no ill intent and that on another night, she would be happy to say yes.

Washington, DC

1. The loud ring of cordless phones causes more than 20 complaints.

At 9:00 a.m. on Friday, October 14, 1983, in Washington, DC, the Consumer Product Safety Commission and the Electronic Industries Association issued a joint consumer alert urging owners of so-called cordless or portable telephones to exercise caution when using the product. The CPSC and EIA acknowledged the convenience of people placing or receiving calls in their home or in the immediate vicinity outside their home using a cordless telephone. However, the organizations cautioned users "always to place the phone in the talk position before moving the telephone to their ear. Otherwise, they may be exposed to a loud and possibly painful ring."

The organizations issued this alert based on more than twenty consumer complaints about the loud sound made when the telephone rings or when someone near the base station of these telephones presses the intercom or page button while the handset was close to the user's ear.

The problem, according to the alert, was a misunderstanding about which part of a cordless telephone produced the ringing sound.

"Currently most cordless telephones are designed so that the ring or page signal comes through the earphone of the unit. From the information provided in the complaints it is clear that the users were not expecting their telephone to ring and had placed it against or near their ear without placing the phone in the talk position." In one case, a phone rang unexpectedly when a user was preparing to place a call. A physician reported that a patient experienced hearing loss because of the loud ring.

Each organization announced that it was tackling this problem in its own way. The CPSC advised consumers who had one of these telephones in their home or office to be sure that everyone using the product was thoroughly familiar with its proper operation. A number of EIA-member manufacturers and distributors of cordless telephones began attaching labels to their products alerting the user about the loud ring.

2. Ronald Reagan hurts the feelings of his top aides and watches a poorly reviewed movie.

At 9:05 p.m. on Friday, October 14, 1983, in the Oval Office of the White House in Washington, DC, President Ronald Reagan began a twenty-four-minute meeting in which he hurt the feelings of his Chief of Staff, James A. Baker III, and his Deputy Chief of Staff, Michael K. Deaver.

Baker wanted the position of head of the National Security Council, which would soon be vacated when its current occupant, William Casey, assumed a new role as Secretary of the Interior. Reagan had been willing to accede to Baker's desire and planned to promote Deavers to Chief of Staff. However, in discussing the possibility of putting Baker in the NSC position, Reagan "found great division and resistance in certain quarters." Thus, this morning, Reagan told Baker and Deavers that the change would not take place.

Although Baker was exhausted and dispirited in his current role, he tried to hide his disappointment behind blandness, although the ever-ambitious Deaver didn't bother.

"Jim took it well. but Mike was pretty upset," Reagan reflected in his diary that night. "It was an unhappy day all around."

3. A White House staff member writes a somewhat snippy memo to his boss.

At 9:20 a.m. on Friday, October 14, 1983, in the flamboyant French Second Empire-style Old Executive Office Building across the street from the White House, in an office down the hall from the southernmost of eight curving granite staircases, Faith Whittlesey, Assistant to the President for Public Liaison, was reading the *Washington Post.* Whittlesey, whose brief was to more fully engage support for the Reagan administration from religious conservatives, found her face feeling warm when she saw the headline "Poll of Evangelicals Finds Glenn Matching Reagan."

According to the article, "the survey of voter preference for president, conducted by Republican pollster Lance Tarrance, found that Reagan led Glenn by a slim 41 to 37 percent among all evangelicals, and actually trailed Glenn among 'biblical literalists,' those who believe the Bible is literally true." Apparently, at the press conference, the Free Congress Foundation's founder and president, Paul Weyrich, usually a friend of the Reagan Administration, said that the administration should not count on the support of evangelicals.

"Religious conservatives not only have somewhere to go but are strongly considering going.... This should be a warning bell that evangelicals are not in Reagan's hip pocket."

As irksome as she found these remarks, they supported her own sense that evangelical groups had done little to get ready for the 1984 presidential campaign and that the Reagan administration had done little to spur on that support.

She fired off a memo to her assistant, Jack Courtemanche, asking for details of the survey and information on why the staff's efforts, if indeed such efforts were underway, were not more successful in energizing evangelicals to support the president.

Courtemanche forwarded the memo to staff member Morton Blackwell, Special Assistant to the president, a veteran of political culture who understood that his role generally was to respond to questions from superiors about why he hadn't done things he had no power to do, and that they had no power to do either. He made only a minimal—and, he knew, unsuccessful—effort to keep the eye rolling he did while composing his reply, which echoed what he knew to be Whittlesey's existing beliefs, from coming through in the memo that he sent to Courtemanche to forward to Whittlesey (surely, he thought, this roundabout way of communication suggests why we don't see more results):

> Attached per your request is the Lance Tarrance poll of evangelicals discussed in this morning's newspapers.
>
> We have a very good personal relationship with the leaders of most of the fundamentalist and evangelical organizations.
>
> We give them good access and cordial Presidential comments.
>
> In my view, the reason why the good personal relationships do not translate into grassroots enthusiasm from their followers is that there are no ongoing legislative battles and record votes on many of the issues which relate to their concerns as committed Christians.
>
> Without such battles and votes, even the most supportive religious leaders can do little more than occasionally say nice things about the President. The Bible, after all, calls for prayers for those in civil authority.
>
> Without those battles and votes, we just will not have working for us next year most of the "Onward Christian Soldiers" support otherwise available.

4. Lobbyists hunt through FBI files on Martin Luther King, Jr. At 10:20 a.m. on Friday, October 14, 1983, in a nondescript—except for its large ground-floor windows—two-story suburban office building on 450 Maple Avenue East in Vienna, Virginia, sixteen miles west of the U.S. Capitol Building, Howard Philips, founder and president of The Conservative Caucus, and other members of the lobbying firm studied a file titled "Security Matter—Communist" containing declassified information compiled by the Federal Bureau of Investigation in the 1960s pertaining to Martin Luther King, Jr. The files contained many redactions, making their task at times seem like putting together a puzzle more than reading documents, but they kept to their task because time was pressing.

At the same time, in the Federal Bar Building at 1815 H Street NW in Washington, DC, a ten-minute stroll from the White House, home of the Federal Bar Association, the luxurious National Lawyers Club, and offices of many law firms doing business with the federal government, in the conference room of the law offices of Smiley, Olson, Gilman, and Pangia, William J. Olson and Lawrence J. Straw Jr., attorneys for The Conservative Coalition, prepared for Monday's emergency hearing requested by Senator Helms in order to secure access to still-sealed tapes and transcripts of FBI wiretapping of Dr. King prior to a vote on Wednesday, October 19, on establishing a national holiday to honor Dr. King. Bent over a conference table. Straw and Olson polished the following sentences:

> Now, legislation is pending which seeks to elevate Dr. King to the status of a national hero, on a level above our founding fathers. Dr. King would thereby become a role model for future generations. In extraordinary circumstances such as these, a senator must have access to all records which would relate to the character of the proposed hero. The constitutional duty of a member of the United States Senate is to thoroughly and dispassionately review all information which could influence his vote.

At the same time, in his office in the West Wing of the White House, Vice President George H.W. Bush reviewed remarks that he planned to deliver on Saturday in Charleston, South Carolina, where he would participate in the installation of former Energy Secretary James Edwards as president of the Medical University of South Carolina. Knowing that he would likely be asked about Senator Helms' pursuit of legal action to undermine establishing a national holiday for Dr. King, Vice President Bush sought to draft an appropriate response. He came up with the following:

> I wouldn't do it myself, what Senator Helms is doing, but I believe Dr. King would understand that this is a free country. His whole thing was peaceful change and standing up for what he believed and taking risks in the process. People are entitled to court remedies or to do anything they want in our country, whether we agree or not. That's one of the prices, or one of the assets, of freedom. Far be it for me to stand here and tell a United States senator or any other citizen what rights he has or how he can exercise it. Our concept of freedom is too broad.

5. Georgetown University refuses to recognize a gay student group

At 1:35 p.m. on Friday, October 14, 1983, in a small courtroom on the second floor of the H. Carl Moultrie Courthouse, a seven-year-old, seven-story building that was the largest courthouse in Washington, DC's Judiciary Square neighborhood, Superior Court Judge Sylvia Bacon dismissed a lawsuit brought by an organization of gay students at Georgetown University after the Catholic university denied the group recognition.

In announcing her decision, Judge Bacon said, "There was no evidence that the beliefs on which the University acted were bizarre, without foundation, or otherwise not entitled to recognition as sincerely-held religious beliefs...."

6. President Reagan calls an old acting friend and watches a poorly reviewed movie.

At 6:06 p.m. on Friday, October 14, 1983, from the presidential retreat in Camp David, Maryland, President Reagan's secretary placed a call to Pat O'Brien, the actor who played the title role in the film *Knute Rockne, All American,* alongside Reagan, who portrayed George Gipp.

Earlier that day, O'Brien, who in recent years had performed a one-man show in small theaters and nightclubs, leaning heavily on Irish-related anecdotes, had a cancerous prostate removed. During the six-minute call, O'Brien told Reagan a joke. "Irish, of course," recalled Reagan.

That evening, Ronald and Nancy Reagan watched the movie *Romantic Comedy,* an adaptation of the recent hit Broadway play written by Bernard Slade. The movie starred Dudley Moore and Mary Steenburgen. Gene Shalit, film critic of *The Today Show,* always dependable for a positive review, called the movie "very funny stuff." However, the *Washington Post* called it "dismal" and focused on the relative height of the two leads: "Steenburgen continues her statuesque staring exercises while Moore bickers at her from an absurdly lower elevation." Mary Steenburgen is five feet, eight inches tall; Dudley Moore was five feet, two inches tall.

Peoria, Illinois

1. A cook sautés onions contaminated with botulism.

At 8:45 a.m. on Friday, October 14, 1983, a man named Jason Cook, who also happened to be a cook, although he thought of himself primarily as an electric bass player, walked through a narrow, employees-only hallway on the lower level of the Northwoods Mall in Peoria, Illinois, past a metal door labeled Kinney Shoes and opened a nearly identical door labeled Skewer Inn.

Fourteen minutes later, wearing his cook's uniform and apron, he clocked in and elbowed his way around a cluster of employees toward the stove. Crowding was a perpetual problem at the Skewer Inn, with between ten and fifteen staff continually striding or reaching or gesturing in a back-of-house space as small as the backroom of Kinney Shoes next door, a fact that Jason had long suspected and finally confirmed one evening when after closing, he was invited to drink a paper cup of whiskey with the assistant manager and high school sales boy who were taking inventory next door.

Jason removed a large pan hanging from a pegboard, placed it on the stove, and turned the burner to medium. While the pan preheated, he removed from the refrigerator a plastic tub heavy with whole onions and placed it at the prep station. He then brought a tub of margarine to the stove and scooped three spoonfuls into the pan. While the margarine melted, Jason returned to the prep station and began chopping onions. The station was designed for someone much shorter than Jason, who was six feet tall, and while his eyes threatened to tear from the onion fumes, he could feel his back muscles beginning to clench, which he knew would get worse as the day continued.

From an open shelf over the stove, he retrieved containers of paprika, garlic salt, and a chicken-base powder, portions of which he added to the now-melting butter. Into this mixture, he stirred the results of this first round of onion chopping. He chopped a few more onions while the mixture heated. He then turned the temperature to the lowest possible setting, which was below 60 C, or 140 F.

From that uncovered pan, Jason and other cooks used tongs to withdraw sauteed onions contaminated with botulism because of their cooking process for the fifteen patty melt sandwiches the Skewer Inn served that day and for no other dishes.

2. A woman buys a celebratory skirt, visits her husband, and eats a patty melt sandwich contaminated with botulism.

At 11:05 a.m. on Friday, October 14, 1983, in Peoria, Illinois, Linda Peavler was enjoying her first outing without her children since giving birth to her third, Tiffany, in August. From her home in Dunlap, Illinois, Linda drove nine miles south to the Peoria home of her mother, Sandra Spore, whom her friends called Sande, and the two proceeded another two miles south to the Northwoods Mall.

At Casual Corner, on the Montgomery Ward side of the upper level, as a small gesture toward feeling like an individual human rather than solely a mother, Linda bought a turquoise stretch miniskirt, which she could tell her mother didn't approve of by the set of her lips. They window-shopped across the mall to the JC Penney side, stopping at Richman Brothers, where Linda's husband, Jan-Paul, was assistant manager.

At Richman Brothers, a pull-up sign near the cash register featured the store's slogan, "700 Fussy Tailors," and a photograph of grim-looking men in suits with their arms crossed, staring at the camera. While Linda waited for Jan-Paul to be finished with a customer, she counted the men in the photograph, and there were only twelve; she imagined the other 688 standing nearby but off camera. In the corner of the sign was the more traditional logo that was on the tags of many of the Richman Brothers garments: the slogan plus two tailors, one older and one younger, studying a man's suit jacket. A very crowded logo, Linda thought, for a clothing tag. She had occasionally wondered if the older tailor was evaluating the work of the younger tailor, or if the two tailors were evaluating the work of another tailor. In any case, she felt bad for Jan-Paul working in this world of scrutiny.

Jan-Paul gave Sande a brief hug and Linda a cheek kiss. Linda told him "Grandpa," Janet's father, was watching the kids and that she and her mother were headed for quick lunch at the Skewer Inn. Janet pulled the miniskirt partially from the bag to show Jan-Paul and he winked inexpertly. One of the things about Jan-Paul that Linda liked the most was his wink, which he knew he did badly but did anyway as a kind of in-joke with Linda.

As Linda and Sande waited in line at the entrance to the Skewer Inn, Linda watched a parakeet fly out of Noah's Ark pet store two stores down, a glistening blue and yellow blur especially vibrant in contrast to the whiteness of the mall, describing an arc that rose to half the height of the nearby escalator and ended inside Brown's Sporting Goods across the way from the Skewer Inn, followed by a Noah's Ark employee running, carrying a long-handled net. Linda turned to see if her mother had witnessed the event, but she was facing the entrance to the restaurant.

Once seated, both Linda and Sande ordered patty melt sandwiches. Neither Linda nor Sande had ever eaten a patty melt sandwich, but the menu's description, one-third pound of hamburger topped with a slice of American cheese and sauteed onions served on toasted rye bread with pickles on the side, sounded appetizing, and everything they had ever ordered at the Skewer Inn had been tasty.

Linda finished her sandwich at the table. Sande took half of her sandwich home in a foil wrapping. She ate the leftover sandwich for dinner and tossed the wrapping in the kitchen garbage, which her husband later took to the can beside their house, which he would take to the curb for pickup on Wednesday.

3. Two students enjoy a break from dorm food.

At 12:15 p.m. on Friday, October 14, 1983, inside the Skewer Inn but out of the line of sight of both Linda Peavler and Sande Spore, Shiela Whitfield and Marsha Hampshire, two 20-year-old Bradley University freshmen, placed their orders, thrilled to be anywhere other than a campus building and especially to be anywhere other than their dormitory and even more especially to be on the cusp of eating something other than dormitory food.

Shiela ordered a burger platter. Marsha ordered the patty melt. When the dishes arrived, Sheila pointed to Marsha's patty melt and said, "That looks good."

"Here," Marsha said, lifting the plate, "let's switch."

4. A copyeditor reviews an editorial.

At 2:10 p.m. on Friday, October 14, 1983, in the combined office and printing plant of the Peoria *Journal Star* almost overlooking Peoria Lake, five miles east of Northwoods Mall, Mike Major sat at the newspaper's copy desk. He had completed proofing the first part of the next day's editorial—that's all he was really allowed to do to with pieces from the editorial board, proof, not change anything that wasn't a flat-out spelling or grammatical mistake—which praised Ronald Reagan's choice of William Clark as the next Secretary of the

Interior. Pen raised and ready, Mike continued past the subheading "Casual Comment" and read the following:

> The federal government says that all cars made after Sept. 1, 1985, must have a third red brake light atop the trunk lid or thereabouts. It decided that this will prevent 900,000 rear-end collisions and 40,000 injuries a year. That represents a lot of people who can't see two lights but could see three. Why not make the whole rear end one big light and save everybody?

Mike considered himself a realist, not an idealist. He had to make a living, he was a skilled copyeditor, he lived in a city with minimal publishing opportunities, and working for the city newspaper had a measure of dignity, even value. If from time to time he had to lend his skills to ensure that an opinion piece from the editorial board disavowing the importance of preventing forty thousand injuries was grammatically correct, well, then that's what he had to do.

5. A high school gym teacher contemplates a Greek restaurant and bank tellers real and automated.

At 5:55 p.m. on Friday, October 14, 1983, Mary Lou Dobrydnia, who went by Lou rather than Mary, rode the down escalator at the Northwoods Mall in Peoria, Illinois.

Lou had parked on the upper-level parking lot, a habit she couldn't shake, even when her business in the mall was on the lower level, as it was this evening. As a high school gym teacher, Lou recognized the fitness benefit of not being stingy with her steps. At the mall, however, her motivation in choosing inconvenience in her route was less pragmatic.

She loved the Northwoods Mall. It had opened ten years ago this past August, Lou's last summer before college. It was the first indoor shopping center in Peoria, Illinois—bright, clean, huge, and dazzling, crammed with so many signs and displays and chrome and tile that these inanimate objects seemed more kinetic than the moving steps of the escalators and the shoppers. The mall felt to Lou, just two weeks away from her first day in college on the day of its opening, like a sign of all the excitement to come for her on campus and in life beyond.

Now, at age 28, as she entered the mall on the side anchored by department store JC Penney, she felt the same excitement and brightness, and would feel nostalgic even if a standing sign in the corridor hadn't reminded shoppers that Northwoods Mall was celebrating its tenth anniversary.

It being Friday, Lou had a paycheck in hand, and although she would normally stand in line to deposit it at Home Savings and Loan—which closed at 6:00 p.m. on Fridays—just to the right of the entrance, and, if she was lucky, be served by the short teller with the thick brown bob and proceed to flirt with her in a barely perceptible way, today she was running a little late, so Lou thought she would try, for the first time, on her way back to her car after dinner, the automatic teller machine that had been installed just outside the bank's sliding glass door.

Anyway, Lou suspected that she was more interested in the teller's bob than the teller was in Lou's hi-low.

Six years ago, when she was 12 years old, Lou had announced that henceforth, she was to be called Lou rather than Mary. Announced to her parents, that is, because her two closest school friends had known for a year, and Lou herself had known for many years before that. Mary made her feel queasy, and Lou made her feel healthy. Settling on a name to be called wasn't a decision or a choice, but a natural occurrence, such as that tonight, Friday, October 14, 1983, the sun would set at 6:20 p.m. in Peoria, Illinois, twenty minutes after she met her friends at the Skewer Inn on the lower level of Northwoods Mall. The decision was to simultaneously expose to her parents something private about herself and to lay down the law, knowing that she would receive from her mother a tight-lipped nod and military-style obedience and from her father a self-consciously goofy smile, no eye contact, and inconsistent obedience, although he would always say "Mary" with such affection that Lou found it hard to fault him.

Which is exactly what happened. Funny how easy it can be to know what people are thinking and how people will react to things. Not being surprised by people and their reactions was a great comfort for Lou as she had gone through life these twenty-eight years. It was the comfort that made getting her job at Limestone Community High School in nearby Bartonville, Illinois, not a surprise but an inevitability, and that made her an unflappable gym and driver's ed teacher and softball coach to restless teenagers, not to mention a captain of an amateur field hockey team.

As Lou stepped off the escalator onto the lower level, facing Montgomery Wards, and turned to face the mall's other side, anchored by JC Penny, she thought she could already smell the Skewer Inn, although that may have been a manifestation of her eagerness. It was hard to overstate the importance of the Skewer Inn to the Northwoods Mall and consequently to the city of Peoria, at least from Lou's perspective. The Skewer Inn introduced Lou to contrasting flavors and textures she had never experienced or imagined. The rich puffiness of pita bread. The slippery firmness of chickpeas. And especially the tangy spiciness of the thin slices of beef in the gyros—a new word for her, one that some people pronounced "gee-roes" and other pronounced "gy-roes," an ambiguity that Lou planned someday to clear up with the owner behind the cash register—a flavor that crawled all around her mouth and the inside of her head and was coupled with cold, plain yogurt—who would ever think to do something like that! Along with the French cigarettes in the window of The Tinder Box, the Skewer Inn was the most exotic thing in the mall, and perhaps in the entire city.

Lou's roommate and two other friends were already seated in a booth, and Lou slid in beside her roommate. She thought about apologizing for being late, but she was, if anything, only two or three minutes late, and one of the rules she lived by was not to apologize when she had nothing significant to apologize for. Her roommate handed Lou a menu, and Lou's eyes fell to the patty melt sandwich. She had heard of patty melts but had never eaten one. She vaguely understood that a patty melt was not Greek, and not exotic, and she felt sad that the Skewer Inn would feel the need to add something so pedestrian to its menu, presumably in an attempt to widen its appeal to the Peoria-area citizens.

However, Lou knew she was forming conclusions based on not much evidence, and perhaps the Skewer Inn could turn out a very tasty patty melt indeed. More interested in having evidence for her thoughts than anything else, Lou ordered her first patty melt sandwich, along with a sangria, which was a specialty of the house. When the sandwich arrived, she tried it, and it tasted okay, like a highly seasoned cheeseburger. Her companions said none of them had ever tried a patty melt. Lou offered them a taste, but all declined.

On the way to her car, Lou stopped outside the bank and for the first time worked through the procedure of depositing her check into the automatic teller. Aside from the concern that her week's wages would be eaten by this machine leaving no record, she found that the process required at least twice as much time and concentration as depositing the check in person. But Lou persevered, as she always did.

6. A pressman's wife decides to forego her husband's pickles.

At 6:10 p.m. on Friday, October 14, 1983, in the Skewer Inn at Peoria's Northwoods Mall, John Mason, a press operator at the Peoria *Journal Star,* having eaten with his wife Leslie dozens of meals at the restaurant, ordered a roast beef sandwich.

"I have to tell you," the waitress replied, "the roast beef isn't very good tonight."

John scanned the menu. Well, he thought, you can't go wrong with a hamburger, and he ordered a patty melt.

John did not like pickles and so was not disappointed when his plate arrived lacking the pickles promised in the menu description. Leslie loved pickles, and she loved eating pickles served with John's meals. She thought of this as a simple and lovely way in which she and John complemented one another. Sad about the lack of pickles on John's plate, Leslie considered alerting a waitress and asking her to bring some, but as she raised a hand to begin the flagging-down process, she saw that the waitresses all seemed unusually busy and decided not to bother them with what was, after all, she told herself, a trivial desire, all things considered.

Having finished their meal, John left a larger-than-usual tip to thank the waitress for warning him about that night's roast beef.

7. An electronics engineer, in a room next to a stuffed, dyed bear, shows 48 people a movie about a spaceborne missile defense system.

At 6:45 p.m. on Friday, October 14, 1983, Ralph Westberg, executive vice president of AutoMeter Products Inc. of Sycamore, Illinois, previously an electronic engineer in the guided missile industry and currently president of Citizens Against Nuclear War, walked past a nine-foot-tall, stuffed, dyed-black grizzly bear in the lobby of Jumer's Castle Lodge in Peoria, Illinois, on his way to the Alps Ballroom to deliver the opening keynote presentation, titled "High Frontier," of the Conservative Seminar, sponsored by the Central Illinois Constitutional Caucus.

Having been to Jumer's Castle Lodge several times before, Ralph did not pay attention to the bear, the wall-mounted replicas of Leviathan Viking axes, or the wine-red velour chaise longue, instead thinking about the size of the audience and whether the audio-visual equipment would work.

At 7:02 p.m., lapel mic clipped on and introduction by the host completed, Ralph stepped to the lectern and explained to the audience of forty-eight that "High Frontier" was a "non-nuclear answer to the nuclear threat that involved spaceborne ballistic missile defense systems that would intercept Soviet warheads." High Frontier, Westberg said, "is a positive alternative to either a buildup or a freeze of nuclear weapons, one that offers America its best assurance for survival and improved living for this and future generations."

At that point, Westerberg gestured to the audio-visual professional, a young man named Darryl Windrift, a radio and television communications major at Bradley University with a wispy mustache, dressed in black, who leaned back and flipped a switch that turned off about two-thirds of the overhead lights in the room, then leaned forward and pushed a button to launch the film that showed from a projector on a card table pointed at a screen.

The film was twenty-five minutes in duration and described the three phases of High Frontier.

In Phase I, America develops "a non-nuclear point defense system" for the nation's intercontinental ballistic missile silos. In Phase II, America develops 432 satellites, each with forty to fifty non-nuclear infrared homing "kill" vehicles, "which would destroy at least eighty percent of any ballistic attack launched, including an all-out attack on the United States or a Soviet missile attack on Europe." In Phase III, the system's capabilities expand to include "mid-course intercepts of hostile warheads" along with "peacetime objectives" such as "improved space transportation, solar power systems in space, industrial applications, and research and development."

Ralph was rather pleased that he had developed an approach to this presentation that was so informative and dynamic and that required him only to speak for fifteen minutes.

Jumer's Castle Lodge, both its exterior and interior fashioned to resemble a German castle, sat atop Peoria's west bluff, alongside the city's oldest and largest homes on Moss Avenue and High Street. The ballroom offered a view from the bluff to the city's valley, adjacent to downtown, which earlier that afternoon Darryl had heard the Jumer's Castle Lodge concierge call "the rougher part of town."

Once Darryl was confident that the film was playing correctly and that the speaker was watching the film and not looking back toward the AV table, Darryl stood and turned toward the window in the back of the ballroom. The lowered lights minimized the reflection of the room in the window that would normally preclude a clear view outside. Not that even a clear view yielded much. Still, Darryl enjoyed looking at the wash of blackness dotted by occasional and unsystematically placed dots of dim lights too far away to determine whether street lights, store lights, or house lights.

8. Lou and Linda watch late-night TV.

At 9:05 p.m. on Friday, October 14, 1983, in their apartment a block and a half north of Bradley University, Lou Dobrydnia's roommate, Gwen Thomas, watched the TV show *Dallas*, which Lou couldn't stand, but then Lou joined Gwen to watch Maureen McGovern perform George Gershwin's "Strike Up the Band" on *The Tonight Show.* Lou had been a senior in high school when she heard McGovern sing "The Morning After" in the disaster movie *The Poseidon Adventure,* and the song and performance tugged deliciously at her heart, but she hadn't heard anything about McGovern since. Lou was glad to see McGovern redirecting herself away from an inevitably short-term career as a singer of pop hits and toward what promised to be a steadier, if less gravity-defying, career as a singer of old standards.

Linda and Jan-Paul Peavler had recently moved into a newly constructed home in the village of Dunlap, and although money was tight, they treated themselves to a cable TV subscription, including what the company called a "premium" channel, HBO, which showed movies that were relatively new, that were not edited to eliminate racy content, and that were free of commercials. Those characteristics were particularly important to Linda, but nonetheless, the novelty was appealing. After watching the drama *Dallas* with one eye while getting the kids to sleep, and after the 10 o'clock news, and after the first half of Johnny Carson's *The Tonight Show* at 11:10, an odd time for a television program to begin, Linda turned to HBO to watch a movie titled *The Exorcist*. This was not exactly a recent film—in fact, it was ten years old—but Linda and her high school friends had loved it for its sheer gross glory, particularly the scene in which the possessed girl threw up what everyone soon discovered was pea soup. Linda, whose first name was the same as the child star of the movie, the girl possessed by the devil, found that, ten years later, the scene made her feel not giddy but queasy.

Saturday, October 15, 1983

New York City

1. Two men pretend to rescue two victims of a fire.

At 3:45 a.m. on Saturday, October 15, 1983, in an apartment at 157 Smith Street, just two doors from Wyckoff Street, in the Prospect Heights neighborhood of Brooklyn, William Trenton was sitting up in bed reading a Bible by candlelight when he felt a cramp in the big toe of his left foot. Shifting the Bible from his left to right hand, keeping his eyes on the text, William reached down to rub his toe. In the process, he bumped the candle, which fell into a small and rather full garbage basket on the floor next to his nightstand.

At 4:15 a.m., one and a half miles away at the corner of Carlton Avenue and Pacific Street in an industrial section of Prospect Heights, on the street outside the New York *Daily News* printing plant, Mervin Bernstein and Prescott Davis stole a newspaper delivery van. Having no purpose or destination in mind, but confident that the illicit possession of a newspaper delivery truck would bring productive possibilities to creative minds, they began to drive.

Six blocks west and slightly north on Atlantic Avenue (in this part of Brooklyn, it was impossible to go straight west or straight north), Mervin and Tim saw, illuminated by streetlights on the still-dark morning, smoke, not a lot of smoke, but enough to be worth a look. Mervin, driving, glanced at Tim, who nodded, and the two navigated one-way streets past and then around the source of the smoke until they were parked directly behind the firetruck beside the three-story building at 157 Smith Street, the top floor of which was the source of the smoke.

Both exited the van. Tim, a bit of an introvert, stayed near the van's back door, while Mervin, a people person, approached police officers and firefighters, in uniform, and the building's residents, in dishabille—some bent over and coughing, some looking around for a way to be helpful. From his wallet, Mervin withdrew the first card that his fingers touched, which happened to be a Suffolk County fishing license from a wallet he had stolen, and flashed it at the group, briskly announcing himself to one and all as Red Cross rescue specialist Porfirio Ramirez, hoping that none of the group would wonder why a Red Cross worker would be wearing jeans and sneakers and a varsity jacket, but also not particularly caring if they did.

He approached two of the stunned-looking residents, Gloria Roman and Cristobal Marques, saying, "You sure as heck won't be going back in there for a while," and telling more than asking them to accompany him to a Red Cross shelter. Overhearing the exchange, the building's landlord, Emanuel Lorenzo, who lived around the corner on Wyckoff Street, eager to do something that comported with his sense of the landlord's paternal role, offered to accompany his tenants. Mervin took Gloria and Cristobal each by one elbow and, with Emanuel trailing, led the group to the van, noting that none of the group seemed to notice the replica of a New York *Daily News* front page with the screaming headline "World's Largest Newspaper" on the van's side.

"Hold on," Emanuel said, "can you wait for me to get a pack of cigarettes?" He pointed toward another apartment building, a dozen yards away on Wyckoff Street.

"But of course," Mervin said. "Your physical comfort is the top priority of the Red Cross." He patted Emanuel's shoulder and left his hand there. "I'm sure our refugees won't mind waiting. In fact"—Mervin slid his palm from Emanuel's shoulder to his elbow—"we'll go with you." Mervin, shifting his gaze to Prescott, dipped his head and raised his eyebrows.

"Oh, not necessary," Emanuel said.

"My dear man, the Red Cross is here to help all those in need," Mervin replied, as Prescott appeared at Emanuel's other side.

Inside the first-floor apartment, Emanuel reached up to a high shelf of his kitchen pantry for a carton of cigarette packs, while Mervin made a circular gesture with his head to Prescott, meaning he should look around. After Prescott left the room, Mervin withdrew a paring knife from the silverware drawer. When Emanuel turned around, a pack of cigarettes in his hand, Mervin stabbed him first in one eye and then, after Emanuel fell onto the peel-and-stick tile floor, in the other eye. Prescott appeared in the kitchen, flashing a small roll of bills. When he saw Emanuel on the floor, he winced, and Mervin and Prescott returned to the van.

Back outside, assuming that the bloodstains on his jacket would not be visible in the dark, Mervin waved placatingly at the two women in the van and called, "Sorry for the delay, ladies." As Gloria was asking, "Where is Mr. Lorenzo?" Mervin shut the back door and got into the driver's seat. Next to Mervin in the passenger seat, Prescott leaned his head back against the headrest, which was adjusted a little too high for Prescott, but Prescott didn't bother to move it. As they drove, Mervin sang, loud enough for the women in back to hear, "We're gonna rock down to Electric Avenue."

They headed south, and were a few blocks from the Red Hook ferry pier when Prescott mumbled that he was going to throw up.

"Well I don't want to smell it, and neither do the ladies," Mervin said, pulling to the curb. When Prescott got out, Mervin leaned across the passenger seat, pulled the door shut, and continued driving.

When he finished vomiting, Prescott looked up, saw the van pulled over a few blocks ahead, turned in the opposite direction, and started the twenty-five-minute walk to the Smith and 9th Street subway station.

Mervin had pulled to the curb where Conover Avenue ended at a forced left turn and became Pioneer Street. He stepped out of the van, withdrew the paring knife from his jacket pocket, and opened the back door, declaring, "Electric Avenue, our last stop." He jumped into the back and, it being dark inside, he stabbed Gloria and Cristobal more or less randomly in the chest and abdomen until they stopped moving. He grabbed Gloria's purse, which miraculously she had retained hold of. Next he felt around for a purse belonging to Cristobal but found nothing. He hopped out of the van, took off his jacket, and turned it inside out to hide the now-considerable bloodstains. The sun had not yet risen, nor was there any sign of its impending appearance.

When, later that morning, George Ortiz heard the story of Gloria being killed by the fake Red Cross rescue workers, he thought to himself that if they had gone out dancing, she might be alive now, not stopping to consider that he was wrong, that she would have been back from the club before the fire started, and that everything that happened to her would have happened just the way it did.

2. Philippe Petit draws a circle.

At 7:00 a.m. on Saturday, October 15, 1983, across the upper bay from Red Hook, the sun strengthening as it began to rise over FDR Drive, the East River beyond, and, across the river, Brooklyn Heights, on the plaza of the South Street Seaport in lower Manhattan, Philippe Petit drew a large chalk circle on the pavement. From a canvas bag, surprisingly small considering all it contained, he withdrew a twenty-inch unicycle, which he placed on its side, and a small and very worn-looking suitcase, which he opened and from which he withdrew three white balls. He left the suitcase open next to the unicycle and the canvas bag, which, based on its lumpiness, seemed still to contain more items, in the center of the circle.

As he walked slowly around the perimeter of the circle, always staying within the chalk line, he held two of the balls in his left hand and tossed the third ball up and down, up and down, with his right hand. He then caught and held the ball and began tossing one ball from his left hand up and down, up and down, the second ball he had held in his left hand now, magically, in his right hand. Two parents and a small child appeared outside the circle, and then an elderly couple, and then a young woman with a mohawk.

Philippe worked all three balls into his juggle, their heights higher then lower, adjusting as needed for occasional breezes. Soon, he would sling a knapsack over his shoulder and mount his unicycle, juggling all the while. Later he would replace the balls with three torches, then while still juggling, offer items from his knapsack to the growing audience—a mirror into which children or the stuffed companions they held were invited to gaze, a pair of toy scissors with which the audience was invited to snip Philippe's hair. Then from his canvas bag would come a threadbare top hat, which, as he walked around the circle, never stepping outside it, he would with head motions and eye blinks suggest that the audience drop bills into. Always, the crowd stayed outside the chalk circle, even when he invited the young woman with the mohawk to stomp all over it. All this with no words.

Yet before any of this transpired, while he was merely tossing one ball and then another into the air, strolling around the circle and watching one and then another person wander into position as his audience, Philippe felt he had achieved a kind of stillness, a kind of perfection fully equal to what he had felt the morning of August 7, 1974, as he danced on a cable he had strung between the roofs of the World Trade Center towers.

3. A car drives through the front window of a dentist's office.

At 10:00 a.m. on Saturday, October 15, 1983, in the office of dentist Dr. Sydney Norman at 909 East 107th Street in the Canarsie section of Brooklyn, New York, Nora Heidelberg, the practice's receptionist, noticed something extraordinary. All the patients in the waiting room were sitting on the side of the room away from the front window. Nora looked through the open panel beside her desk at the rows of chairs, their emptiness revealing the uniform upholstery of small, angular geometric shapes.

The people did not amass in the one area, Nora thought, so they could have a view of the sunny day, because the chairs faced different directions, some toward the window and some not. It was as though the patients, largely strangers to one another, had entered into a silent pact, or perhaps had a sudden and unspoken need to huddle together for solace or safety. Then a black Chevy Impala drove through the front window. The shattered glass resting on the empty chairs looked like simply an embellishment of the pattern of the upholstery. No one was injured.

4. Miss Davies has nuptials.

At 11:00 a.m. on Saturday, October 15, 1983, at the Brick Presbyterian Church at the corner of 92nd Street and Park Avenue on the Upper East Side of Manhattan, after the hair and makeup services, the arrival of the photographer, the individual portraits, the wedding party group photos, the portrait photos of the couple together, the wedding party and family photos, the processional, the words of welcome by the Reverend Herbert B. Anderson, the introduction, the readings, and the address to the couple by Reverend Anderson,

Wendy Anne Wilding Davies exchanged marriage vows with Philip Caldwell Bowers.

A few facts about the bride: Wendy Bowers née Davies was presented at the 1974 Debutante Ball of the Junior League of New York. She was an alumna of the Spence School and Smith College. She received an MBA from Columbia University. At the time of her marriage, she was a financial analyst at W. R. Grace & Company in Manhattan.

And a few facts about Edward Alfred Davies, the father of the bride: He was director of the department of pediatrics and president of the medical board of Lenox Hill Hospital and professor of pediatrics at New York University School of Medicine. About the mother of the bride, less was evident in the public record.

A few facts about the groom, Philip Caldwell Bowers: He graduated from St. Mark's School and the University of Virginia. Like his bride, he received an MBA from Columbia University in New York, where he and his wife were in a statistics class and related study group together. At the time of his marriage, he was an associate—an entry-level position—in the corporate finance department of the Merrill Lynch Capital Markets Group.

And a few facts about the mother of the groom: Philippa Bowers lived in Washington, DC, where she was a broker with Chesapeake Investment Brokers. And about the father of the groom: Alexander Stewart Bowers lived in Manhattan and in Earlysville, Virginia; in the latter, he operated Hickory Ridge Farm, a stable where old coaches were restored and horses trained.

Truth be told, shortly after vows were exchanged, the newly christened Mrs. Bowers found herself wondering whether those among the guests who would be attending both the wedding ceremony and the reception would be inconvenienced, or perhaps annoyed, or even angry because of the four-hour gap between the end of the ceremony and the beginning of cocktail hour followed by dinner and reception at the Carlyle Hotel on Madison Avenue and 76th Street. Although her concern spoke well of her character, the new Mrs. Bowers need not have worried. Those in the wedding party, even those who lived on the Upper East Side, had been provided with rooms at the Carlyle, where they enjoyed resting, room-service lunches, and ample time to change into their formal evening wear. Others were perfectly happy to begin the festivities at cocktail hour and were delighted with the choice of venue, two or three of the couples even stealing away from the reception to see Eartha Kitt in the Café Carlyle and to spot in the audience the famous actor couple Goldie Hawn and Kurt Russell, the latter who had recently starred in a movie about a labor union activist who had blown the whistle about alleged wrongdoings at a plutonium plant and died mysteriously.

The wedding and reception went according to plan, although Mr. Bowers noted that, when he told inquiring guests about his role at Hickory Ridge Farm, he received no requests for further information.

Washington, DC

1. President Reagan makes a straw-person argument and collects acorns.

At 10:30 a.m. on Saturday, October 15, 1983, President Ronald Reagan was informed that actor Pat O'Brien had died earlier that morning of a massive heart attack.

At 12:06 p.m., the president recorded the weekly radio address. This week's broadcast was on the topic of the quality of life in America. The address began as follows:

"My fellow Americans: I know I court trouble when I dispute experts who specialize in spotting storm clouds and preaching doom and gloom. But at the risk of being the skunk that invades their garden party, I must warn them: Some very good news is sneaking up on you. The quality of American life is improving again."

On the morning of Saturday, October 15, 1983, Ralph H. Johnson opened a box that he found on his doorstep. Inside the box were ten complimentary author copies of the second edition of the book he had written with J. Anthony Blair titled *Logical Self Defense*, published by McGraw-Hill Ryerson. On page 103 of this book, in the first section of the chapter "Fallacies of Diversion," Johnson and Blair wrote:

> A cardinal principle that governs all argumentation is this: *The position criticized must be the position actually held.* This principle is particularly prone to violation in adversarial contexts, where each side may want to make the other side look bad. The temptation to distort the opponent's view is strong. What we call the fallacy of *straw person* is the direct result of a violation of this principle.... When you misrepresent your opponent's position, attribute to that person an implausible or inaccurate version that you can easily demolish, and then proceed to argue against the trumped-up version as though it were your opponent's, you commit the fallacy of *straw person.*

In the preface to the 2006 reprinting of *Logical Self-Defense* by the International Debate Education Association, reflecting on the relevance of the book over time and on what they had learned over their long careers, the authors wrote:

> [D]ialectical theories of argumentation have shown that some of the traditional fallacies, or some versions of them, are really violations of norms of productive dialogue rather than violations of canons of good reasoning. A prime example is the straw-person fallacy.... The argument critical of the falsely attributed position can be fallacy-free, but the false attribution violates norms of fair discussion.

In a chapter titled "Diagnosing Misattribution of Commitments: A Normative and Pragmatic Model of for Assessing Straw Man," published in the 2019 Springer anthology *Further Advances in Pragmatics and Philosophy: Part 2 Theories and Applications, Perspectives in Pragmatics, Philosophy & Psychology*, Douglas Walton and Fabrizio

Macagno proposed the following nine-step process for determining whether a straw-person argument has been put forth:

1. Identify P1, the proposition attacked
2. Determine whether P1 is the conclusion of the argument, one of its premises, or the inferential link (the argumentation scheme) joining the premises to the conclusion.
3. Search for some original text of the argument, such as a quotation, attributable to the arguer that can be used as evidence to compare P1 and P2.
4. If no evidence is available a burden of proof is set in place for the attacker to find a suitable quotation or text that can be used as evidence for P1.
5. If the attacker fails to meet this burden of proof, his straw man is defeated.
6. If evidence is available, a comparison needs to be made to determine whether P1 and P2 are close enough to equivalence to support the straw man attack.
7. Proving that P1 is equivalent to P2 can be carried out by deriving P1 from the text or quotation containing or indicating P2.
8. If the two propositions are not close enough to show equivalence, and the party with the burden can show this by using the textual evidence, a straw man fallacy has been committed.
9. If the two propositions are close enough to show equivalence, as indicated by the evidence, no straw man fallacy has been committed.

At 12:11 p.m. on Saturday, October 15, 1983, President Reagan closed his radio address as follows: "Our critics may never be satisfied with anything we do, but I can only say those who created the worst economic mess in postwar history should be the last people crying wolf one thousand days into this administration, when so many trends that were headed the wrong way are headed back in the right direction. Thanks for listening, and God bless you."

At 2:25 p.m. on Saturday, October 15, 1983, President Reagan rode his quarter horse, Whistle, around the Camp David compound. During the ride, he paused, dismounted, and picked up acorns from the ground, depositing as many as would fit into Whistle's side saddles, which also contained an attaché case containing nuclear launch codes, with the intention of transporting the acorns back to Washington and giving them to the squirrels outside the Oval Office.

At 3:30 p.m., the president telephoned Eloise O'Brien, Pat O'Brien's widow, and they spoke for one minute. After the call, President Reagan directed that a statement be released, which said, "The president and Mrs. Reagan are deeply saddened by Mr. O'Brien's death."

During the day, the president received and made numerous calls as he continued to grapple with the feelings of his aides, his aides' ability to get along with one another, and the appropriateness of their placement in new administrative roles, particularly that of National Security Council head. A thorny problem it was. Some associates asked that the president consider Jeane Kirkpatrick for the NSC job; however, President Reagan was concerned that Ms. Kirkpatrick would not get along with Secretary of State George Shultz and the State Department as a whole. Yet President Reagan knew that Ms. Kirkpatrick was eager to leave her current position as United States Ambassador to the United Nations, and he wondered if she had her heart set on the NSC role.

Some colleagues suggested Brent Scowcroft, currently Chairman of the President's Commission on Strategic Forces and previously NSC head under President Ford. But President Reagan doubted that Mr. Scowcroft would become a problem if he did not get the job.

The president himself preferred Bud MacFarlane, a solid and competent man who would not make waves or demands, but still was concerned about disappointing Jim Baker. Well, the president told himself, he would try to find some new role for Ms. Kirkpatrick, and would ask Jim Baker whether he wanted the UN job, and he would see how that played.

That evening, Ronald and Nancy Reagan watched the movie *A Star Is Born,* the 1954 version starring Judy Garland and James Mason, both of whom were guests on General Electric Theater, which broadcast on CBS television Sunday at 9:00 p.m. and which Ronald Reagan hosted, making introductory and concluding remarks, from September 26, 1954, through June 3 1962.

Unlike most episodes, which were narrative drama, the Judy Garland episode, directed by famous fashion photographer Richard Avedon, featured Judy performing seven songs against starkly designed sets. After the first song, Judy said, "I have a feeling that there's much too much talk going on in the world today so you're going to get very little from me, but I'm a singer and I just like to sing."

2. A man remembers his Christian drive-in movie theater.

At 11:00 a.m. on Saturday, October 15, 1983, 75-year-old Mildred Myrtle Masser Rice heard a rap on the front window of the restaurant portion of the Dan-Dee Country Inn and Restaurant, just outside the entrance of the Gambrill State Park, six miles northwest of downtown Frederick, Maryland, fifty-five miles north of the White House in Washington, DC, and fourteen miles south of Camp David.

The restaurant was not due to open for another thirty minutes, and Mildred instinctively felt her hackles go up at anyone who would presume to get her attention in a manner that bordered on bumptious, but when Mildred looked up and saw through the window the woman waving between the "open" sign (turned inward so those outside saw "closed") and the back of a sign advertising (Mildred knew but could not at this moment see) today's event, Mildred's annoyance, not very intense to begin with, relaxed.

Unlocking and opened the front door, Mildren was met by the friendly, almost too friendly, woman with large, thick tortoise-shell-frame glasses who had checked in last evening at the eleven-unit motel portion of the property. Mildred gave a "well, hello there" that she hoped was adequately welcoming for someone who was causing Mildred a fair amount of additional work this morning, not to mention fielding phone calls about the event all the previous week.

When Mildred noticed that beside the woman on the porch were two medium-sized cardboard boxes, she called for her 56-year-old daughter, a retired hospital nurse who went by the name Thelma Shafer Pryor, having kept the name of her first husband, George C. Shafer, now deceased, and added to it the name of her current husband, Glenn J. Pryor. Tomorrow, Thelma would turn 57, and she wondered if that were an age at which she might finally stop working at the Dan-Dee Country Restaurant and spend more time with Glenn, who had retired a few years ago after thirty-five years as a brakeman for the C&P Railroad and now was working part-time as a stonemason at Gambrill State Park.

Thelma had spent the past twenty minutes setting up as separate a space as was possible in the open and undifferentiated ten-thousand-square-foot restaurant for the event that the Dan-Dee was hosting today in service of the woman that both Mildred and Thelma had heard about through the Parkway Church of God, of which both were devoted attendees.

Thelma had not met the visitor the previous evening, but knew of her and, after helping her with one of the boxes, which was extraordinarily heavy, waved an arm toward the setup—tables and chairs for sixty, turned so most could see a head table.

"Hello, dear," the woman said, removing a hat, revealing a tall arrangement of tight brown curls, and removing a wool coat to reveal a chocolate brown poly-knit skirt and vest suit and a blouse with a bold print that was somehow, at least at a glance, both floral and aquatic. She handed her hat and coat to Thelma, who, after a moment to realize what was happening, held her arms out to accept the garments.

Thelma was tempted to introduce herself to this woman as a way of pointing out that the woman had not bothered to introduce herself to Thelma, but suddenly Thelma was too weary to bother. Instead, she said, "Well, Mrs. Gabler, I hope these arrangements meet with your approval. We tried hard to follow your instructions."

Mrs. Gabler, whose first name was Norma, but who rarely referred to herself as anything other than Mrs. Gabler, scanned the setting, taking a beat or two longer than seemed necessary, and said, "Well, dear, I'm sure that this will work out just fine," in a way that made it clear that the setup wasn't fully up to her expectations and in a careful enunciation and accent that reminded Thelma of an actress on television pretending to have a Texas accent.

Thelma having been dismissed and forgotten, Norma removed from one of the carboard boxes a roll of masking tape from which she tore five strips and attached one end of each to the yellow plastic sheet covering the head table. She next withdrew from the box a cylinder that, when unrolled and attached with the masking tape to hang from the front of the head table, revealed itself to be a hand-painted sign with the words, "Sex Education encourages abortion, illicit sexual activity and homosexuality." From the other box, Norma withdrew hardbound books of varying sizes and colors, stacking them so high Thelma would have been concerned they would topple if Norma were not handling them in such a way that suggested the confidence of both experience and God's will.

When Mildred unlocked the front door at 11:30 a.m., the people lined up outside took one of two paths upon entering the restaurant: either toward the hostess to the right for seating or toward a small table on the left, where they paid Thelma fifteen dollars in cash for today's luncheon and workshop, half of which would go to the Dan-Dee Restaurant and half to Norma's and her husband's organization, Educational Research Analysts.

Thelma and two other wait staff expertly served platters of ham (regular and country), apple fritters, home-baked rolls, bowls of coleslaw, cottage cheese, three-bean salad (which the Dan-Dee menu called "chow-chow"), and pitchers of water, tea, and milk, all served with ice. Norma offered a prayer. As attendees began scooping portions onto individual plates and taking first bites, Norma, her voice projecting wonderfully not just to breach the distance between herself at the head table and the fifty-five people seated in front of her but also to be heard over the chit-chat of the diners not part of today's presentation, spoke:

"If I may ask you to pause for just a moment in your enjoyment of this wonderful meal, I would like to pose to you a most important question." Murmuring stopped immediately, although a few utensils continued to clink. "That question is this: Who is the father of our country?"

Perhaps half of those in the audience felt a momentary panic. Some required a moment to locate in their minds the answer filed away during first grade or perhaps kindergarten, some feared that the answer was so obvious perhaps a joke was being played, some combated apprehension about the potential of being asked to speak in front of a group, and still others were concerned that everyone's apprehension would preclude even one person from responding, thus getting this well-meaning woman's presentation off to an awkward start.

In contrast, about half of the audience felt excited anticipation, having heard Norma, accompanied by her soft-spoken husband, Mel, do this same bit on *The Phil Donahue Show* or *Firing Line with William F. Buckley* or NBC's *The Today Show* or CNN's *Crossfire* with Patrick J. Buchanan.

A white-haired man, who had seen Norma on both ABC's *20/20* and CBS's *Morning News,* said in a voice even clearer and more confident than Norma's, "George Washington!"

"Sir," Norma said, "I thank you for voicing so beautifully the answer that is surely obvious to every single person in this room, having been instilled in us during the early years of our education by our wise teachers and loving parents."

Without taking her eyes from the audience, Norma lifted the book from the top of the pile an arm's length from her. "However, according to Mister"—she pretended—and everyone knew she was pretending, as all were intended to be in on this joke—to read slowly from the book's cover—"William Jay Jacobs, author of"—Norma fake-glanced again at the book's cover—"*Search for Freedom: America and Its People*, which just happens to be a civics textbook for middle-school pupils, each of us in this room, and each of our teachers and parents, are, in fact, incorrect."

Norma widened and then narrowed her eyes. "No, according to this"—Norma used a nanosecond pause to indicate the phrase "so-called" without needing to say it—"textbook, the father of our country is not George Washington. You may all consider yourselves corrected by the author, Mister Jacobs, who is, let's see"—the fake glance this time was at the book's back cover—"author, historian, and professor, who received his doctorate from the fine institution of Columbia University, which if I'm not mistaken is located in New York City." The audience emitted a few mumbles and knowing chuckles.

"No, if this book is to be believed, the father of our country is none other than"—here she took a pause for obvious, overly obvious, dramatic effect—"Marilyn Monroe!"

Amid laughter, Norma went on. "This textbook about America and its people mentions George Washington, whom we all had in our woeful ignorance assumed to be the father of our country, only three times, while Mister Jacobs devotes *six pages* to the, well, let us say, charitably, the *actress* Marilyn Monroe."

At this point, Norma shifted deftly from the diction of entertainment to that befitting a topic of the utmost seriousness. "Our children are being totally controlled. Can you imagine a sex symbol being given more time than the father of our country? I don't think it's fair that our children be subjected to this kind of information. They are being totally indoctrinated into one philosophy."

Norma settled back in her chair for a moment, letting her words sink in, aware that she was seated with her back to a window, making her a silhouetted and thus mysterious and powerful figure to the audience, something she had noted when reviewing Thelma's setup of the room, but had not complimented Thelma on, assuming the positioning was fortuitous rather than clever.

At exactly the moment that, at the Dan-Dee Inn and Restaurant in Frederick, Maryland, Norma was sitting back in her chair to let her statement settle on her audience, her husband, Mel Gabler was rising from the chair behind his desk in the office he and his wife shared in what had been intended as the master bedroom of their home in Fairview, Texas.

Viewing this room, one might understandably conclude that God's will had overridden the natural law that the contents cannot be of greater volume than their container. The room held fourteen five-drawer filing cabinets, with books stacked on top of each all the way up to the drop ceiling, eight six-shelf bookcases, six ten-drawer cabinets for correspondence, and four columns of narrow, open shelves containing mimeographed handouts.

The books were texts from around the country, but a plurality from Texas, that Mel and Norma, mostly Mel, either had assessed or were in the process of assessing to ensure they included, among many other features, the scientific weaknesses of evolutionary theories, phonics-based reading instruction, principles and benefits of free enterprise, original intent of the U.S. Constitution, respect for Judeo-Christian morals, and emphasis on abstinence in sex education. Mel and Norma filed their findings with the appropriate bodies of the appropriate states or school districts and distributed their criteria to other individuals and groups for use in their own assessments, along with ranked lists of published textbooks.

This morning, Mel had been reviewing an American literature text based on his and Norma's criteria that such texts must base coverage on contemporaries' relative esteem of various authors' works, as well as on modern editors' and critics' opinions. In the text at hand, he had already noted nine pages devoted to the writings of abolitionist Olaudah Equiano but nothing from The Federalist Papers, and eight pages on Emily Dickinson and only a half page on Longfellow—clear examples of anti-intellectual pandering to special-interest groups.

Mel was happy to focus on the analytical side of their endeavors and let Norma take the lead in their public appearances. He knew she had an affable presence that he could never hope to equal. However, on the occasions that he did not accompany Norma for a public appearance, he missed her.

It was lunchtime, but Mel wasn't terribly interested in eating. When Norma was home, he generally sat with her and each had a sandwich, but when she was not, the Lord sometimes called him to use the lunch hour to take a drive.

No number of lamps and no amount of wattage could make Mel and Norma's office bright, and Mel, when he pulled his car from the attached garage, enjoyed the contrast of the noontime sunlight that exploded through his windows.

Mel and Norma's house was at the lower edge of their neighborhood, and just a few hundred feet brought Mel to an anomaly for Texas: a road surrounded by trees and brush thick and tall enough to block his view, a road that ended soon and deposited Mel onto Birdsong Street, which led to West Loop 281, both offering unobstructed views of several truck equipment, rigging, scrap metal, and storage companies—most, Mel was always proud to note, locally owned and not franchises, and therefore indicated by signs that had a handmade quality.

Three miles further on, at the West Loop Church of Christ, Mel took the fork to the right, which almost immediately fed him into a right turn onto Jaycee Drive, and Mel felt, as he did every time he entered this intersection, a sensation—nervousness? excitement? longing?—that he could not ever quite classify.

A few feet before the Longview Police Station, Mel made a left on Lake Lemond Road. To his left was a pleasant subdivision of relatively new, decidedly modest homes. On his right, well, on his right was what Mel thought of as The Beginning.

A couple hundred feet on, at Tex Pack Road, Mel turned right and pulled onto a concrete slab that looked like a driveway but led to nothing. He turned off the car's ignition. He rolled the driver's side window down for the air, but kept his eyes straight ahead at the view through his windshield.

He supposed that the view could be described as nothing. That would be typical of how some northern smart-alecks described the landscape of Texas, but in this case Mel could accept that description as fair. Ahead of him, for almost as many yards as he could see, was a swath of scrub grass and dirt.

In the far distance, he could sense more than see the Jaycee-owned Longview Exhibit Center, the almost-ready-for-christening Maud Cobb Convention Center, and the agricultural pavilions and rodeo arena of the Longview Fairgrounds. It was, however, the swath of scrub grass and dirt that Mel was here to see. For here, from an entrance that no longer existed at the corner of Tex Pack Road and Lake Lemond Road—and if an entrance were there now, to what would anyone be entering?—was where, on another Saturday thirty years ago, dozens of people assembled in their automobiles, facing a screen constructed at no charge by the carpenters' union and painted at no charge by the painters' union, at the launch of the product of Mel's passion: the Longview Christian Drive-In Theater.

On the screen that night, Mel and Norma, alongside all the people hidden in their own cars, having their own private experience of the event, had watched the feature of the evening: a movie titled *Great Awakening.*

The film starred Colleen Townsend, who had recently retired from Hollywood to focus on her Christian works, as Connie, a student at Westmont College, a Christian liberal arts institution in California—and a real place, Mel was happy to note—who for the first time was finding purpose in life by taking Jesus Christ as her savior, and who for the first time was falling in love, with Dave, whose goal was to become a pastor. Connie had recently returned to the States after working for the Allied High Commission for Occupied Germany; Dave had recently returned to the states after working as a missionary in Germany.

As Mel let the landscape, which two weeks from today would be an overflow parking lot for the Longview Fair, blur in his vision, he did was he always did when he visited this place. He let the final moments of the film play through in his mind. Connie and Dave were standing together on a flowing lawn of the campus, Connie in a crisp white blouse and Dave in a rather ill-fitting blue-and-black-checked sportscoat that seemed too informal for the occasion and always threatened to sully Mel's memory of the scene. Having graduated from Westmont, Connie and Dave were excited about their futures, but were also concerned. For both, their priority was to follow the calling of Jesus Christ. But what if He called each to different paths and different places? What a disappointment that would be.

To this point, both had kept their plans private, but now, clearly, those plans would have to be revealed. Who should speak first? And would the plans of one influence the plans of the other? How could they ensure that they were truly following the path of Christ and not a different path, one that would keep them together but contradict the Lord's wishes?

Connie came up with a simple and elegant solution. She asked Dave for a piece of paper and pencil, which he supplied from his inside jacket pocket (he was in the habit of jotting down his thoughts and kept notebook and pencil handy). Using her handbag as backing, and turned so Dave could not see, she wrote a few words and folded the paper in half. Turning back to face Dave, she said, "Now, we will both know that I will not change my calling to match yours. You tell me your calling, and then I will read you mine."

Their eyes and faces glowed with anticipation, with fear, with longing—with the actorly and cinematic expression of the sensation that Mel felt on his solitary visits to this site.

Dave took a breath and said, "Preach in Germany."

Connie, her face betraying nothing, unfolded her paper and read, "Teach in Germany."

Arm in arm, they walked from the lawn, toward a roadway. Orchestral music swelled, and superimposed over the couple appeared words: not "The End" but "The Beginning."

The Longview Christian Drive-In, which continued its Saturday showings for five years, was Mel's project. It was his calling. He gathered his backers. He spoke with the Jaycees, which owned the lot.

He spoke with the union representatives. He sketched the layout—where the projection booth would be, the screen, the cars. Norma placed the ad in the newspaper and created a poster. But it was Mel's, and of course the Lord's, project.

Educational Research Analysts, on the other hand, was a beautiful, wordless, and lasting convergence of Mel, Norma, and the Lord. It was a bond among the three as exhilarating, even after two decades, as the convergence of Connie, Dave, and the Lord. And like Connie and Dave, Mel felt that he and Norma were always poised at The Beginning.

At the Dan-Dee Inn and Restaurant, Norma's voice inevitably carried to those merely enjoying a lunch—by now, a rather late lunch. Truth be told, the habitues of the restaurants were mostly older, tending even toward the older end of older. However, one threesome was quite a distance from this norm: a woman named Helen Tyson; her husband, Jim; and their 9-year-old daughter, Melinda. Helen and Jim wore jeans and work shirts, having taken a spontaneous break from gardening for this lunch, and Melinda's hair was a mess, not for any particular reason other than it was always a mess.

Jim and Melinda had been kidding one another through most of the meal, but Helen had been listening on and off to Norma's words and thinking about a letter she had mailed two weeks previously to the school board overseeing Melinda's middle school about a social studies text that included overt references to the preference of women to motherhood and housework over careers. In Friday's mail, she had received a letter from the school board chair, a woman, sounding mortified and asserting her commitment to eliminating sexism from the school district's curricula.

Melinda in the lead, Helen and Jim paid their check to Thelma at the register near the front door, and Helen got her first look at Norma, her smiling cheeks as round and inviting as the fresh-baked rolls so recently consumed by both Helen's family and Norma's audience.

Seeing Helen staring at her, Norma paused in her remarks, and said, "Have a wonderful day, dear. May God be with you."

Not sure what else to do, Helen smiled and nodded.

3. Dot Helms, wife of Senator Jesse Helms, polishes a story about a deaf lifeguard.

At 1:00 p.m. on Saturday, October 15, 1983, in a simple two-story brick colonial house, a small rectangular structure with a steep, saltbox roof, on South Glebe Road in the Douglas Park neighborhood of Arlington, Virginia, Dorothy Coble Helms, known to friends and intimates as Dot, was serving coffee to her husband, North Carolina Senator Jesse Helms; to John Porter East, also a U.S. Senator from North Carolina; and to Jeremiah Andrew Denton, Jr., a U.S. Senator from Alabama, in the living room. Although she had known John for several years, she still found herself taking extra care to avoid bumping into his wheelchair, to which he had been confined after contracting polio as a young man.

Jesse, seated on an armchair, held a hand-painted, blue fluted full lace porcelain coffee cup by pinching its tiny handle in his thick fingers, the cup hovering over the similarly designed saucer, which lay on his lap. As both host and leader of this small gathering, Jesse was setting the context and agenda: "My people are still digging through the files, and my lawyers are still working on a delay, but in the absence of a bombshell discovery or a sudden fit of good sense among certain Democrat-appointed judges, I'm afraid we will be having a vote on Wednesday."

He was stating the obvious, but that was the way among legislators, Dot knew, to lay out a case carefully, using more words rather than fewer, the opposite of the advice of the journalism professors who taught both her and Jesse at the University of North Carolina in Chapel Hill.

Jesse took a sip of coffee, lifted the saucer from his lap with his other hand, and set cup and saucer together on the table at his elbow. Dot started back toward the kitchen, hearing Jesse's voice behind her saying to his fellow Senators, "So if we can't beat them, we'll annoy the shit out of them."

Dot got herself a regular-sized mug—she hated the fussy little cups that seemed required for polite political gatherings—poured it half full from the drip pot, leaving enough for the men in case they wanted more, and headed into her study.

She could never concentrate on new composition while Jesse was entertaining, so she contented herself with refining an existing piece for her book in progress, titled *Interesting Deaf Americans.*

Dot's interest in deaf people began when she attended a Sunday school class for the deaf taught at the First Baptist Church of Raleigh by a friend of hers. She had even learned sign language, although it was difficult to stay in practice here in Washington, where many people behaved as if they were deaf, but few people of her acquaintance actually were.

After an hour and a half, she had heard from the other room only voices raised and lowered as one might expect, and working with pencil on a typescript she had created with her 1971 battleship-green IBM Selectric II (which was also shaped rather like a battleship) at her tiny desk, had completed the following to her satisfaction.

> Leroy Columbo left his lifeguard post. He walked slowly down the beach. Many people were sun-bathing on the sand, and they spoke to him. Leroy nodded and smiled to them.
>
> But, he always kept his eyes on the water.
>
> You see, Leroy Columbo was a lifeguard, and he was deaf. He could not hear cries for help; so he had to use his eyes all the time. He could spot a person in trouble in the water quickly.

Leroy Columbo was a familiar sight on the Galveston, Texas, beaches. He was a lifeguard there for 40 years. During those years he saved 907 people from drowning in the waters around Galveston Island. Leroy Columbo was the world's greatest life-saver!

Many people in Galveston still remember the year 1928 when a boat blew up at a dock and a nearby barge full of crude oil caught fire. Mr. Columbo saved two people from the burning boat, and he rescued several more from drowning. He saved the captain and first mate of a tugboat when the tugboat sank after bumping into another boat. Once, he dived into the icy waters of Galveston Bay to save the lives of two men.

Leroy Columbo was born in 1905. He lost his hearing when he was seven years old. When he was ten, he entered the Texas School for the Deaf at Austin. Six years later, his father died.

Leroy decided to leave school and help support his family. However, Leroy didn't need much money to swim in the waters around Galveston Island; so he spent most of his free time swimming. He became an expert swimmer.

When Leroy was eighteen, his brother asked the Surf Toboggan Club to let Leroy become a member. He had to take a test first before he could be accepted. He had to swim for three hours without stopping. He couldn't even rest by floating or swimming on his back. Leroy took the test and passed it easily.

In 1924, Leroy beat a man named Herbert Brenan in a one-mile race. Mr. Brenan was then the national endurance champion of the Amateur Athletic Union. Mr. Brenan could swim longer than anyone else without stopping. But Leroy beat him.

The next year, September 5, 1925, Leroy finished a mile ahead of Mr. Brenan in a ten-mile race. He set a new record for Galveston; he finished the race in six hours and fifty-five minutes. Fourteen swimmers started the race. Leroy and Mr. Brenan were the only two to finish it. During the years from 1929 to 1939, Mr. Columbo won all distance races held in the Gulf of Mexico.

Leroy Columbo never won a scholarship. He never went into training for serious sports competition, instead, he used his talents to save the lives of other people. He became well-known. When he died on July 2, 1974, members of the Texas State Senate stood for a moment of silence in his honor. The people of Galveston have had a plaque made in his memory. His name was included in the Guiness Book of World Records.

They will never forget this very brave and famous deaf swimmer.

Peoria, Illinois

1. Four people play a game of chance before dawn while another watches.

At 1:00 a.m. on Saturday, October 15, 1983, in Dunlap, Illinois, *The Exorcist* ended. Linda and Jan-Paul Peavler looked in on their two boys in one bedroom and infant, Tiffany, in another, and retired to their master bedroom, Linda reflecting that "master" may seem too fine a word for a bedroom just a few square feet larger than the others, but if you add the word "and mistress," a perfectly fine term for a room that was hers and Jan-Paul's own, no children in cribs or squirming between them. Linda, although faintly queasy from the movie, fell asleep quickly and Jan-Paul soon after.

At 2:05 a.m. on Saturday, October 15, 1983, just southwest of downtown Peoria, Reginald Hale began to turn from Elm Street into Meyer Alley and hit another car exiting the alley. When police officers, who had been cruising only two blocks away, arrived at 2:10 a.m., Reginald told them that he had been having trouble with his brakes.

At 2:15 a.m. on Saturday, October 15, 1983, in the parking lot behind an apartment building at 529 SW Adams Street in downtown Peoria, Illinois, Charlie Alexander, kneeling with three other young men between two parked cars, two pairs of dice and a roll of bills on the pavement by his knees, was trying to convince Leha Young, who was standing and leaning against one of the cars, to take a turn.

She snorted. "Turn myself over to chance? Not likely. My goal in life is to stay in control of events."

At 2:40 a.m., a man none of them knew stumbled, perhaps a bit too theatrically, past the five, mumbled, "Hey," and continued on his way. At 2:45 a.m., two police cars pulled into the parking lot, arrested the four dice players and Leha, and took them to the Peoria County Jail.

At 4:20 a.m., on Saturday, October 16, 1983, Terry Hanson was driving south on the 1300 block of Northeast Jefferson Street in Peoria, Illinois. His car left the street, went onto the sidewalk, returned to the street, and ran into a parked car, pushing that car into the center of the street and coming to rest behind it. Fortunately, the lack of traffic at that hour prevented any other cars from colliding with the two stopped vehicles.

2. Linda Peavler declines her husband's suggestion that she attend their neighbor's garage sale.

At 8:30 a.m. on Saturday, October 15, 1983, in Dunlap, Illinois, Jan-Paul woke, looked at the clock on his bedside table, then looked to his other side, saw Linda, and registered surprise that kids had woken neither of them.

Knowing he should get up and check on the children, Jan-Paul instead lay on his back, listening to the unusual morning silence.

Soon, through the window to his left, which faced the driveway of their neighbors to the south, Jan-Paul heard voices from one and then two and then another adult, followed by a hard-to-define scraping and creaking. Jan-Paul rose, stood in the foot-and-a-half space between his side of the bed and the wall, and peeked through the side of the curtain, seeking two racks of clothes; three picnic tables covered with books, toys, and shoes; and a smattering of chairs.

He looked back to the bed, and Linda's was staring at him with an odd fixity.

"The neighbors are having a yard sale," he said.

She blinked and sat up.

"Maybe you should go over there," he said. "Get to know the neighbors. Pick up some cheap toys."

Linda, looking straight ahead toward their closet rather than toward Jan-Paul, said, "How many doors does our closet have?"

3. Linda Peavler calls her mother.

At 10:50 a.m. on Saturday, October 15, 1983, Linda was on the phone with her mother, Sande, saying, "Jan-Paul just left for work and he took care of the kids this morning but now it's just me and I'm seeing double so I don't know if I have three kids or six and I think I'm going to throw up."

Sande, short of breath, recounted her morning, being as economical with her words as possible: Dewey waking with back pain from lifting something he shouldn't have lifted at the post office, he was a supervisor after all; Sande, like Linda, seeing double and queasy. Sande didn't mention that she couldn't quite fill her lungs when she breathed.

4. Dewey Spore calls Jan-Paul Peavler at the Richmond Brothers store.

At 11:50 a.m. on Saturday, October 15, 1983, in northern Peoria, Illinois, Dewey Spore was looking for the telephone book. He didn't use it often and could never quite remember where they kept it or even if they had a specific place for it, but he knew it was large enough—well, not coffee-table-book large and probably not as large as the Chicago phone book, but still, large—to be fairly easily spotted. He didn't remember what its cover looked like, especially because it changed every year—or was it every six months?—but he knew the cover was always some sort of collage of Abe Lincoln and tractors and parks and Bradley University and children playing.

It was buried in the back of the bottom portion of the dining room credenza, and Dewey noted that on the cover of this issue, Abraham Lincoln was absent but Ronald Reagan and his alma mater, nearby Eureka College, were represented, along with the usual tractors and children playing. Dewey pulled their new push-button-in-the-handset phone from the top of the credenza, placed it on the dining room table, opened the book to the yellow pages, looked for a section headed "Men's Clothing," found none, and then located "Clothing—Men's," where he ignored the display ads and ran his finger down the listings until he found Richmond Brothers in the Northwoods Mall.

Thinking he would have found the number quicker if he had looked in the White Pages, he held his left index finger under the phone number and with his right hand removed the handset from its cradle, placed it upside down so the buttons showed, and began pushing in the number, having some difficulty because the significant pressure required to press the oddly protuberant buttons tended to make the handset squirt away.

Trying to keep from his voice the crabbiness he was starting to feel because of his back pain, his anxiety over Sande's mysterious condition, and the difficulty of executing even the simplest of tasks like making a telephone call, Dewey asked the young lady who answered the phone, and who seemed to lisp the "s" in "Brothers," to speak to Jan-Paul Peavler, who came on right away, so Dewey assumed he had been standing by the front counter chatting with the girl, which seemed to him rather an easier job than working at the post office and apparently also paid enough for a new house, even if it was in the middle of nowhere.

"Listen," Dewey said, "it sounds like Linda is feeling worse. I'm going to pick up the kids and bring them here. I think you'd better go home and look after Linda."

Jan-Paul asked whether it wasn't just the flu, and Dewey barely restrained himself from saying that his lack of a medical degree would make his opinion on the matter worthless.

The truth was, Jan-Paul was just as happy to leave work. Saturdays were busy, often bringing people not just from Peoria but also families from surrounding farming towns, the men and boys in need of wedding or church suits. Also, Jan-Paul had to admit that he rather liked the dramatic feeling of hinting to his coworkers at an emergency.

At home, Linda was dressed for the day but lying on the couch. Seeing Jan-Paul, she struggled to sit up and then to use both her hands to push herself up off the couch, saying "I need to go to the bathroom." On her feet, she wobbled in such an erratic and helpless way that Jan-Paul suddenly felt terrified. She reached a hand down toward the couch and guided herself slowly back to a sitting position. With the same hand, she reached toward Jan-Paul and said, "I really need to get to the bathroom."

At their house, Dewey looked in on Sande in the bedroom. She lay on her back with her eyes closed, breathing through her mouth. She said, "I feel like a beach ball is inside my lungs," and she felt as if that might be the last thing she would say for a while, not so much because she needed to marshal her strength, but because she suspected she was running out of oxygen.

5. Lou Dobrydnia hates being short of breath, really hates it.

At 7:30 a.m. on Saturday, October 15, 1983, in her Peoria, Illinois, apartment, Lou Dobrydnia woke with a headache. When she was a child, she had experienced one migraine headache, and in diagnosing it, the doctor had asked Lou—then called Mary—how bad the pain was, showing her simple pictures of faces with varying expressions on a continuum from serenity to agony. Lou remembered pointed toward the next-to-most agonized face, not because she didn't think the most-agonized face was warranted, but because she wasn't sure what would happen if she pointed to the most agonized face—surgery?—and also because even as a child, she was pretty confident that she could deal with discomfort herself, and also she thought that the polka-dot bow tie the doctor wore made him look like a clown, and she didn't want a clown doing anything to her head.

The headache Lou woke up with this morning didn't fit with any of the faces. It wasn't shooting and stabbing and blinding pain like her long-ago migraine had been, which isn't to say it wasn't painful. It was like having a head full of catsup that somehow carried an electrical charge. It didn't flat-out hurt as much as her migraine, but it was more troubling because it was a sensation she had never experienced, and because it was unlike a traditional headache or even her one migraine, which she understood to be temporary, like her brain was telling her that she was in pain, but no real damage was being done. This sensation was different—less painful, but more frightening, more like something was fundamentally wrong. Also, if this didn't go away, it would be a damned nuisance at today's field hockey game, or maybe the game would allow her to forget her head.

One of the assistant coaches picked up Lou at the front door of her apartment building, and together they drove on Route 24 first to Bartonville, where they picked up some equipment they were borrowing from the high school and stuffed it into the assistant coach's station wagon. They continued on Route 24 for an hour and a half west across central Illinois past one small town after another—Mapleton, Glasford, Canton, Cuba, Smithfield, Marietta, and Lou's favorite, New Philadelphia—at each Lou thinking maybe they should stop at a gas station and buy some aspirin, but then thought, why bother? This wasn't the kind of pain that she had used aspirin to quell in the past, and anyway, she could live with a headache, even one that made her think her brain might be coming loose from its moorings, even one she couldn't quite forget about when they arrived at the athletic field of Western Illinois University in Macomb, Illinois, met the rest of the team, and headed onto the field for their warmup.

When it came to physical sensations, what Lou hated, what she really hated, was being short of breath. When she had started seriously physically training, she had been too aggressive and too ill-informed to stay sufficiently hydrated, and she had ended up with lactic acidosis, which, she learned later, was caused by impaired tissue oxygenation and which, in its acute phase—because of course she had pushed herself along and ignored the less acute symptoms she experienced in the moment—manifested itself in dizziness leading to delirium and what is called respiratory compensation, also known as the feeling that you're going to die at any second from not being able to breathe.

Which goddammit to hell was what she was starting to feel in the first quarter of the game in which the team was depending on her as one of its most reliable strikers. Ridiculous, she thought. It was almost as if she were out of shape, which she knew damn well she wasn't. But she couldn't see clearly what was happening on the field. And she felt as if her chest was between two slabs of wood squeezed by a giant vise, and there was still that headache, worse now in its weird, not-quite-a-headache way.

For the first time in her playing life, Lou took herself out of the game. She lay down on the grass behind the half-filled bleachers, then sat up, then tried to walk, then lay down again. Eventually, she made her way to a garbage can near the parking lot into which she thought she would vomit, but she didn't.

6. A ladder is a dangerous thing when the person climbing it is seeing double.

At 10:00 a.m. on Saturday, October 15, 1983, John Mason and his 13-year-old son went to a football game, which thank goodness was at Peoria Stadium, only six blocks straight north from their house, because John was feeling a little woozy.

After the game, John took his son to McDonald's on War Memorial Drive, but didn't order anything for himself and got his son's meal to go.

Back home, while his son ate, John stirred a can of paint resting on a drop cloth covering half their living room floor, removed the plastic from a new brush, opened the ladder that was leaning against the wall, poured paint into the tray, and rested the tray on the ladder's fold-out shelf.

As he mounted the steps, he found his eyes on the living room windows, and he noticed that the number of windows transformed from two to four, then he looked down at the ladder slats and steps, and they began to multiple to something John couldn't quantify. He held onto the ladder, waiting for the episode to pass, but it didn't. He eased himself down and lay on the couch. He closed his eyes, thinking that would erase the multiplying images, but it only made him feel sick to his stomach, so he opened his eyes again.

7. A bass player reflects on bass playing.

At 10:15 a.m. on Saturday, October 15, 1983, in the kitchen of the Skewer Inn on the lower level, Montgomery Ward side, of Peoria's Northwoods Mall, as he scooped margarine into the pan and chopped onions for that day's patty melts, his mind never fully absorbed by the rote tasks before the lunch rush, Jason Cook thought about last night's band rehearsal. More specifically, he thought about the sensation of playing the bass in a rock band. The bass player, Jason thought, had to be a perfect balance of follower and leader. To keep the beat, the bass player sometimes had to follow the drummer, but sometimes if things started to drag even the tiniest bit, the bass player had to lead the drummer, and each note required a snap-decision, total confidence, doubt disintegrated to nonexistence, on whether to follow or lead. For the bass player, each session brought a thousand or more moments of precariousness, each of which Jason loved.

8. Some people eat at the Skewer Inn and some people do not eat. At 12:02 p.m. on Saturday, October 15, 1983, Ruth Burroughs and her daughters Susan and Sally were in line at the Skewer Inn, the line extending into the common area of the mall. For the most part, Ruth didn't mind standing in lines. When her children had been young and on some rare occasion Ruth was able to go shopping alone, she always thought of standing in line as guilt-free resting time—time she couldn't do any of the chores piled up around the house and time she couldn't be attending to her daughters' needs. Not that she resented any of these draws on her time. Just the same, she rather liked having a bit of rest and independence forced on her by the circumstance of a long, slow line at the A&P or Szold's or Belscot or Woolworth's.

However, with her daughters now adults and with Ruth 60 years old and—she hated to admit it, even to herself—an intermittently aching right hip, she was less attuned to the virtues of a long line. And this one at the Skewer Inn was not moving quickly.

Ruth turned to her grown daughters, Susan and Sally, and said, "Let's go somewhere else."

At 12:12 p.m., standing in line at the Skewer Inn, Dianne Hollister, whose friends called her Happ, and her daughter Amy, 11, were in the process of doing something they become quite adept at: communicating without words. They didn't use sign language or any private system of signals. Rather, where most people used words and facial expressions together, at some point Happ and Amy discovered that the facial expressions said pretty much whatever needed saying without the words. Happ thought this may have been the result of the wonderful descriptions of facial expressions and the meaning behind those expressions in one of her favorite children's books, Marjory Schwalze's criminally little-known *Mystery at Redtop Hill.* She had underlined many of those descriptions in one of the two copies she owned of the book. Once in a while, Happ used the expression-but-no-words technique with her boss, the fire chief, and it was surprisingly efficient.

Today, having driven from Bloomington, Illinois, thirty miles from Peoria on Route 74, to the Northwoods Mall, intent on starting their lunch with the Skewer Inn's famous flaming melted cheese appetizer, they stood in line outside the restaurant, or rather in front of Coach House Gifts because the line was long enough to reach the storefront adjacent to the restaurant.

Taking their position in line, Amy rolled her eyes and smiled at her mother: What a line!

Happ pursed her lips and shook her head: A nuisance, but we'll live.

In front of Happ and Amy, two older women stood side by side chatting, and two older men stood side by side and not chatting but not seeming discontented by their silence. Happ hoped that the women were one romantic couple and the men another, rather than two husbands and wives taking the social outing as an opportunity to momentarily split from one another.

One of the women said, "That Bob Evans just opened on War Memorial."

Happ, looking at Amy, tilted her head to the left: Listen!

The other woman said, "Bob Evans?"

The first one repeated. "The restaurant. Bob Evans restaurant. Like the one in East Peoria. It must have just opened. We passed it on the way here. It looks like a house, but bright red and shinier. Actually, I think it's supposed to look like a barn."

Amy, looking at Happ, raised and lowered her eyebrows and pushed out her lower lip: Well, what do you think of that?

Happ widened her eyes and smiled: Sounds good to me!

Amy raised her right eyebrow—something Happ couldn't do—and tipped her head to the right: Let's get out of here.

They went to Bob Evans.

Had they stayed in line, Happ and Amy may have been seated at the table where Beverly Ratter, in line behind Happ and Amy, was eating a patty melt sandwich.

9. Senator Ron Paul suggests that the gold standard would be a steadying force for American society.

At 1:45 p.m. on Saturday, October 15, 1983, in the Alps Ballroom of Jumer's Castle Lodge, Darryl Windrift, wearing the same black clothes he had the evening before, black clothing being a requirement of his job so that he would blend into the background, was clipping a lavalier microphone to the lapel of Texas Senator Ron Paul. Standing next to the Senator, Darryl, who was five-foot-seven, was surprised to find that the Senator was at least four inches taller than Darryl. When Darryl had seen the Senator across the room, talking with the conference organizer, he had looked about Darryl's height.

At 2:05 p.m., the introduction having been completed, Senator Paul began a presentation with a title that Darryl found surprisingly lacking in drama, "Federal Reserve System/Gold Standard/Legal Tender Laws."

At a lectern on the front of which was mounted an oval sign reading "Jumer's Castle Lodge" in the Germanic-looking and not very legible font called Breitkopf Fraktur, Senator Paul leaned forward, not from the waist but from the neck, and read from typed sheets resting on the lectern:

> We live in an age of inflation. Punctuated by brief moments of austerity and declining prices, the world of work hurtles without compass toward a rendezvous with catastrophe. As those in this room well know, inflation is usually defined as too much money chasing too few goods. Essentially, inflation is the depreciation of money, a process of monetary destruction. But a stable monetary standard is essential in a market economy—it is the indispensable standard of commercial value. Stable money is, in fact, bound up with civilization itself. The depreciation of the commercial standard of civilization—money, as with the depreciation of moral and legal standards of value, brings chaos and disorder. For a generation, we have seen the debasement of these standards not only in commerce, but also in our public life, our schools, our families, our art, and our science.
>
> It is no exaggeration to say that the survival of Western civilization in general, and America in particular, is at stake in the struggle over standards of value.
>
> More and more people are asking if a gold standard will end the financial crisis in which we find ourselves. The question is not so much if it will help or if we will resort to gold, but when. All great inflations end with the acceptance of real money—gold—and the rejection of political money—paper. The stage is now set; monetary order is of the utmost importance. Conditions are deteriorating, and the solutions proposed to date have only made things worse. Although the solution is readily available to us, powerful forces whose interests are served by continuation of the present system cling tenaciously to a monetary system that no longer has any foundation. The time at which there will be no other choice but to reject the current system entirely is

fast approaching. Although that moment is unknown to us, the course that we continue to pursue will undoubtedly hurtle us into a monetary abyss.

10. The City of New Philadelphia, Illinois, does not exist.

When, at 3:35 p.m. on Saturday, October 15, 1983, Lou Dobrydnia and her friend the assistant coach, on their way back to Peoria from the field hockey game at Western Macomb University, passed the historical marker at New Philadelphia, Illinois, Lou was not feeling well enough to attend to its words. Come to think of it, on previous trips to and from Macomb to play field hockey, she had never been able to, from her moving car, read the text below the heading "New Philadelphia." Therefore, Lou did not know that New Philadelphia, Illinois, no longer existed.

Before the Civil War, Free Frank McWorter had saved enough money, in part by selling lots in New Philadelphia, to buy his wife's freedom and then his own. At its largest, the town had a population of 160. However, when the railroad bypassed it, the town eventually disappeared, becoming farmland with a two-sided historical marker rather than people.

11. The first victims of botulism arrive at Peoria hospitals.

At 5:00 p.m. on Saturday, October 15, 1983, Dewey Spore took his wife, Sande, to the Saint Francis Medical Center emergency room just north of downtown Peoria, Illinois.

At 6:00 p.m., Jan-Paul Peavler drove Linda to the same emergency room. As they drove, Linda was astonished to realize that she had no clear idea where her children were—in the back seat, at her mother's house, somewhere else?

At 6:00 p.m., Sande was transferred to the intensive care unit.

12. A man feels unwelcome at the Skewer Inn.

At 6:15 p.m. on Saturday, October 15, 1983, Ray Brown, standing with his 8-year-old daughter in line to be seated at the Skewer Inn watched as a man wearing a short-sleeved white shirt, presumably the owner given his confidence and propriety voice and gestures, greeted and seated the two parties in front of Ray in line. The owner did so with great crescendos and decrescendos of welcoming words and with tooth-showing smiles of gratitude and comradeship.

When Ray Brown and his daughter advanced to first in line, the owner did not meet Ray's eyes and did not say anything. Which did not surprise Ray. In the couple dozen times he had eaten at the Skewer Inn, Ray was used to the white people in line getting hearty welcomes while he received a reaction that could be called civil only if your definition of civil included nonverbal rudeness. Ray decided this would be his last trip to the Skewer Inn.

He ordered and ate a patty melt sandwich.

13. At the hospital and at home, the situation deteriorates.

At 7:00 p.m. on Saturday, October 15, 1983, at Saint Francis Medical Center in Peoria, Illinois, Linda Peavler was transferred to the intensive care unit.

At 7:30, both Sande Spore and Linda were on respirators, their condition critical. Although the cause of their condition was not clear, physicians included botulism as among the possibilities.

Four months earlier, Saint Francis had broken ground on a $47 million, seven-story addition to the medical center. The building would house a new emergency department, five intensive care units, radiology department, main lobby, coffee shop, patient registration, shuttle lobby, central supply, thirty-six-bed cardiac stepdown unit, thirty-six-bed medical nursing unit, and inpatient/outpatient recovery rooms for surgery. But it was far from complete on October 15, 1983.

14. Health investigators ponder the evidence.

At 8:00 p.m. on Saturday, October 15, 1983, the Peoria City/County Health Department, in consultation with the Illinois State Health Department, began investigating the Skewer Inn, but determined the existing evidence did not warrant closing the restaurant or making its name public.

After speaking with Dewey Spore, public health investigators ask his permission to retrieve from the garbage can beside the Spores' garage the foil in which Sande's leftover patty melt had been wrapped.

15. More people suffer at home.

At 11:17 p.m., on Saturday, October 15, 1983, Sheila Whitfield arrived at Peoria, Illinois' Methodist Medical Center emergency room complaining of nausea, dizziness, double vision, exhaustion, and difficulty breathing. A physician examined her and told her to go home and to return if her symptoms got worse.

John Mason vomited periodically throughout the night, using the hall bathroom rather than the one off of the master bedroom so he would not disturb his wife and eventually moving from their bedroom to the couch in the living room.

Sunday, October 16, 1983

New York City

1. Mayor Ed Koch will work out the details later.

At 8:00 a.m. Eastern Standard Time, 9:00 a.m. Atlantic Standard Time, on Sunday, October 16, 1983, in Santo Domingo, capital of the Dominican Republic, Santo Domingo Mayor José Francisco Peña Gómez, on the last morning of what José described to his aides and several local reporters, off the record, as "un poco de turismo político por parte del gran fanfarrón" (or "gran pendejo," depending on his mood), Mayor Gómez was attempting to nail to the wall the ass of New York City Mayor Ed Koch.

José's requests to purchase used equipment of various types had met with good results from Italian Prime Minister Bettino Craxi, Swedish Prime Minister Olof Palme, and French President François Mitterrand. Last May, Mayor Gómez had achieved more modest results from Mayor Koch—five used garbage trucks for $5,000 each.

Now, after a day of sightseeing at which José had arranged for cheering crowds holding banners with Ed's picture and sick-making words like "Welcome, Mr. Mayor" and "We Love Mr. Koch" and a luxurious dinner in Ed's honor at which he was given the keys to the city, and with this motorcade to the city center getting ready to begin and more crowds and banners already visible, Ed was slipping out of every attempt by Mayor Gómez to grasp him.

Used equipment, *used* equipment. Equipment that they'd *pay* for. That was all Mayor Gómez was seeking. He could barely imagine the great heaps of used equipment lying in lots scattered throughout New York City. Yet every time Mayor Gómez mentioned another deal, Mayor Koch would smile and say, "We'll get into the details later."

As the motorcade started to roll, Mayor Gómez said, quite accurately, "You never see this kind of love in New York, I don't believe."

Mayor Koch smiled and started to rise from his seat, preparatory to sticking his head out of the roof of the car.

Mayor Gómez grabbed Mayor Koch's scrawny arm through the sleeve of his gray suit jacket and squeezed. "I can arrange for these people to hate you just as much as do the citizens of New York City."

Mayor Koch smiled, made a patting motion of placation with his free hand, and jerked his other arm loose with an ease that made Mayor Gómez grind his teeth.

In Colonial City, the motorcade deposited the two fellow mayors in back of a stage with red, white, and blue (conveniently, the colors of both the Dominican Republic and United States of America flags) bunting set up in front of the Catedral de Santa Mariá de la Encarnación, the first cathedral in the Americas. As Mayor Gómez drifted a few steps from Mayor Koch, an on-site aide approached Mayor Gómez, who muttered to his aide, "*New York Times*?" Yes, he was assured. "New York *Daily News*?" Another yes. "*New York Post*?" Yes again.

On stage, the mayors smiled, joined hands, and raised their arms to the cheering crowd. They stepped to their separate lecterns, and Mayor Gómez began. Speaking in English, he thanked Mayor Koch for the visit, for New York City's dedication to the welfare of those from the Dominican Republic who lived in that great metropolis, and for the mayor's personal friendship.

"And," he said, "I would like to further and especially thank Mayor Koch for personally promising to sell to the city of Santo Domingo *two* tractors and *twenty* trucks!"

As the audience applauded, Mayor Koch, beaming, said into his microphone, "We'll get into the details later."

2. Pretending to be the son of actor Sidney Poitier, a young man experiences the elegant Upper East and Upper West sides of Manhattan.

At 8:45 a.m. on Sunday, October 16, 1983, from his townhouse on 72nd Street between Madison and Park Avenues on the Upper East Side of Manhattan, Osborn Elliott, former editor-in-chief of *Newsweek* magazine and current dean of the Columbia University Graduate School of Journalism, called his friend John Jay Iselin, former national affairs editor of *Newsweek* and current president of WNET channel 13, New York City's public television station, at John's townhouse on 96th Street and Columbus Avenue on the Upper West Side of Manhattan. Both had attended Harvard, but at different times, Osborn being nine years John's senior.

Osborn asked Jay if his daughter Josephine, a student at Harvard, and a friend of Osborn's daughter Dorinda, also a student at Harvard, might be home.

John found this an odd question, given that the fall semester was in progress and so naturally, Josephine would be on campus, and besides, what would his friend Osborn want from John's daughter? Yet he only said, no, she was at school.

Osborn explained that he had tried to call his daughter without success and was hoping to reach Josephine as the next best source of the information he sought. And he began this tale:

The previous morning, a rather distraught-seeming young man had appeared at their door, giving his name as David Poitier, saying he was a friend of Dorinda at Harvard, that he had just been mugged, and that he had no money or identification or place to stay until his father, the famous actor Sidney Poitier, arrived in New York the next day. As the young man was telling this story, Osborn was joined at the door by his wife, more precisely his second wife, Inger McCabe Elliott, founder of China Seas, a company that provided batik fabrics from Indonesia to exclusive designers and a handful of celebrities.

Osborn and Inger glanced at each other and, almost as one, invited David in. That day, David told Osborn stories about the social circle at Harvard and about life with his famous father. Osborn and Inger insisted that David stay the night, laid out some clothes for him to wear the next day, and gave him fifty dollars spending money.

That evening, over cheese, crackers, and wine, David mentioned a favorite restaurant where he and Dorinda enjoyed the cheese selections on the charcuterie board. The problem was that Dorinda was allergic to cheese.

Osborn and Inger's suspicions of the gregarious young man having grown overnight—a young man whom, now that Osborn thought about it, his daughter had never mentioned—Osborn moved to a room out of earshot of the young man and tried calling Dorinda again, but again got no answer. Thus, this call to his friend John, to see if his daughter Josephine might corroborate or dispute the young man's account.

John was known among his circle as a good listener, and he proved it this morning. He could have interrupted Osborn's story early on, but he understood that Osborn needed not only information, but also the assuagement of anxiety that comes from sharing an experience. When Osborn concluded with an uncharacteristically limp, "Well, what do you think?" John explained that the young man, having arrived at his door on Friday with the same story and also being offered a room for the night, had aroused John's suspicions this morning and been shown the door this morning.

"Apparently," said John, "he went right from my door to yours."

After a "No," an "I'll be damned," and a longish pause, Osborn said, "He does seem to be a very nice young man, though. Very verbal. Obviously very creative. I wonder if we should help him in some way."

Osborn and Inger decided to confront the young man. They approached his room, knocked on the door, and not waiting for a reply, opened it. Inside, the young man they knew as David Poitier was in bed, the covers reaching the middle of his bare chest. Beside him, somewhat less covered, was another bare-chested young man.

3. A new law brings some handy cash for industrious New York City children and their families.

At 1:05 p.m. on Sunday, October 16, 1983, Ramón Martinez, 9 years old, and his brother Zé (short for José), 14 years old, were leaving the A&P grocery store on 80 West End Avenue in New York City, Ramón holding two dollar bills, one quarter, one dime, and one nickel, which they had been given at the service desk in exchange for forty-nine cans they had collected on Broadway south of Columbus Circle, mostly from gutters, washed at home on 56th Street and 10th Avenue, and taken a mile north to the grocery store. Zé let Ramón hold the money because Zé recognized that Ramón was genuinely excited about this project.

Several weeks ago, Ramón's and Zé's mother, Leonora, had heard on the radio that a new law required a deposit of five cents on every container of carbonated beverages, the concept being that people would return the containers to claim their deposits rather than littering. She had told Ramón and José (she called him José, not Zé) what she had heard, and Ramón had at once wanted to collect cans, and Zé, encouraged only by a meaningful glance from his mother, had gone along. This was their second week of work.

Back home at their apartment, Ramón handed Leonora their $2.45, and the boys immediately headed back out. Ramón's announced goal for the day was twenty dollars, but based on what they had collected this morning, Zé knew that was unrealistic. He wasn't sure whether Ramón would be more disappointed to have his hopes dashed now, by Zé, or later, by their inevitable failure. In any case, they would return with some extra money, which Leonora would take with her on the bus to that same A&P to buy groceries for the three of them.

4. A man finds a perfect view on Madison Avenue.

At 2:30 p.m. on Sunday, October 16, 1983, Andre Backar set out to prove, or in any case exemplify, the adage that nothing much happens in New York City on a Sunday afternoon, especially one as bright and crisp and perfect as today. Andre was a senior vice president at E.F. Hutton and Company; a member of the Founders Club, Chairman's Club, Blue Chip Club, Doubles Club, Le Club, St. James Club, Club of Clubs (in Cologne), and Harry's Bar (in London); as well as an Honorary Consul General of the embassies of Tunisia and Turkmenistan. His birth name was Omar Ayachi Backar, but even more than his chosen first name, Andre, he liked when he was referred to as The Mayor of Madison Avenue, an honor he earned, he believed, by his habit—no, his joy—in greeting all his many acquaintances, whether royalty or commoner, by their first names, by his good cheer and fair tipping, and by his frank but always decorous admiration of pretty girls and beautiful women.

This afternoon, Andre left his gray-and-black 1980 Rolls Royce Silver Shadow double-parked on Madison Avenue, a privilege he accorded himself as the street's mayor, near the corner of 63rd Street outside Le Relais, where he, his second wife, Heather, and his E.F. Hutton colleague Samir Beydoun were shown to a miraculously empty sidewalk table, and Andre was positioned so he had an excellent view of both Heather and the sun glinting off the hood ornament of his Rolls Royce.

To each sidewalk passerby whose eyes he could catch, and to the driver whose eyes he could catch of each car inching around his double-parked Silver Shadow, Andre smiled, and to a person they smiled back, in part, Andre knew, in response to his special smile, and in part, Andre believed, because New Yorkers always smiled, especially on a day as bright and crisp and perfect as today.

5. An attorney from Vermont wants to be the guardian of a Long Island newborn, although the baby already has parents.

At 8:00 p.m. on Sunday, October 16, 1983, at Tweed's Restaurant and Buffalo Bar, an elegant and much-loved three-story Queen Anne-style structure built in 1896, in downtown Riverhead, Long Island, New York, after the waiter had served them after-dinner coffee, Lawrence Washburn, whom his family and friends called Larry, removed from his suit jacket pocket a set of vertically folded papers and, aided only minimally by the text on his papers, began telling a story to his dining companion, New York State Supreme Court Justice Frank DeLuca.

Washburn, a 47-year-old attorney who lived and practiced in Dorset, Vermont, was formerly a bond lawyer on Wall Street who had been instrumental in helping New York City keep its financial footing during the fiscal crisis of 1975 and 1976, the era of the famous *Daily News* headline, "Ford to City: Drop Dead."

While still practicing on Wall Street in December 1971, Washburn, along with Robert Byrn and Thomas Ford, brought a case against the New York City Health and Hospital Corporation in which Robert Byrn was appointed guardian ad litem (that is, guardian only for the purposes of a legal action) of an infant referred to as "Roe" as well as all unborn infants of less than twenty-four weeks gestation who were scheduled for abortion in hospitals controlled by the corporation, which comprises New York City's public hospitals. Once named guardian, Byrn, along with Ford and Washburn, asked the courts to declare the New York State law allowing for abortions unconstitutional and to permanently restrain the NYC Health and Hospital Corporation from performing abortions except when the mother's life was in jeopardy.

Now, Washburn rested both forearms on the edge of the table, leaned forward, and said, "Frank, I think we have another Byrn v NYC Health and Hospital, but with a twist."

DeLuca nodded but did not speak. By both personal and professional disposition, DeLuca tended not to reply when no question had been asked. Why should he bother? He knew that Washburn would continue with the story he had promised when scheduling the dinner, and so he did.

Two days ago, Washburn had received a call, an "anonymous tip" (DeLuca knew that Washburn had a network of kindred spirits—he himself sympathized with Washburn's causes, but somehow the idea of any kind of secret network made him shudder, in this case inwardly), about a baby born on October 11 at St. Charles Hospital in Port Jefferson (which Washburn called "Port Jeff" in talking with DeLuca, more of a North Shore cognoscenti than Washburn was) on Long Island. Washburn knew the infant's and the family's names, but didn't use them at this moment, for which DeLuca felt himself unaccountably grateful.

The infant was born with spina bifida. Her spinal sac was exposed. She had an abnormally small head. Her brain stem was malformed. Fluid had accumulated in her cranium. Her limbs were spasmodic. She couldn't close her eyes. She couldn't suck. Her rectal, bladder, leg, and sensory functions were impaired. The examining physician at St. Charles said she was at high risk for severe retardation to the point that she would not be able to interact with others in any meaningful way.

At the physician's advice, the infant was transferred to University Hospital (Washburn did not have to say "in Stony Brook"—DeLuca would know), six miles away. There, physicians and the broader care team proposed two possible courses of action.

DeLuca was surprised but still, knowing Washburn, not surprised at how infrequently Washburn consulted his papers as he spoke.

One course of care was surgery to excise a sac of fluid and nerve endings on the spine and close the opening that allowed the buildup, then implant a shunt to relieve pressure in the cranium. These surgeries, the medical record indicated, were expected to prolong the infant's life, although not to correct most of the handicaps, including mental retardation, that the condition had or would cause.

The second course of care proposed, an alternative to corrective surgery, was to administer antibiotics, which, in conjunction with good nutrition and dressing the exposed spinal sac, was intended to prevent infection.

To this point, Washburn had avoided any overt editorializing. Here, however, he pursed his lips and wagged his head slowly back and forth in the universal gesture for "what the fuck is wrong with people."

Washburn sipped his now-cold coffee. Odd, he thought, that Tweed's would allow anyone's coffee to get cold, but perhaps the waiters recognized the sensitivity of the conversation and did not want to interrupt. Washburn prided himself on always striving for the most charitable construction of the available evidence.

He returned the cup to its saucer, lifted the papers from the table, and handed them to DeLuca. "Read that."

Here is what DeLuca read:

I. This court may act to protect the infant Baby Jane Doe. (*Matter of Storar,* 52 NY2d 363; *Jehovah's Witnesses v Kings County Hosp.,* 278 F Supp 488, 390 US 598; *Matter of Cicero,* 101 Misc 2d 699; *Matter of Vasko,* 238 App Div 128; *Matter of Sampson,* 29 NY2d 900.)

II. The infant Baby Jane Doe has a reasonable chance to live a useful, fulfilled life. (*Matter of Storar,* 52 NY2d 363; *Matter of Cicero,* 101 Misc 2d 699.)

III. The infant Baby Jane Doe is in imminent danger of death as a result of the failure to render ordinary medical care and treatment notwithstanding any quality of life considerations. (*Whalen v Roe,* 429 US 589; *Prince v Massachusetts,* 321 US 158; *Jehovah's Witnesses v Kings County Hosp.,* 278 F Supp 488, 390 US 598; *Matter of Hofbauer,* 47 NY2d 648.)

IV. If the court would order similar treatment for a "normal" child, but allow it to be withheld from a child with a handicap, then this would constitute invidious discrimination on the basis of disability.

V. The discriminatory denial of treatment to Baby Jane Doe violates the common law, New York and Federal statutes and the Constitution of the United States. (*Matter of Storar,* 52 NY2d 363; *Matter of Sampson,* 65 Misc 2d 658, 37 AD2d 668, 29 NY2d 900; *Matter of Cicero,* 101 Misc 2d 699; *Matter of Vasko,* 238 App Div 128; *Jehovah's Witnesses v Kings County Hosp.,* 278 F Supp 488, 390 US 598; *Totro v State of Texas,* 625 F2d 557; *New York State Assn. for Retarded Children v Carey,* 612 F2d 644; *Roe v Wade,* 410 US 113.)

"Byrn v NYC with a twist," Washburn concluded. "You have the complaint in your hands. We need to get it in front of the right judge. Obviously, Tannenbaum would be ideal. We need to appoint a guardian ad litem. I'd like it to be me, but if not me, it could be Billy Weber."

Still not having heard a question, DeLuca did not reply. He did, however, respond in one way. He glanced at his half-full cup of coffee and decided to allow himself to finish it, knowing that he would not have to worry about the caffeine interfering with his sleep, because he would be working tonight. And so would his clerk, come to think of it.

Washington, DC

1. President Reagan assuages his aides.

At 11:04 a.m. on Sunday, October 16, 1983, from Camp David, Maryland, President Ronald Reagan spoke by telephone with Secretary of Defense Caspar Weinberger. President Reagan told Weinberger, calling him "Cap," that Bud McFarlane would be nominated tomorrow for the position of National Security Advisor rather than Weinberger's choice, Jeane Kirkpatrick. President Reagan assured Weinberger that McFarlane would have direct and regular access to the president in order to voice the conservative views that Weinberger valued and as a counterbalance to the more moderate Secretary of State George Shultz. The conversation lasted four minutes.

At 11:50 a.m., President Reagan spoke by phone with Director of the Central Intelligence Agency William Casey. President Reagan told Casey that Bud McFarlane would be nominated tomorrow for the position of National Security Advisor rather than Casey's choice, Jeane Kirkpatrick. President Reagan assured Casey that McFarlane would have direct and regular access to the president in order to voice the conservative views that Casey valued and as a counterbalance to the more moderate Secretary of State George Shultz. The conversation lasted six minutes.

At 12:07 p.m., President Reagan spoke by phone with conservative businessman Donald Kendall, Chairman of PepsiCo, Inc. President Reagan told Kendall that Bud McFarlane would be nominated tomorrow for the position of National Security Advisor rather than Kendall's choice, Jeane Kirkpatrick. President Reagan assured Kendall that McFarlane would have direct and regular access to the president in order to voice the conservative views that Kendall valued and as a counterbalance to the more moderate Secretary of State George Shultz. The conversation lasted four minutes.

At 12:18 p.m., President Reagan spoke by phone with Director of the CIA William Casey, letting him know that the president had had a positive conversation with Cap Weinberger. The conversation lasted one minute.

At 12:22 p.m., the president had a brief lunch.

At 1:15 p.m., President Reagan spoke by phone with conservative philanthropist and businessman Jacqueline (Jack) Hume, president of Basic Vegetables. President Reagan told Hume that Bud McFarlane would be nominated tomorrow for the position of National Security Advisor rather than Hume's choice, Jeane Kirkpatrick. President Reagan assured Hume that McFarlane would have direct and regular access to the president in order to voice the conservative views that Hume valued and as a counterbalance to the more moderate Secretary of State George Shultz. The conversation lasted five minutes.

The president did not speak with Jeane Kirkpatrick, whom the president had heard felt that her nomination had been blocked by Secretary George Shultz, was angry that the president planned to offer her a newly created foreign policy advisor position that she perceived as an empty and insulting gesture of conciliation, and she planned to reject any such offer.

At 1:58 p.m., Ronald and Nancy Reagan boarded a Marine helicopter, and by 2:30 p.m., they were in the second-floor residence of the White House, where, both settled into armchairs, Nancy said, "Ronnie, you are the most powerful man in the world. You can put any person in any position you want them in. If they're a little miffed, so what? They will always be on your side no matter what. I mean, what are they going to do, support John Glenn?"

"Well," Ron said, "after tonight's gala they might."

That night was the Washington, DC, premier of the movie version of *The Right Stuff.* The film's showing would be followed by a party at a huge airplane hangar at National Airport. The event was widely considered in political circles to be an opportunity to boost former astronaut and current Senator John Glenn, depicted heroically in the movie, as a presidential candidate in 1984. The only prominent Republican expected to be present was American Film Institute President Charleton Heston.

2. An anecdote about being left-handed doesn't quite work.

At 7:16 p.m. on Sunday, October 16, 1983, in the Hillandale Forest neighborhood of Adelphi, Maryland, ten miles north of the White House, four days after his 62nd birthday, Roland Edward Nairn, Jr., whose nickname was Lefty, heard a shout from the street outside his home. The shout, thought Lefty, must have been loud at its source, considering that Lefty's home was behind a bulwark of flowering dogwoods (not flowering at the moment, but still quite leafy), and a lawn that while far from grand put at least three hundred feet between Lefty's front window and the curb. However, pedestrians were rare on the sidewalk-less street, and more importantly, Lefty was a member of the one-year-old—its anniversary was yesterday—Hillandale Neighborhood Watch Network, which comprised 143 block organizations and more than 1,600 households. The motto of the network, printed on posters at yesterday's anniversary celebration, held at the nearby Naval Weapons Research Center, was, "A nosy neighbor is a good neighbor."

Lefty called the relatively new 911 emergency dispatch number, and when, four minutes later, he saw the Mars lights, he advanced to the end of his driveway to witness the situation, which was two police officers handcuffing a truly huge man who, clearly inebriated, was making unintelligible explanations to the officers.

Once the man was, with some difficulty, inserted into the back seat of the police sedan, Lefty advanced to within a few steps of the car.

Officer Martin Douglas, who, with Montgomery County Police Chief Bernard Crooke, had attended yesterday's celebration, said, "Hey, Lefty. Were you the one who called this in?"

"Yes, sir," said Lefty. "Thanks for getting here so fast."

"Whatever we can do for the Hillandale Neighborhood Watch. Say, Lefty, I don't think you know Boris here." He gestured toward his partner, who, now that Lefty studied him, appeared to be almost as huge as the man they had arrested, staring dolefully straight ahead in the back seat. "Officer Boris Stendak, this is Lefty Nairn."

"Hiya, sir," said Boris.

Martin continued, "Lefty here is our local war hero. Tell him, Lefty, tell him how you got your nickname."

Lefty wasn't wild about being asked to tell this story. Not that he wasn't proud. In March of 1945, Lefty, then a staff sergeant stationed in Horham, flew in B-17 bomber crew runs over Germany. Lefty was a togglier, the man who armed and released the bombs over their targets.

On March 21, during Lefty's tenth mission, he was hit by flak in his left arm. Even with this injury, Lefty maintained his post and dropped his load at the required moment. For this feat, Lefty was recognized with the Air Medal, Distinguished Flying Cross, and Purple Heart.

The punchline of the story, a punchline that Lefty had been using for almost forty years now, was this: "German intelligence must have known everything if they even knew I was left-handed."

It's not that the punchline didn't get a positive reaction—chuckles, a bit of laughter, expressions of awe. And the punchline had a bit of unstated self-praise, as if Lefty's will had managed to overcome German intelligence.

Still, Lefty always found himself thinking that a better story and a better punchline would be this: "The flak hit me in the *right* arm because German intelligence was too dumb to realize I was *left*-handed." That would have better symmetry, would play better, almost like the figure of speech called antimetabole, a term Lefty had looked up some years back.

3. President Reagan's call to the victorious Baltimore Orioles is a case study in intrapsychic communication.

At 7:31 p.m., on Sunday, October 16, 1983, President Reagan, who, with Nancy, had been eating dinner while watching the last innings of what turned out to be the final game of the baseball World Series (referred to as "World" despite its teams all being affiliated with cities in the United States of America), interrupted his dinner in the White House residence to speak on the phone with the Commissioner of Major League Baseball and with the owner, general manager, manager, and series Most Valuable Player from the winning Baltimore Orioles, which was practically the hometown Washington, DC, team, the Orioles' home field of Camden Yards being only forty miles from the White House.

Edward Bennett Williams (owner of the Baltimore Orioles): "Hello, Mr. President. I'm sorry you missed this game, Mr. President. We have to get you back."

Ronald Reagan: "I've been sitting here watching on TV. When I was at your game, in the seventh inning and you were leading, and then you lost, I thought you'd never let me back into the ballpark again."

Williams: "Anytime you want to come, we'd love to have you at our park. I'm sorry you missed this great series in Philadelphia. It was magnificent baseball."

From 1976 to 1977, Edward Bennett Williams, Democrat, high-profile attorney with clients from Frank Sinatra to the *Washington Post* (during the Watergate scandal, no less), part-owner of the Washington Redskins professional football team, and sole owner of the Baltimore Orioles, was a member of a body called the President's Foreign Intelligence Advisory Board. Ed's fellow members included the actress, socialite, editor, playwright, and former Republican Congresswoman Clare Luce Booth; wealthy former Governor of Texas John Connally; head of Motorola Bob Galvin; and co-founder of Polaroid Ed Land.

Not long after assuming the office of the presidency in 1977, Jimmy Carter found out about this group's existence and asked several mostly rhetorical questions: What do these people do? Don't we already have a state department and a department of defense with tens of thousands of staff? Aren't these VIPs just going to lobby me for their pet projects?

So President Carter abolished the President's Foreign Intelligence Advisory Board. And here is how he—or in any case, one of his staff, but the buck always stops at the top—did it: He sent each member a mimeographed letter telling him or her that he'd abolished the committee, and attached to the letter an application for unemployment insurance.

In 1980, Williams was, no one's surprise, a delegate to the Democratic National Convention. Faced with the choice of being a delegate for President Carter or supporting an open convention, which would allow Senator Edward Kennedy to challenge Carter for the nomination, Williams hesitated not a moment before deciding to support the latter.

After Ronald Reagan defeated Jimmy Carter and took office on January 20, 1981, one of his first acts was to restore the President's Foreign Intelligence Advisory Board and to reinstate Edward Bennett Williams as a member.

Reagan: "Is this Hank Peters? Congratulations."

Hank Peters (General Manager of the Orioles): "Thank you sir. This is a great organization and a great team and that's why we won. Good people. We're proud of everyone."

Rick Dempsey (Orioles catcher): "Mr. President, you go tell the Russians that we're having a good time over here playing baseball."

Reagan: "Congratulations, Rick, on being the Most Valuable Player."

Dempsey: "It was a pleasure talking to you."

Reagan: "Well, it was a pleasure talking to you."

Rick Dempsey described himself as a "blue-collar catcher, down there in the trenches with the fans, fighting and scrapping just to break even." When Dempsey was acquired in 1976, Orioles manager Earl Weaver refused to play him, until Hank Peters intervened. From that point on, said Dempsey, "Weaver tried to humiliate me every day. When he got tired of yelling at the pitchers, he came looking for me. Every single day, he pounded on me as hard as anyone's ever pounded me. He always said things to me so that the pitchers and other players could hear him." The Orioles' first-year manager Joe Altobelli, however, "Gives us a little praise and stays off our backs. Joe's a smiler. And we won the Series."

Joe Altobelli (manager of the Orioles): "Mr. President, we met in May on the South Lawn for the Little League baseball game when you named the month of May National Amateur Baseball Month. It's just awfully nice of you to call. It's a little difficult to hear you, but I thank you for calling on such a big day for us. We really appreciate it. After we met, I would never miss a Ronald Reagan movie on television."

Reagan: "Joe, I thought Eddie Murray's two home runs were terrific. Thirty-three was my number when I played football. I just knew it was going to be his day."

The scholarship on the effect of praise in conversation is vast. Yet, it focuses almost exclusively on praise as interpsychic—more specifically, the effects of different types of praise on the person who receives it.

Largely lacking in the literature is the phenomenon of praise as an exclusively intrapsychic phenomenon. Michael Yeomans, Maurice E. Schweitzer, and Alison Wood Brooks, in their paper "The Conversational Circumplex: Identifying, prioritizing, and pursuing informational and relational motives in conversation," which appeared in the April 2022 issue of *Current Opinion in Psychology 2022*, offer many examples of recently studied conversational behaviors they classify as intrapsychic, including backhanded compliments, prosocial lying, name dropping, and hiding failures.

However, they characterize these as resulting from the quick decisions required by pressure inherent in conversation and, in many if not most cases, "errors." Perhaps because those studying the phenomenon of praise have not studied the case of the presidential congratulatory phone call to the winning team through 1983, or perhaps because the authors have not spent much time in competitive venues such as business, politics, and sports, or perhaps because they have skillfully managed to avoid conversational manifestations of the competition in academia, no studies have been done on praise as a rhetorical stalking horse for reflexive statements of self-worth—in this case, a statement praising a person not present being a means of saying, "I played football and the fact that I had the same number as the person I am praising may play some part in his success"—

that are so complete they transcend the need for any reaction by the nonentity who is on the receiving end.

Bowie Kuhn (Commissioner of baseball): "Mr. President, you are really great to call, and we appreciate it a lot. It's been—well, for you to come to a game and to follow it as you have on television—thank you on behalf of all of us."

Ed Williams thought that Bowie Kuhn was a buffoon. "What do you think it does to me," he said, "when we get the following letter [from the commissioner's office]: 'We have received word that on an Oriole telecast of August 30, one of the announcers said to the other in discussing the answer to a baseball trivia quiz, 'I'll bet you a necktie.' And the other replied, 'So long as it's only a ten-dollar tie." We get a letter from the baseball establishment saying, 'We are trying to maximize the distance between baseball and gambling." They sent it to [General Manager Hank] Peters and Peters calls me. I thought some nut stole the stationery from the commissioner's office." On November 1, 1982, the owners voted not to renew Kuhn's contract, although he had not yet left his position.

At 10:40 p.m. on Sunday, October 16, 1983, the president and First Lady retired to the Lincoln Bedroom for the evening.

Peoria, Illinois

1. A resident of Dwight, Illinois, is admitted to a hospital in Peoria.
At 3:21 a.m. on Sunday, October 16, 1983, Barbara Clapp, 53, of Dwight, Illinois, was admitted to Methodist Medical Center in Peoria and listed in serious condition.

2. An acceptable work of public art makes its way to the Peoria Civic Center.
At 6:40 a.m. on Sunday, October 16, 1983, on Washington Street in downtown Peoria, Illinois, a large, uncovered flatbed truck, pilot cars ahead and behind, crept east on the 0.8 mile trip from Van Buskirk Construction Company to the plaza in front of the newly built Peoria Civic Center on SW Jefferson Street.

On the truck, visible to the two pedestrians walking home in two different directions, one from a bar called The Judge's Chambers and the other from a bar called Club El Dorado, and four drivers heading to work at soon-to-open restaurants, was a sculpture, uncovered, fifty-one feet and nine inches long, twenty-six feet high, and four feet wide painted in a matte black and forming a large, simple hook resting at an angle.

The work was conceived by the minimalist sculptor Ronald Bladen, whose public works, before this one, consisted of simple, flat surfaces. Bladen, after visiting Peoria, said that he wanted the sculpture to capture the city's industry—which was the manufacture of tractors, steel, bourbon, and beer—and the bend in the Illinois River, which was visible to people in Bureau Junction and perhaps Hennepin, and of course on a map of the state of Illinois, but would not have been visible to Bladen or to people in Peoria or its outlying communities. The piece, titled Sonar Tide, was Bladen's last public commission.

Bladen was the second name among three finalists chosen for Peoria's commission. First was the sculptor Richard Serra, who proposed a minimalist work sixty-four feet tall, consisting of two slabs of weathering steel, sometimes called corten steel. Weathering steel does not require paint; rather, over a relatively short time, exposed to the air and elements, it forms a dark-brown coating that has the color and texture of rust, but actually functions to resist rust. In Serra's proposed work, one slab of steel leaned against a larger slab of steel, a rough weld at the intersection. The two slabs were to be mounted on a cracked foundation.

When a model of the work, covered by a mauve fabric, was placed on the conference table at which sat members of the Civic Center Authority, and when the fabric was removed, no words were spoken for three minutes.

3. A man tries to cry for help, but fails.

At 6:45 a.m. on Sunday, October 16, 1983, in his home on Elmhurst Street in Peoria, John Mason fell off the toilet. On the floor, he found himself only barely able to move his arms and legs. He tried to call for his wife, but he was unable to make a sound. Eventually, he crawled back to the couch.

4. Sheila Whitfield gets a phone call from the hospital that sent her home.

At 9:05 a.m. on Sunday, October 16, 1983, in the Bradley University dorm room of Sheila Whitfield and her roommate, Laura Trenton, the telephone rang. Laura answered, listened, said Sheila could not come to the phone, listened, and called out to Sheila, "It's Methodist Hospital. They want to send an ambulance for you." After hanging up the phone, Laura said, "Fuck this, we're going," and drove Sheila to the emergency department of Saint Francis rather than Methodist, where she was admitted and subsequently listed in serious condition.

5. Lou Dobrydnia plays with words while her eyes are closed.

At 10:30 a.m. on Sunday, October 16, 1983, at her apartment on North Underhill Street in Peoria, Illinois, Lou Dobrydnia, wearing gym shorts and a t-shirt, lay on her back. She lay on top of the bed covers rather than under them because she imagined the covers' weight would feel massive. She lay with her head on three pillows to help fend off dizziness and nausea. She kept her eyes closed because of the distortions she saw when they were open.

Lou's roommate, Gwen, approached the open doorway and watched Lou for a moment. It was impossible to imagine Lou immobilized by anything. Even now, she looked only like she had paused in the performance of one hundred fifty sit-ups. Lou was long and taut and the most physically present person Gwen had ever seen. At the same time, she was the calmest person; even while watching Lou play field hockey or basketball, while moving as quickly as it seemed any person could move, she seemed completely still.

Without opening her eyes, Lou said, "About that chest," and lifted her arm to point to the tall chest of drawers against the opposite wall.

"The chest?"

"The problem with that chest," Lou said and paused, "is that I feel like it's lying on my chest." Again she paused. "Get it? A chest on my chest."

"Ah," Gwen said.

"Kind of funny," Lou said.

"Kind of funny," Gwen said.

"And when I open my eyes and see it," Lou continued, "on the bottom it looks okay, but on the top it's blurry." She tried to take a deep breath but a shallow one had to suffice, then opened her eyes and looked at Gwen. "You too," she said.

"Me too?"

"You too. The bottom of your face is fine, but the top, it's a blurry mess." She closed her eyes again. "Nothing personal."

6. People eat lunch at the Skewer Inn.

Between 12:00 p.m. and 1:00 p.m. on Sunday, October 16, 1983, Margaret Riley ate a patty melt sandwich. Laurie Fryman ate a patty melt sandwich. Cincy Clasen ate a club sandwich that was placed on her plate with tongs that had been used to place onions on Laurie Fryman's patty melt.

7. Health department decides to allow the Skewer Inn to remain open.

At 1:50 p.m. on Sunday, October 16, 1983, at the Northwoods Mall, representatives of the health department spoke with the owners of the Skewer Inn about the restaurant's patty melt sandwiches. According to the restaurant, the only foodstuffs used in the sandwiches or served with the sandwiches, that had not already been consumed were the pickles, which were stored in large plastic containers. The restaurant had three containers of pickles on hand. The owners gave one container to the health department officials for analysis and agreed to not serve any pickles from the other two.

On their way back to the office, Thomas F. Jackamore, acting director of the Peoria City and County Health Department, revisited a topic he had discussed yesterday with John W. Parker, PhD, associate director of the Health Department: whether the Health Department should make public the name of the restaurant involved.

Jackamore said, "You draw a fine line between protection of a community and being a stormtrooper."

To the media, Jackamore and Parker said the following: The pickles are being examined. Of the people hospitalized, three ate pickles, two did not, and one may have; those who did not eat pickles may have ingested pickle juice absorbed by the sandwich. At this time, they would not name the restaurant but the potentially dangerous food items all were either consumed or, in the case of the pickles, put aside. Pickle samples were sent to the national Centers for Disease Control in Atlanta, along with specimens from some victims; results were expected in two to four days. Patients were being treated with an innovative drug flown in from Washington DC; treatment required one vial to be injected into a vein and one to be injected into a muscle. Jackamore said that "at the present time, we do not feel" the restaurant was at fault; he noted that proper food preparation cannot stop the bacteria. Parker said, "We have had good cooperation with the restaurant." Jackamore said that if people had symptoms such as blurred vision, dizziness, difficulty breathing, and nausea, they should go to their local hospital's emergency room.

8. "Authorities suspect the pickle."

At 3:20 p.m. on Sunday, October 16, 1983, Cliff Caldwell, a reporter at WQRX radio station in Peoria, Illinois, put down the phone and intoned to the room at large, "Authorities suspect the pickle." Cat Kouns, a 22-year-old clerk at the station, stifled a laugh. Later, Cat and a friend were at the coffee machine. Cat said, her voice deep and radio-serious, "Authorities suspect the pickle," and they both started laughing, then looked up and saw Caldwell approaching.

9. Radio stations broadcast the botulism story.

At 3:30 p.m. on Sunday, October 16, 1983, Peoria radio stations began broadcasting news of a botulism outbreak, naming the restaurant involved as the Skewer Inn and the likely source of botulism as pickles served with patty melt sandwiches.

Twenty minutes later, the owner of the Skewer Inn picked up the ringing cordless phone from its cradle on the front counter next to the cash register. He heard a muffled voice, or perhaps more than one voice. The ambient sound of the restaurant always made distinguishing voices on the telephone difficult. He said, "Yes, hello?" One voice, deeper than a typical woman's voice but higher than a typical man's voice—perhaps, the owner thought, a teenage boy—said, "Can I get an order of pickles to go?" followed by a gust of giggles from the caller and other voices in the background.

Listening to the report in the car on the way to visit her husband, John, in the hospital, Leslie Mason said out loud, "You morons, it can't be the pickles. John didn't have any pickles."

10. A decision: Skewer Inn or Denny's.

At 5:30 p.m. on Sunday, October 16, 1983, in Metamora, Illinois, having just finished decorating her brother-in-law and his future bride's wedding cake, Jerra Nimmo decided to go out to dinner. Planning to go to the Skewer Inn, Jerra, her mother, and her baby got off Route 74 at the War Memorial Drive Exit and were about to take the left exit to Scenic Drive, which would take them to the mall, when Jerra's mother spotted the saturated yellow sign of Denny's and suggested the family go there instead. They did.

11. More people with symptoms of botulism are admitted to Peoria hospitals.

At 6:00 p.m. on Sunday, October 16, 1983, Beverly Ritter, 45, of Washington, Illinois, was admitted to Saint Francis Medical Center and listed in serious condition. At 6:30 p.m. on Sunday, October 16, 1983, Clifford Yakley, 73, and Viola Yakley, 64, of Davenport, Iowa, ninety-eight miles from Peoria, were admitted to Methodist Medical Center and listed in serious condition.

At 6:40 p.m., after John Mason's wife had coaxed a nod from John Mason resulting in a phone call from John's wife to his doctor's answering service, and after his doctor had phoned back twenty minutes later, and after John's wife had driven him to the Saint Francis Medical Center emergency entrance, and after John Mason was admitted to the intensive care unit and placed on a respirator, John signed a consent form with an X, which was all he could do by way of signing, for administration of the antitoxin that had been flown in from Washington, DC.

12. Lou finally goes to the hospital only to be sent home.

At 7:05 p.m. on Sunday, October 16, 1983, having just heard a news report on a local radio station, Gwen, looked again through the open bedroom door at Lou. She didn't really need the news story as a catalyst; she had been looking in on Lou every few minutes all day, bringing her water, which Lou drank, and food, which Lou only nibbled. Now, Lou was still lying on top of the bed covers. The room was chilly, but Lou said, more with gestures than words, that she didn't want any weight on her chest. Gwen said Lou's name, and Lou opened her eyes, but let the lids fall closed again.

"Lou, Lou, on the radio just now, they talked about the Skewer Inn, they even mentioned the patty melt sandwich. You have the symptoms. I think you have botulism."

Gwen drove Lou to the Saint Francis Medical Center emergency room, where they spent twenty minutes in a waiting room crowded with, Gwen discerned from overheard conversations, people worried they had botulism. Finally shown to an examination room, and having waited another twenty minutes, Lou's door was opened, not preceded by a knock, by a young white male physician in a wrinkled suit, ill-fitting in the way suits are ill-sitting on young men who have not yet learned how to buy clothes. The physician said to Gwen, "And you are…?" When it became apparent it would take Gwen more than a nanosecond to formulate her replay, the physician turned to Lou, lying on the examination table, and asked her symptoms.

"I'm having trouble breathing," Lou said, with obvious difficulty.

The physician umm-hmmed.

"I have this weird headache."

"How bad does it hurt?"

"It's not so much that it hurts bad, but it hurts weird. Like my brain is bruised. And on fire. I've never felt anything like it."

The physician asked what else.

"My vision is like I'm looking through a prism."

The physician umm-hmmed.

"I feel faint."

The physician asked, "Did you faint?"

"Well, no."

"Then you're not faint, you're lightheaded. What else?"

"I feel nauseous."

"Did you vomit?"

"Well, no."

"Then you're not nauseous, you're queasy."

The physician told Lou she may have the flu or she may have botulism. He told her to go home and return if her symptoms worsened.

Goddammit, Lou thought, why is it I feel cowed by a doctor who I could take down in about three seconds?

13. The Skewer Inn receives another phone call.

At 8:00 p.m. on Sunday, October 16, 1983, the Skewer Inn phone rang again. It was Jackamore from the Public Health Department. "We'd like you to consider voluntarily closing the restaurant tomorrow. If you don't close voluntarily, we will need to make this official."

14. The Peoria *Journal Star* makes two decisions.

At 9:00 p.m. on Sunday, October 16, 1983, from his position on the copy desk of the Peoria *Journal Star*, Mike Major overheard a discussion between two editors. Do we name the restaurant? Not if the Health Department won't. Do we run it on the front page? Not if we don't want to alienate a regular advertiser.

An hour later, Mike was handed copy to edit, written by Ray Long. Mike was glad that Ray was reporting this story. His copy was always clean. And Mike made no changes to the lede: "Suspected botulism—possibly from a local restaurant's pickles—left six people hospitalized over the weekend." Alas, in the rush to write the article and revisions to keep the article current, the third paragraph, which named the victims, listed seven people rather than six, and omitted Barbara Clapp, who had been admitted before dawn that morning. While Ray had been writing the article and while Mike was copyediting the article and while it was being laid out and placed on page A6 and plates were being made, Beverly Ritter, 45, of Washington, Illinois; Tracy Dearing, 23, of Peoria; Anne Hiter, 72, of East Peoria; and Marie Schwenk, 53, of London Mills, Illinois, were admitted to Peoria hospitals. All were listed in serious condition, except for Marie Schwenk, who was listed in critical condition.

15. A lot of people eat at the Skewer Inn and a lot of people eat patty melts.

From Friday, October 14, 1983, to Sunday, October 16, between nineteen hundred and twenty-four hundred people ate at the Skewer Inn restaurant on the lower level of the Northwoods Mall, located on the Montgomery Wards side between Coach House Gifts and Kinney Shoes. Of those, forty-five people ate patty melts.

Monday, October 17, 1983

New York City

1. If they can do it, we can too.

At 9:00 a.m. on Monday, October 17, 1983, in his office on the thirty-eighth floor at 51 West 52nd Street in midtown Manhattan, Walter R. Yetnikoff, president of the CBS Records Group, was, as he was wont to do, thinking out loud on the telephone, leaning back, feet on his desk, shirt open to expose three buttons' worth of chest hair cascading in a continuous stream starting with his full beard—this morning with a reporter from the *New York Times,* an appointment with whom had been set to coincide with a press release from CBS Records announcing that it was actively seeking to acquire "one or more major record companies."

What did Walter think about the recently announced intent to merge by CBS Records' biggest competitor, Warner Communications, with Polygram Records, a deal that would give Warner greater market share than CBS Records, which owns the Columbia record label?

"I never thought this sort of thing was legal."

And if it is approved?

"If it is legal, we'll do it too."

Which record companies would CBS Records want to buy?

"Obviously, it must have a certain level of revenues to make sense."

Like RCA or Capitol?

"Yep, they would fit into that category."

How actively are you pursuing a deal?

"Today's announcement is a wedding invitation. It's a serious statement of current intentions. It promises to change the worldwide competitive landscape of the record business in significant ways."

2. Justice DeLuca gets to work.

At 9:30 a.m. on Monday, October 17, 1983, in the dominating stone and pillared structure that was the New York State Supreme Court of Suffolk County at 1 Court Street in Riverhead, in the region called North Fork in Long Island, New York City, Justice Frank DeLuca assigned Washburn's petition to Justice Melvyn Tanenbaum, who had run for this office the previous November as the nominee of the Right-to-Life Party.

Justice Tanenbaum appointed as guardian ad litem William E. Weber, known by his friends as Billy, who previously was court-appointed attorney for the man accused of the "Amityville Horrors" murders.

Justice Tanenbaum received Billy's petition, William E. Weber, as Guardian ad Litem for Baby Jane Doe, Appellant, v. Stony Brook Hospital et al., Respondents, and scheduled a hearing for the coming Thursday, October 20, 1983.

3. C. Douglas Dillon steps down from chairmanship of the Met.

At 10:00 a.m. on Monday, October 17, 1983, in the Metropolitan Museum of Art on 1000 Fifth Avenue, covering the space on the west side of the avenue between 80th and 84th Streets, in a boardroom on the second floor, a room not visible on any public map of the museum, its gleaming mahogany and mixed exotic woods fifty-person oval table alongside a window the length of the room overlooking Central Park, at a slim lectern to a group of thirty people—including some members of the executive committee of the museum's board, the director of public relations and other administrative executives, two assistants in the museum's public relations department, three newspaper reporters, and two television reporters (without cameras)—several statements were made.

First, C. Douglas Dillon, 76 years old, announced he would step down after fourteen years as chairman of the board at the Metropolitan Museum of Art.

Douglas' mother was Anne McEldin Douglass, who was descended from the burgesses of Virginia, and his father was Clarence Dillon, co-founder of investment bank Dillon, Read & Co., and one of the richest people in the United States. After their marriage in 1908, they honeymooned in Europe, their trip paid for by a railroad line because of an event that had transpired before the marriage. Clarence had been visiting Anne at a resort near her family's home in Milwaukee, Wisconsin, and they happened to be standing one day near a railroad station. As a train approached, a St. Bernard dog walked onto the tracks and was hit by the train, the engine's cow catcher throwing the dog into Clarence's stomach. Clarence fell backward, first into his fiancée, breaking her arm, and then into a lamp post, striking his head, the injury requiring weeks of care. When he recovered, the two married, and the railroad paid for their European honeymoon as compensation. Not that Clarence and Anne couldn't have afforded to fund their own honeymoon. A year later, in Geneva, Switzerland, Douglas was born.

Douglas attended Pine Lodge School, Groton School, and Harvard College, from which he graduated in 1931, the year after his father and mother moved into a townhouse they had built at 124 East 80th Street, between Park and Lexington Avenue, two and a half blocks from Central Park and four and a half blocks from the Metropolitan Museum of Art.

In 1938, Douglas became a vice president of Dillon, Read & Co.

In 1946, Douglas became chairman of Dillon, Read & Co.

In 1950, Douglas became a trustee of the Metropolitan Museum of Art.

In 1952, Douglas was an organizer, fundraiser, and contributor for Dwight D. Eisenhower's presidential campaign.

In 1953, Douglas was appointed United States Ambassador to France.

In 1958, Douglas was appointed Under Secretary of State for Economic Growth, Energy, and the Environment.

In 1959, Douglas was appointed Under Secretary of State.

In 1961, Douglas was appointed Secretary of the Treasury.

In 1970, Douglas became president of the Metropolitan Museum of Art.

In 1972, Douglas was named chairman of the Rockefeller Foundation.

In 1977, Douglas was named chairman of the Metropolitan Museum of Art.

Over time, Douglas donated $20 million to the Metropolitan Museum of Art.

Second, C. Douglas Dillon commented on his long-time collaboration with former museum director Thomas Hoving.

In 1931, Thomas Pearsall Field Hoving was born in New York City to Walter Hoving, controlling owner of Tiffany & Company, and Mary Osgood Field, who were married on November 4, 1925, in St. Bartholomew's Church on 325 Park Avenue in New York to "a large contingent of the old Knickerbocker families, for the Fields family for generations has been prominent in the social life of New York," according to the *New York Times*.

In 1949, after attending the Buckley School. Eaglebrook School, and Exeter, Thomas graduated from the Hotchkiss School.

In 1953, Thomas graduated with a bachelor's degree from Princeton University.

In 1958, Thomas graduated with a Master of Fine Arts degree from Princeton University.

In 1959, Thomas graduated with a PhD from Princeton University.

In 1959, Thomas began to work in the medieval department of the Metropolitan Museum of Art.

In 1965, Thomas was named curator of the medieval department of the Metropolitan Museum of Art.

In 1966, Thomas was named Parks Commissioner of New York City.

In 1967, Thomas was named director of the Metropolitan Museum of Art.

Third, J. Richardson Dilworth was announced as Dillon's successor as chairman.

On June 9, 1916, J. Richardson Dilworth was born in Long Island, New York, to Edith Logan Dilworth and Dewees Wood Dilworth, who was an investment banker.

In 1938, after attending the Buckley School and St. Mark's School, Richardson graduated with a bachelor's degree from Yale University.

In 1942, Richardson graduated from Yale Law School.

In 1952, Richardson became a partner in the investment bank Kuhn, Loeb & Co.

In 1956, Richardson became a senior financial advisor to the Rockefeller family.

In 1964, Richardson and his wife, Elizabeth, gave 577 drawings and three sketchbooks by the eighteenth-century English painter George Romney to the Yale University Art Gallery in New Haven.

In 1966, Richardson also was named chairman of Rockefeller Center.

In 1981, Richardson retired from his role with the Rockefeller family.

In 1982, Richardson retired from his role as chairman of Rockefeller Center.

Fourth, Guy Philippe Henri Lannes de Montebello, Director of the Metropolitan Museum of Art, announced the following:

C. Douglas Dillon would continue to be a trustee, a member of the executive committee, and chairman of the acquisitions committee of the museum board.

The board room in which they were seated would be renamed the Douglas Dillon Boardroom.

4. Children find skulls.

At 1:20 p.m. on Monday, October 17, 1983, in the Bushwick neighborhood of Brooklyn, New York, 10-year-old Sylvia Marshaun, 11-year-old Harold Justice, and 11-year-old Martin Santos, left their school building at lunch with no intention to return that day, in part because the temperature was an unseasonal sixty degrees.

They met at one of their favorite places, a vacant lot bordered by Randolph Street and Gardner Avenue, and only vaguely aware of the bog-like smell surrounding them, engaged in one of their favorite activities: picking through the garbage routinely dumped in the lot for things that they liked and things that they needed. For Sylvia Marshaun, the things that she liked were old radios or electronic toys that she would turn into musical instruments; for Harold Justice, the things that he liked were paperback books, his treasures being the works of Donald Goines; for Martin Santos, the things that he liked were action figures missing limbs or heads, which he arranged on a rotating basis on the window ledges of the apartment; for all, the things that they needed were cans and bottles that could be cleaned and taken to the Associated supermarket, a thirty-minute walk to Hart Street, and exchanged for cash.

Today, Sylvia assumed she had hit the motherlode when she found, in a corner near the wall of a burned-out building, two boxes, both medium-sized, their corners soft from age, both with the return address of Williamsburgh Electronics, Inc. and a shipping address of Eastern District High School on Marcy Avenue, a now-vacant four-story box of a building across from the Williamsburgh branch of the Brooklyn Public Library, its windows facing the BMT Jamaica line elevated train.

Both boxes were unsealed. When Sylvia pulled back the flaps of one, she was disappointed to see not electronics but dirt. She poked around in the dirt and then called Harold and Martin over.

Eventually, laid out next to the boxes on a patch of ground they cleared for the purpose, were seven human skulls and 14 other bones of various sizes.

After a heated conference during which they weighed the likelihood of their getting in trouble if they did not take the bones to the police versus the likelihood of their getting in trouble if they did take the bones to the police, the three carried the boxes to the castle-like 83rd Precinct headquarters on the corner of Wilson and Dekalb Avenues, about a twenty-five-minute walk, only to see a sign that headquarters of the 83rd had moved to Knickerbocker Avenue and Bleecker Street, a half mile away. There, in what turned out to be a squat, unfriendly building, they deposited their boxes on the front desk, and when they told the desk sergeant what was inside, he called down a man in plain clothes and oddly wide-open eyes—not wide open in astonishment, because they were wide open when he arrived at the desk and wide open the whole time he was there—who looked inside the box, dug around with his fingers, wiped his fingers on a paper towel requested from the desk sergeant, took down their names, and thanked them as if he meant it.

5. A nominee wants to quell hostility.

At 2:40 p.m. on Monday, October 17, 1983, at the World Trade Center during a confirmation hearing before the State Senate Transportation Committee, Robert R. Kiley, nominee for chairman of the New York Metropolitan Transportation Authority, noted public frustration resulting from the many train derailments over the summer and delays caused as trains were forced to slow to a crawl when they traversed portions of track in need of repair. He suggested holding public hearings about decisions to improve the rail lines.

"If people feel involved," he said, "they are less hostile."

6. A woman gets bad news about her lawsuit.

Also at 2:40 p.m. on Monday, October 17, 1983, the phone rang in the first floor studio unit occupied by a 60-year-old woman named Ruth B. Watt. The unit was in a two-flat clapboard house in a Queens neighborhood sometimes called Southside Jamaica and sometimes called South Suicide. The house was at 145-40 120th Avenue, five blocks from the Baisley Park Houses, headquarters of Kenneth "Supreme" McGriff's Supreme Team street gang.

Ruth's attorney was on the phone, or rather, a female assistant to the attorney Ruth had most recently been handed off to, letting her know in cadence even more rapid than her most recent attorney's gallop (it seemed that each attorney spoke more quickly than the last) that, in the matter of Watt v. New York Transit Authority, the New York City Appellate Court, which, Ruth had learned, in New York was the top court while the Supreme Court was the lowest, had just ruled that she could not proceed with her claim for damages from the injury she suffered from a fall caused by a defective grating at a subway station that occurred in June 1, 1974, because she had mailed the original complaint to the Corporate Counsel of the City of New York rather than to the New York City Transit Authority.

Washington, DC

1. Two bicycle messengers don't quite make a promise to each other.
At 6:15 a.m. on Monday, October 17, 1983, Patty Styles and her boyfriend, Mitchel Frederick, having lifted their bicycles from the side-by-side wall mounts in their 450-square-foot apartment in the Mount Pleasant neighborhood of northwest Washington, DC, and having slung bicycle-messenger bags over their shoulders, made their usual admonition to one another on their way to work:

"Be safe."

"You be safe."

Because these were admonitions rather than promises, both felt relatively clear consciences about the fact that both took some pride in never having stopped for a red light. If they obeyed the traffic laws, each would make twenty dollars per day as bicycle messengers. Because they did not obey the traffic laws, each made fifty dollars per day.

2. Ronald Reagan wears light-yellow pajamas and a light-blue robe that complements the work of an interior designer who is the most powerful person in the nation.
At 6:30 a.m. on Monday, October 17, 1983, at the kitchen island in a four-bedroom, two-story brick home at 9508 Linden Avenue

in Bethesda, Maryland, Jonda Riley McFarlane graded papers on Thoreau's *Walden* from one of the high school English classes she taught, careful not to spill her coffee on the papers.

She was grading papers for two reasons: first, because they needed to be graded, and second, to project a normalcy onto such a big morning for her husband, Bud, who sat next to her, drinking coffee and eating toast, having responded to her suggestion that today might require a big breakfast by saying that he didn't think he could handle anything more than toast.

They sat quietly, backs to the sink and stove, facing the sliding glass door to the backyard, but neither looking up, Jonda from her papers nor Bud from his coffee cup. If they had looked up at the still-dark outside, they would have seen their reflections.

Jonda knew that Bud's silence was only a tiny bit of nervousness. Far more, it was the way Bud always prepared himself for an important duty.

Bud continued looking at his coffee mug, a sturdy white one with the emblem of the United States Marine Corps, the words "semper fidelis" held in the eagle's beak so tiny as to be almost undecipherable.

Bud said, the faintest of chuckles in his voice, "This job is way beyond me. They should have gotten somebody better, like Kissinger."

Jonda knew that Bud didn't really mean that, and she knew she didn't have to say that.

At 7:30, the sun still not risen but light beginning to leak over the horizon, Bud was driving on the Clara Barton Parkway along the Potomac River toward Washington. The long way, but what were they going to do if he was late, fire him?—not Bud McFarlane's usual way of looking at things, but today was not a usual day, but one he was not quite sure how to think about.

From 8:30 to 9:50 a.m., while Bud sat in the office down the hall from the corner office that Bill Clark now occupied and that Bud would move into after his appointment was announced, President

Reagan spoke with George Shultz and met with Bill Clark, James Baker, Edwin Meese, Michael Deaver, John Poindexter, and Douglas McMinn about how to announce Bud's selection as the next Assistant to the President for National Security Affairs, which was scheduled for 3:30 that afternoon.

At 10:00, Bud was called to the Oval Office. In the outer office, he was intercepted by Michael McManus, Deputy to the Deputy Chief of Staff and redirected to the West Wing Lobby, where from a sofa, Bud stared at an eighteenth-century mahogany bookcase, although the glare on its glass doors prevented him from reading the spines of the works within.

At 10:06 a.m., Bud entered the Oval Office, where Bill Clark was sitting on one side of the president's desk, President Reagan on the other side. Invited, Bud sat.

"Are you ready for this afternoon?" the president asked.

"Yes, sir," Bud said.

"Bill, you think he's ready?"

"Oh, he's ready," said Bill.

"But is he ready for this?" the president said, reaching toward his desk drawers.

From the top left drawer the president removed a flat, rectangular, item, which he placed on the desk almost near enough for Bud to reach without rising from his chair.

"The first thing," the president said, "to hang on the wall of your new office," as Bud lifted the item from the president's gleaming desktop.

The photograph was horizontally oriented, color, beautifully reproduced, carefully matted, and elegantly framed.

Stepping back:

In a largely human-centric society, we may be forgiven for first simply identifying the three people in this photograph, although their identities are only important in so far as they interact with other, more powerful elements seen around them in the picture. The people were, from left to right, Bud McFarlane, George Shultz, and Ronald Reagan.

In a society that largely assigns the value of humans by their professional roles, we may be further forgiven for next describing these humans by that indicator. At the time of the photograph, Bud McFarlane was Deputy National Security Advisor, the president's Special Representative in the Middle East responsible for Israeli-Arab negotiations, and a member of the National Security Council Deputies Committee. George Shultz was Secretary of State, a member of the president's Cabinet, and a member of the National Security Council Principals Committee. And Ronald Reagan was president of the United States of America.

Independent of and in conjunction with professional role, another initial method used by humans to judge the value and character of other humans is choice of apparel. In this photograph, Bud was wearing a white dress shirt and beige dress slacks, no suit coat or tie, which was the uniform for staff members doing before-dawn weekend work in the White House circa 1983. George Shultz was wearing the same, with the addition of a brown cardigan sweater, the uniform for before-dawn weekend work in the White House of one of higher rank than one who wore no sweater. The president was wearing light yellow pajamas, a color that Bud thought of as "sweat-stain yellow," surprisingly unwrinkled, along with an unbelted baby-blue robe with ultramarine border, and royal-blue backless slippers. His hair was sleep-tousled. This was, if not the uniform, the accepted attire of the most powerful man in the world doing pre-dawn weekend work in the White House.

We might next be moved to judge these men by their posture in the picture. Would we all not prefer to be judged by our actions than by our appearance? Bud, who we see in one-quarter profile, was seated, leaning forward, elbows on his knees, a thin sheaf of papers on top of the open manilla envelope from which the papers likely came, his right hand clutching a writing implement of some kind, staring intently at the president, not speaking, but perhaps just having spoken, perhaps to explain some point on the papers he was grasping.

George Shultz, seated on a sofa, was also leaning forward, elbows on knees, his reading glasses in both hands, staring at Bud, his posture suggesting the importance of what Bud was communicating, but his lack of document or writing implement suggesting the importance may be either passing or the information already well understood.

The president was also seated, but on the far end of the sofa, and he was leaning back, right leg crossed at the knee over the left. He was holding papers that we may assume were the twin of those Bud was holding. He was looking at Bud, and he was speaking, but his expression, a touch sleep-addled, made it difficult to infer whether he was making an observation or asking a question.

This information—the names, positions, attire, and actions—of these men, plus the darkness through the window behind them, suggested that they were discussing weighty matters. Given Bud's role at the time the photograph was taken, these matters may have involved escalating military tension in the Middle East.

Although all this information amply attests to the import of these men and this moment, in this photograph, that import falls shockingly and completely asunder to a person of less repute than these men, but of a person whose might that transcends rank, and who wields a weapon more powerful than any policy document or a top secret memo that Bud and the president may be clutching.

This person was Ted Graber.

Ted's office was in Beverly Hills on a quiet street off Rodeo Drive. The name on the door was William Haines, but Billy died in 1973, and the business was Ted's now. Although Billy's reputation as bon vivant and interior decorator to the stars remained vivid in

Hollywood, Ted was carrying on admirably, if somewhat more quietly. At least, until the morning after election day, November 4, 1980.

At that point, Ted and Nancy Reagan, having had only brief conversations, began to toss back and forth color, fabric, and furniture ideas for the family quarters, accompanied by bon mots and understanding smiles. Because that darned Jimmy Carter family wouldn't move out early, Ted and Nancy had to wait until the morning after Reagan's January 20, 1981, inauguration-night revelry to start work in earnest—such earnest that Ted moved into the White House. That work consumed them through more festivities during the president's first birthday at the White House, his 70th, after which Ted's live-in partner, Arch Case, joined Ted in spending the night, in the same room and bed, in the White House quarters that he was in the process of designing.

Nancy and Ronald Reagan having found a way to leave the governmental budget of $50,000 on residence quarters decorating in the dust, work was, if not finished—design, being organic, is never finished—at least in a state of momentary repose when the photograph with Bud, George Shultz, and the president was taken.

In the room that was the setting for this photograph, Ted's weapon was deep-sky blue. A sky-blue rug stretched from end to end of the visible floor (one can only determine it is a rug rather than wall-to-wall carpet because of Ted's known dislike of the latter), its pile looking deep enough to tickle the bare ankles of the president, the texture of that pile suggesting the undulation of nearly invisible clouds. Sky-blue floral prints crawled up and all around the sofa on which the president and George Shultz sat, and on the upholstery of the slender Victorian mahogany accent chair from which Bud leaned toward his commander in chief.

An identical sky-blue floral pattern encroached the drapery, relieved only barely because the curtains were partially drawn, revealing a sheer, powder-blue privacy curtain. From the curtain, the sky-blue floral print hopped to the wallpaper and, as wallpaper does, enveloped the room.

The darkness from the window made the interior light of the room especially brilliant and thereby the sky-blue especially saturated.

Within this environment created by Ted Graber, Bud and George Shultz looked like bland men who inexplicably wandered into the backdrop of a technicolor cartoon from the 1940s. They looked like dull mistakes, distracting irrelevancies, they looked like uncomfortable husbands waiting for their wives to try on clothes in a Beverly Hills salon whose couturier is a month away from falling out of fashion.

The president, on the other hand, bore a very different relationship to his surroundings. Far from being inharmonious, the president was as much a subject of Ted Graber's might as the rug, curtain, upholstery, and wallpaper. The sky-blue of the carpet, upholstery, and wallpaper, having seeped into the complementary blues of his robe, appeared to slide up and then strap down the president, while the electricity of the royal blue slippers—the most penetrating color of the photograph—appeared ready to send an electrical charge through his captive body.

Bud looked at the photograph. Politics only belongs in black and white, he thought, the president only belongs in black and white, and I definitely only belong in black and white. Sensing that he had probably stared at the picture longer than the president intended, Bud looked up, and the president and Bill Clark laughed.

At 10:09, the president said, "Out you go, Bill. I'm going to have a few private words with Bud. Don't worry, we won't talk about you behind your back."

When Bill Casey had left, the president turned to Bud. This position was very important, said the president, to the safety of the country, the safety of the world, and to the president, personally. He and Bud, said the president, would have a close working relationship.

The president went on to say that there were some big personalities on the national security team, as Bud well knew, but that he was confident that Bud could hold his own without ruffling too many feathers.

Bud paused to make sure the president was finished speaking, leaned forward slightly, and said, "There's no limit to what a man can do or where he can go if he doesn't mind who gets the credit." The president nodded but otherwise made no reply.

Their meeting ended at 10:19 a.m., at which time the president placed a call to Don Kendall, chairman of PepsiCo.

3. Bud McFarlane gets some reading material.

At 10:21 a.m. on Monday, October 17, 1983, back in his White House office, Bud McFarlane placed the photograph of Ronald Reagan in his pajamas face up on his desk and leaned back in his chair. A moment later, Jack Matlock entered through the open door, a sheaf of papers in his hand.

Bud knew Jack had recently been transferred from his role as Ambassador to Czechoslovakia to Soviet specialist on the National Security Council. Short, round-faced, with severely receding hairline and usually an expression of comic bluster, and wearing no jacket, Jack glanced at the photograph and snorted. Saying, "Welcome to the jungle, boss," Jack dropped the papers on Bud's desk, spun around with surprising grace, and left.

Bud looked down at the top sheet. Under the National Security Council letterhead and the date, October 17, 1983, was this heading:

TOP SECRET INFORMATION
MEMORANDUM FOR ROBERT C. McFARLANE
FROM: JACK F. MATLOCK
SUBJECT: Urgent Items: Europe

Bud flipped to the last page, then back to the first, and began to read:

1. U.S.-Soviet Relations post KAL: Don Fortier and I will be working on a package of "follow-up" measures. In addition, we need to take a comprehensive look at our strategy toward the Soviets over the next 12–18 months. Specific decisions or events include: a. Possibility of major speech by President in November; b. President's meeting with Art Hartman week of October 23, and possibility of activating dialogue through him; c. A proposal by U.S. Customs to ban the import of a large number of Soviet products, which could have a major political impact. I will get a comprehensive memo to you later this week. (S)
2. Poland: A decision must be made on Shultz's recommendation that we agree to discuss the 1981 Polish debt at the October 26 Paris Club meeting and lift the ban on Polish fisheries. (S)
3. Italy: Craxi Visit: Italy's first socialist PM will be meeting the President Thursday. He has emerged as a major spokesman for Western security policies and is supportive of U.S. interests. He has launched an austerity program domestically and views the visit as very important to him. (S)

4. INF: The demonstrations in Germany over the weekend were neither as violent nor large as expected. The relative lack of success may, however, prod the protesters to resort to greater violence in the future. To assist the public campaign in support of deployments, we will be recommending that the President write his NATO colleagues urging them to publicize the upcoming decision—to be taken at the NPG ministerial meeting—to reduce nuclear stockpiles.

Their frustration is heightened by a recognition that the President is in fact successful in achieving his objectives. His defense budgets get passed; the NATO Alliance is holding; the U.S. economy is picking up. And he constantly outmaneuvers them: the President's handling of the KAL "incident" was "absolutely brilliant": it left the Soviet leaders "wallowing in the mud."

The Soviets know that we will succeed in starting INF deployments, and are convinced that the President is very likely to be reelected next year. He implied, however, that their current mood was so truculent and their prestige so much at stake that they are unable to draw the logical conclusions from these convictions.

As for the future, his parting words were that, in his opinion, the Soviets would stonewall all our proposals this fall and would have to react in some fashion to INF deployments, which would require a stonewall well into 1984. However, "about six months into the next year" they might be willing—since the domestic economy remains the priority issue for them—to reassess their stance.

Matlock Comments: Vishnevsky did most of the talking during lunch, but I pointed out repeatedly that the Soviet predicament, as he described it, was the direct result of their own actions and their own aggressive policies, and not of propaganda manipulation on our part. (He did not disagree.) I told him they could not have handled the KAL massacre worse. (He agreed.)

I stressed that, despite everything, we were still prepared to negotiate seriously .to lower arms levels and had made proposals which should interest them, if they indeed do desire a reduction of tension. (This elicited his comments implying that the Soviet leadership, at the moment at least, is incapable of considering them rationally.)

In response to his comment that the Soviet leaders are convinced that they could not deal with this Administration, I told him that Soviet actions across the board created grave doubts that we could deal with the Soviets. All Soviet actions and their propagandistic and one-sided "proposals" seemed designed to acquire or perpetuate Soviet military superiority. There could obviously be no agreements on this basis, and so long as these Soviet policies persisted, we could not take seriously Soviet professions of a desire to improve relations.

Comment: Vishnevsky has held key positions with Pravda for many years, so he clearly has sound Party and (almost certainly) KGB credentials. His trade is propaganda and his specialty the U.S. We must assume that, in general, he was conveying a series of messages someone in the regime wants us to hear. He was so intent on getting his comments off his chest that he carefully avoided debating any points I made, either agreeing with them or letting them pass. There is obviously a heavy potential here for disinformation, and his comments must be treated with caution.

Nevertheless, I would summarize the real messages he tried to convey as the following:

Expect a Soviet stonewall for about nine months, but do not conclude from this that we cannot do business at all in 1984.

> There are still powerful incentives in Moscow to deal realistically with us, but these may not be evident in the months ahead because of the psychological and prestige factors cited.
>
> Andropov is not in complete control: he shares power with Ustinov (the military) and Gromyko (a stalwart of traditional Soviet foreign policy with a large personal stake in it).
>
> Changing policies will not come easy.
>
> If this was the intended message, then it may well be essentially accurate, since there is much corroborative evidence. And if this is the case, it means that we are on the right track and must make sure we stay the course, while keeping channels of communication open.

Taking out a writing pad from his top desk drawer and a pen from his inside jacket pocket, Bud McFarlane turned to a clean sheet and paused. He thought he would write a message for his secretary to distribute to his deputies, something like, "For all future memos longer than two pages, include an executive summary." Then he thought he would write, instead, "For all future memos, have a point." Then he thought, what the hell, and put the pen back in his pocket and the pad back into the drawer.

4. In the Senate, sometimes the morning begins, and ends, in the afternoon.

At 12:00 p.m. on Monday, October 17, 1983, in the Senate chambers of the United States Capitol, Senate Chaplain Reverend Richard C. Halverson, DD, opened the day's session with a prayer that concluded:

> Almighty God, as the Senate resumes its work midst the pressures of serious domestic and international problems, grant that critical and demanding issues will not be sacrificed on the altar of an election more than a year away. Protect the Senate from being governed by pressure groups. Give to all who labor here wisdom

in understanding the issues, strength for the task, and courage to make the moral choice. In the name of Jesus Christ who was virtue incarnate. Amen.

Reverend Halverson received his bachelor's degree from Eureka College, Ronald Reagan's alma mater, eighteen miles from Peoria, Illinois. One of his favorite hymns has the chorus, "Great is Thy faithfulness, Lord unto me."

The Senate then commenced what the body referred to as routine morning business, which continued until 12:30, at which time the Senate recessed until 2:00 p.m., at which time it continued routine morning business until 2:44 p.m., at which time Senator Howard Baker of Tennessee addressed the acting president pro tempore of the Senate with some proactive management and a bit of dramatic foreshadowing:

> Mr. President, I remind Senators and those who may be listening in their offices or their staffs that tomorrow the Senate will convene very early at 8:45 a.m., that at 9 a.m. the Senate will turn to the consideration of H.R. 3706, which is the Martin Luther King bill, under the order entered prior to the Columbus Day recess. At that time, according to the provisions of that order, Mr. Helms will be recognized to make a motion to commit the bill to the Judiciary Committee. There is a time limitation of twenty minutes equally divided on that motion. A vote is expected on or in relation to that motion very early, at 9:20 a.m. or shortly thereafter.
>
> Mr. President, the Senate is expected to remain on that measure then as long as necessary during the day on Tuesday as well as Wednesday, and the order previously entered provides that a vote shall occur on final passage of the bill at 4 p.m. on Wednesday, October 19, 1983. I fully expect that that schedule will be adhered to."

At 2:44 p.m., the Senate adjourned.

5. President Reagan straightens a few things out with a columnist. At 12:07 p.m. on Monday, October 17, 1983, President Reagan began his longest meeting of the day, which lasted until 1:15 p.m., with a break at 12:20 for a two-minute meeting in his private study with James Baker. The meeting was a lunch in the Oval Office with George Will, a syndicated columnist whose columns, according to an article by James A. Nuechterlein in the October 1983 issue of the monthly journal *Commentary,* were written in "confident prose" and "attempt to ground particular political cases in larger philosophic and moral contexts." During their sixty-six minutes together, in President Reagan's words in that evening's diary entry, "I think we are straightened out on some differences about taxes and the Soviets. We parted on very good terms."

The president's second-longest meeting of the day took place just before his lunch with George Will, a sixty-five-minute cabinet meeting about tax reforms pertaining to what the president called "women's issues, such as tax credits and deductions for child care centers."

The president's third-longest meeting started immediately after the meeting with George Will ended, when the president was joined in the Oval Office by Jeane Kirkpatrick, U.S. Ambassador to the United Nations, who had just returned from a diplomatic visit to Panama, where former Secretary of State Henry Kissinger, an observer, had grabbed most of the attention, as Kissinger was so good at doing. To separate Kissinger from the limelight, she would have had to deck him, but she supposed that would just have generated more attention for him in the form of sympathy.

Like most meetings in the Oval Office, and perhaps most meetings anywhere, this one began with a restatement of what was already known to the participants, and in this case, widely and somewhat breathlessly reported in the press: Ambassador Kirkpatrick (or as the president called her, "Mrs. Kirkpatrick") wanted to return to Washington, DC, from the UN position in New York, and Ambassador Kirkpatrick had hoped that she would be given the position of Special Assistant to the President for National Security, which she inferred from press reports would be given to Bud McFarlane.

The president spoke of the Ambassador's important work as UN Ambassador, of the great respect she enjoyed in his administration and the country as a whole, and his desire to facilitate her return to the nation's capital. To that end, the president had a proposal: He would appoint Ambassador Kirkpatrick to a newly created position as Counselor to the President on International Policy. In this role, the president assured Ambassador Kirkpatrick, she would have both the president's ear and significant influence on the international policy—an idea that had already been floated to the ambassador through intermediaries.

The ambassador expressed her doubts about the position's significance, as intermediaries had previously communicated to the president, and the meeting ended at that point, having broken no new ground, except for issues being discussed in person for the first time, albeit a little late to affect the outcome.

6. President Reagan tests Slepian's process model for keeping secrets.

At 3:34 p.m. on Monday, October 17, 1983, in the press briefing area of the White House, after the president announced the appointment of Bud McFarlane and invited questions from the media, the first question was, "Mr. President, what about Jeane Kirkpatrick? What will happen to her now?"

The president replied, "May I say that there was a lot of speculation and declarations that were based, again, on those faceless and nameless sources. Jeane Kirkpatrick is ambassador to the United Nations. She continues there as ambassador to the United Nations where she has done, I think, as magnificent a job as anyone who has ever held that post and probably more so than most. And she is invaluable in what she's doing."

Another reporter asked, "You're not offering her another post here in Washington?"

"Jeane is continuing as ambassador to the United Nations."

Perhaps our finest contemporary scholar on the subject of keeping secrets is Michael L. Slepian, who, forty years after President Reagan responded to this reporter's question, became a tenured associate professor of business in the Management Division of the Columbia Business School in New York City, having been promoted from his 2019–2023 position as Sanford C. Bernstein & Co. Associate Professor of Leadership and Ethics in the Columbia Business School; in those roles, he teaches classes in managerial negotiation and practical research tools. Slepian earned his BA in experimental psychology from Syracuse University in 2009 and his MS and PhD, both in experimental psychology, in 2011 and 2014, respectively, from Tufts University.

Slepian is a prolific researcher and author on the subject of secrets, including sixty-seven peer-reviewed articles in less than thirteen years, as well as a book aimed at the popular audience titled *The Secret Lives of Secrets.* Slepian also consults with Fortune 500 companies, although the focus of his consulting, while we may assume it pertains to secrecy, is itself a secret due to non-disclosure agreements.

Volume 129, number 3 of *Psychological Review,* published by the American Psychological Association in 2022, included a sole-author article by Slepian titled "A Process Model of Having and Keeping Secrets." A lengthy and detailed work, it applies previous experimental research and analysis to create the first "integrative theoretical model that captures this broad experience."

Because President Reagan's answer to the reporter's question constitutes an instance of secrecy, it should be useful in testing Slepian's model.

To a certain point, Reagan's response corresponds so well to the model that one would be forgiven for believing they had collaborated, although Slepian was only 17 years old when President Reagan died.

Wisely, Slepian's model begins before the concealment of a secret actually takes place with the *intention* to conceal. Michael explains, "People inhibit speech in conversations for reasons other than secrecy, and not all secrets need to be concealed. Hence, secrecy should not be defined as concealment. One cannot purposefully conceal without the intent to do so. Thus, secrecy should be defined as the intention to keep information unknown from one or more others."

Reagan's secret was, of course, all the machinations to keep Jeane Kirkpatrick happy.

In the next step, the individual who has formed an intention to keep a secret meets a cue that triggers the intention to action. As Slepian explains, "Forming an intention brings a host of cognitive consequences. Most notably, forming an intention makes people more sensitive to cues in their internal or external environment that are related to the intention. When a cue to one's intention is detected outside of a concealment context, people have mind-wandered to the secret. When detected within a concealment context, concealment may follow."

As one may discern from this explanation, two paths of action may result. One comprises a complex series of actions and reactions that exist largely within the individual's mind, a fascinating approach to the notion of secrecy, but not the path the president is traveling in his very public role and this very public pressure on his secrecy.

The other path, and this is the path within which President Reagan's public remarks fit, is the path of active concealment.

Slepian breaks down this latter path into three phases. The first is deciding whether to implement the intention of secrecy. Slepian acknowledges that the intention of secrecy—the first step in the process—would, in most cases, render the decision to maintain secrecy an obvious one; nonetheless, Slepian writes, "other factors may lead to a sudden change of mind." Fair enough. In the case of the president's engagement with the press, and with the president's conversational patterns and purposes in general, no such last-minute change of mind took place.

The next step in the process is the decision to reveal or to conceal, which seems only very subtly different from the previous step of "implementation decision." Slepian describes the "reveal" option as follows: "Revealing a secret to a person it was intentionally kept from is termed confession, and this would be the end of keeping that secret from that person. In contrast, revealing a secret to a third party is termed confiding, and would not end the secrecy." In the case of the president's conversation with the press, the press and by extension the public functions as "a person [the secret] was intentionally kept from, although one might split a hair and question whether disclosure would be completely properly characterized as a confession. In any case, this is not the decision the president made. Rather, the president chose the "conceal secret" step in Slepian's process.

The act of concealment, which the president embarked on, is carried out, according to Slepian, with a complication of three sub-processes: monitoring, expressive inhibition, and alteration, all three of which come into play in this example.

Slepian's explanation of "monitoring" in this context is as poetic as it is valid, and deserves to be quoted here: "In seeking to conceal a secret, to ensure no information related to the secret is revealed, one must carefully monitor one's own behavior and speech, and also one's interaction partner. Monitoring is effortful, and such vigilance can reduce interaction quality." Taking the second part first, monitoring media interest in this press conference requires only the most crude of sensors. The reporters' questions are boldly stated both in wording and volume.

The president being an experienced movie actor and television host as well as political office-holder, the management of expression is a well-honed skill. Thus, Slepian's definition of "expressive inhibition" may seem overstated in this case: "If one detects the potential for information slipping out during monitoring, the particular response will be inhibited. Inhibition of responses consumes regulatory resources and can reduce interaction quality." First, for an experienced public figure, monitoring of a secrecy situation would rarely detect any potential for information unintentionally slipping out, and the resources required to maintain that posture surely are minimal. Having said that, the result no doubt is, as Michael states, to "reduce interaction quality," as anyone who has witnessed a presidential press conference can testify to.

Metaphorically speaking, the audience is in its seats. The house lights are down. The curtain is up. Slepian has taken us through these preliminaries at what even a patient reader might permissibly call a snail's pace. Yet perhaps that is the role of the scholar—to force those of us eager to rush through a thought process to—what is the expression?—slow our roll.

But now comes the payoff. The central act of secrecy is ready to commence: alteration. Interestingly, this is the last step of Michael's process model even if it the first act of the public display in this case.

Slepian divides "alteration behaviors" into two categories. One is "honest alteration," for example, changing the subject or otherwise distracting the listener.

In the case of the president's press conference, an attempt at distraction and change of subject is indeed the initial tactic. Rather than answer the question, the president attacked the questioners, that is, the media, and their informants for "speculation and declarations" based on "faceless and nameless sources." Although this response certainly attempted to shift attention from the president's actions to the media's actions, it can hardly be classified as "honest alteration." Rather, it is another form of deception, because the president was aware that the press accounts, even if speculative and declamatory and based on unnamed sources, were true and entirely consistent with the president's own knowledge, including first-hand knowledge from his conversation with Kirkpatrick that morning.

Slepian's second form of "alteration behavior" is "deception."

And here, at last, in the case of the president's interaction with the reporters on the question of Jeane Kirkpatrick, we have arrived at the point where the rubber hits the road, at the meat of the issue, or choose your own cliché indicating aptness.

Slepian suggests that in the short term, lying is the easiest (or as he says, "the least effortful") action. The president's simple-to-the-point-of-bald response supports that observation. After his one-sentence diversionary attack on the media, the president responds with simple, declarative sentences: "Jeane Kirkpatrick is ambassador to the United Nations. She continues there as ambassador to the United Nations."

The simplicity and apparent effortlessness of these statements belie a measure of artfulness. By speaking in the present tense when the questions asked about the future, the president's lie was disguised in a narrowly defined truth. Even if Jeane stepped to the lectern at that very moment and announced her resignation, she was, at the moment the president spoke, the United States ambassador to the United Nations. The true art and core of the deception was in the present tense form of the verb to continue. The word "continues" denotes an activity to go on over a period of time. When the verb is used in the present tense, the strong inference is that the action will continue into the future, even if the verb tense could, with some effort and credulity on the part of the listener, be interpreted to include only the period of time ending at the moment the word was spoken.

However, to limit this instance of deception in service of keeping a secret to the sleight of hand of answering-not-answering is to short-change the nature of the interaction. In this case, as in the case of so many conversations involving secrecy, most pervasively public conversations, there is, in fact, no secret. The president is lying. The reporters know he is lying. The president knows that the reporters know he is lying. And the reporters know that the president knows that the reporters know he is lying. The act of concealment is a feint that fools no one, nor is it intended to. Rather, it is a formality expected by the occasion.

Slepian wrote that concealment is the riskiest approach to secrecy. The president's modest effort to avoid an outright lie suggests that he deems the risk of the truth being revealed as similarly modest. Slepian also wrote that concealment is the most taxing approach in the long term because of the potential for "feelings of guilt and feelings of inauthenticity," the presence of which in the president would be speculative.

7. Jeane Kirkpatrick is not allowed to say no.

At 6:14 p.m. on Monday, October 17, 1983, from the second-floor residence of the White House, the president placed a call to Jeane Kirkpatrick. He asked whether she had considered his offer of the position as Counselor to the President on International Affairs. She declined the offer. The president said he did not accept her decision. The ambassador said she would think about it during the two months she would still be ambassador to the UN. The call ended at 6:18 p.m.

At that time, the president went to dinner with Nancy, his daughter Maureen, and interior designer Ted Graber.

Peoria, Illinois

1. A boy excels at the art of folding newspapers.

At 6:30 a.m. on Monday, October 17, 1983, on the east side of Airport Road just south of Airways Road in an unincorporated section in Limestone Township, Illinois, between Peoria and Bartonville, a boy named Sam Somers pulled a rusty red Radio Flyer wagon, glad it was not yet daylight so no one was there to see him pulling a kid's wagon. He was also glad he could pull the wagon in the road at this hour because at precisely this spot, the walkable ground beside the road narrowed and a misstep would send him and the wagon down a gully. And he was glad that he could see Jimmy's pickup truck in the gas station parking lot and Jimmy standing by the open tailgate, and the banded bundles of newspapers in the truck's bed, which meant that Sam would be able to deliver his route on time, which meant that probably—although not for sure, never for sure—no one would call his house and wake his parents complaining their newspaper was late. Holding the bundles by their bands, Jimmy handed one, then another, and then another to Sam, who dropped each into the wagon, which shook under the impact of each drop. Jimmy, in his usual brown insulated vest from which the sleeves of his red flannel shirt emerged, leaned against the side of the truck to wait for the other carriers, which he referred to as "my boys." Sam pulled his wagon to the corner of the gas station lot nearest the street and sat on a rock facing the station.

For a moment, Sam watched the bent-over man getting the gas station ready to open for the day. From his earliest memories, Sam had seen the bent-over man working at the gas station. He was a lot bent over, a ninety-degree angle, Sam had learned in math class, his personal goal of learning the day geometry began being to know the angle of the bent-over-man's posture. The man looked old to Sam, and Sam expected the man at any moment to either die of old age or simply tip over, or maybe both, the danger of both far greater when the man pumped gas for customers, and reduced now that customers pumped their own gas.

Sam took his penknife from his hip pocket, pulled the wagon closer, cut the first bundle's band, and began to fold the papers.

When Sam had first learned how to fold papers, the task had not come naturally. But over time, he felt a very specific change in his execution: from something that required careful intention to something that he did absolutely without thought. How, he often wondered, was it that he performed something better without thinking about it than he did when concentrating on it? And not just better, but beautifully, with the total command of an artist. Whether a thin Monday morning edition like today or a thick Sunday edition, he could fold the paper as crisply as he wanted, tight enough to withstand a toss from the sidewalk to the stoop, but yielding enough to open with the lightest tug. On days when he felt grumpy, he could pack the folds tighter, and on days when he felt at peace with the world, he could make the folds more supple. All without thought—in fact, only by removing thought and allowing something else to take over, something he loved to watch, to experience every day, but something that existed unconnected to logic or words.

The newspapers, of course, came to Sam already folded in half, as they would be displayed in racks in convenience stores. Sam's job, or rather, his art, was to fold them in thirds for delivery. Because the Peoria *Journal Star* (like most newspapers, something Sam did not know, rarely ever having seen a newspaper from another city) is laid out in four columns, that meant Sam's folded newspapers showed on one side the inner half of the two center columns, and on the other side the remaining half of the right center column and the full right column.

The result was that one side was largely gibberish: headlines, pictures, and sentences sliced in half vertically. When Sam stacked his folded papers, this was the side he put face up, and he rather enjoyed looking at the nonsense piling before him. This morning, one portion of this visible panel was one half of an illustrated automobile and small, difficult-to-read numbers indicating percentage change in auto sales from 1982 to 1983. Next to that was a vertical half of a headline, which read:

Ano
Mar
Kill

Below the headline were the words "BEIRUT, Lebanon."

Sam watched as one instance of "Ano Mar Kill" piled on another, translating the syllables into a chant to match the pace of his folding. Ano Mar Kill. Ano Mar Kill.

On the other side, the side Sam placed face down, the remainder of the headline would have been visible had Sam stacked his folded papers with that side face up:

ther
ine
ed

To the right of this half-headline was the one fully visible column of the top half of the front page of this delivery-ready folded newspaper. At the top was a shallow gray bar with the date in reversed type, using an odd combination of capital and lowercase letters: MONDAY, Oct. 17, 1983. Below that was a series of previews of the contents of that day's newspaper. The first item was in its own box sporting an illustration of a ribbon and large bow diagonally across its corner:

Yule ideas
You'll save on
Do you want to wrap
Your own gifts, make
Your own Christmas
Cards or create your
Own bows for
presents this year?
The Peoria Park District is offering
Classes that will help you.
Accent/Your pocketbook A10

Following this item were several headlines and blurbs in tiny type about other stories to be found in that day's paper, not in order of their appearance. The first two alluded to the sports section:

Sports extra: When the historians sit down to rank great World Series, they will determine that the 1983 Philadelphia Phillies were rank and the Baltimore Orioles were great. They won it all. **Page B1. Another opponent** was impressed, as well as defeated, Sunday as the Peoria Prancers scored victory No. 1 in International Hockey League action. **Page B2.**

This was followed by what might be construed as some boosterism of the local university:

> **Scholarship hearing:** University officials and others who want the state to pay more attention to merit when giving out scholarships will testify before an Illinois House committee Tuesday in Springfield. Among them will be Dr. Martin G. Abegg, Bradley University president. **Page A5.**

Finally, just before the weather forecast, was this item:

> **Food poisoning:** Suspected botulism, possibly from pickles at a local restaurant, sent six people to Peoria hospitals over the weekend. They remained in serious but stable condition Sunday night. **Page A6.**

By the time he had finished folding, two other boys had arrived, both in parent-driven cars, dropped their papers in the back seat, and headed off. Sam waved to Jimmy and headed down Airport Road. The sunlight beginning to emerge as he walked, he let his eyes rest across the road on the six-foot-high chain-link fence and beyond that a field of grass that Sam assumed had something to do with the airport, which was invisible at the moment down a hill in the distance.

At the T intersection with Harp Hollow Road, on the west side of the street, the chain-link fence acquired barbed wire at the top and the grass field gave way to the Peoria Air National Guard base. Sam turned left onto Harp Hollow, away from the base, and soon was tossing papers, or placing them inside screen doors if that was the customer's preference. When he emptied his wagon, he would stash it under some brush in the woods just beyond where Airland Street stopped and then head to Monroe School to start that part of his day. On his way home, he would retrieve the wagon and take mostly dirt paths to avoid any of the kids seeing him and laughing about the wagon.

2. Lou Dobrydnia tries to teach driver's education.

At 8:10 a.m. on Monday, October 17, 1983, in Limestone Community High School, a long, smooth-brick building, two stories in some parts and three stories in others, on Airport Road a mile south from where Sam folded his newspapers, across the border from unincorporated Peoria into Bartonville, Illinois, on the second floor, Lou Dobrydnia was attempting to teach a driver's education class.

A friend of Lou's had once commented that from the outside, high schools looked like prisons. To Lou, it was the other way around. In downtown Peoria, they (Lou always wondered, who is this "they" who are building new buildings, replacing street signs, and paving the streets) were building a new juvenile detention facility that looked like Limestone Community High School. And that made sense to Lou: She felt safe at Limestone, if occasionally overwhelmed by the team color of royal blue that permeated the wall lockers, strips of floor tile, and in some rooms, chairs. At Limestone, home of the Rockets, she felt that she had purpose, structure, direction. Today, however, her mind, which felt like it was playing dodgeball and losing, found another relevance in the idea of prison, which is that Lou's body felt like a prison, a prison in which guards who were as apathetic as they were malevolent were beating her.

Lou's lectures made no sense to her, and she could barely perceive how they were being perceived by her students. At 2:00 p.m., she was on the third floor in a three-tier lecture room, teaching driver's ed, which, at the moment, seemed a particularly absurd subject to be teaching through lecture, and she was an athlete, so why was she teaching driver's ed, especially because she liked to look at her students when she lectured and she couldn't see the students on the third tier, well, she could see them, but only as outlines, and then she couldn't see them for a different reason, which was because her eyes were starting to close, and that wiped away those students in the top tier, and Limestone wasn't an overpopulated school so why were her driver's ed classes so large that she needed the three-tier lecture room, although she had to admit she rather enjoyed the performance of it, although, another although, she always thought driver's ed lectures were rather silly because honestly who remembered a lecture when they were under pressure behind a wheel especially for the first time, and speaking of pressure, her bruised brain now felt like something Lou read about somewhere, a book or a magazine article, which was the iron battering ram police use to smash open doors, the way they worked was that the ram is a hollow metal cylinder and inside is a metal weight that slides back and forth and when the police draw the ram back and pause, the metal weight slides back, and when the police swing the ram forward, the weight follows behind, slamming the rod harder into the door, and that sliding weight was Lou's brain, poised to slide forward, to smash into her skull if she tilted her head forward, but now another weight took over, three weights, two casting sinkers, one tied to the eyelashes of each of her eyelids, pulling her lids down, and the other was a fifty-pound version of that plastic bird that dips its beak into the water and out and in, and the fifty-pound plastic bird was pulling her chin down, but Lou was made of sterner stuff than any plastic bird, and she was keeping her head level, keeping it level, but the weight was terrific, pulling her face forward, as if she were bowing to royalty, in the gravest nod on the gravest occasion with the gravest meaning, except that she was going to faint or vomit or have a stroke or die, and if she was going to faint or vomit or have a stroke or die, she was going to do it not in front of her students during a lecture but in the faculty lounge, which was just a few doors down the hall, that was all, just a few doors, but between here and there are those lockers, those electric blue lockers, and the tile floor, with its strip of electric blue, and if she were to fall against those lockers there were the vents in the locker doors, or were they blades of a grater, surely they were, and it was just stupid and sad to fall against those lockers, drag her face along those electric blue cheese graters, even if she was caught by something or someone it really doesn't matter because fainting was an act of erasure and erased she was.

Lou's assistant softball coach carried her downstairs. Laid Lou in the assistant coach's car. Drove Lou to a friend's house. Laid her on the couch, where she barely breathed, barely moved. Waited one hour, watching TV while Lou lay there, another hour, watching TV while Lou lay there, called Lou's roommate, Gwen, for advice, Gwen put words to her bafflement that Lou had been driven by one person to the home of another person and was lying on that person's couch in that person's house unable to breathe and unable to move and was not at a hospital, and having received that bit of insight, the assistant coach drove Lou back to Saint Francis Medical Center, from which she had been sent home yesterday, and where now she was sent to the intensive care unit and admitted and put on a respirator. Lou signed the consent for antitoxin with an X because she couldn't write anything but an X, and Lou wondered why she needed to write an X, why the act of two lines intersecting created veracity where a single straight line would not, or perhaps a single crooked line would do, although who would judge the degree of crookedness that would be sufficient? Someone who looked like a silhouette fiddled with one of Lou's arms and then fiddled with her other arm, and probably it would have been uncomfortable at some other time but now it was only one other thing perhaps real and perhaps imagined to be registered.

3. What the first visitors to the Northwoods Mall today see.

At 10:00 a.m. on Monday, October 17, 1983, security guards unlocked the five main doors to the Northwoods Mall. At the same time, staff at Carson Pirie Scott, JC Penny, Mongomery Ward, Adelyn's, Aladdin's Castle, Bachrach's, Baker's Shoes, B.J. & Co. on Hair, Book Market, Brooks, Brown's Sporting Goods, Burton's Shoes,

Byerly Music Center, Caren Charles, Casual Corner, Chadban's Keepsake Diamond Center, Chess King, Children's Photographer, Claire's Boutique, Coach House Gifts, Construction Equipment Credit Union, Crazy Top Shop, Cutlery World, B. Dalton Bookseller, Diamond Dave's Taco Co., Dipper Dan, Elliot's Children's World, Energy Alternatives, Evenson's Hallmark, Fannie May Candies, Father & Son Shoes, Federal Travel, Ferdinand's Wigs, Flowerama, Foxmoor Casuals, Frontier Fruit & Nut, Gallenkamp Shoes, Garcia's Pan Pizza By the Slice, Garrott Jewelry, General Nutrition Center, Grizzley's, Hardee's, Hertzberg's Diamonds, Holmes Florsheim Shoes, Holmes Shoes-Schradzki's, Household Finance Corp., Jade East, J.R.'s Music Shop, Jeans West, Johnson's, Just Pants, Karmelkorn Shoppes, Kay Bee Toy & Hobby Shop, Kinney Shoes, Karlin's, LeCart Gourmet, Life Stride Shoes, Maurice's, Merle Norman Cosmetics, Midwestern Surveys, Moeckei's Adidas, Motherhood Maternity, Moore's Jewelry, Musicland, National Shirt Shop, Naturalizer, Noah's Ark, Northwoods Management Company, Northwoods Merchants Association, Orange Bowl, Orange Julius, Otto Malik, Paul Harris, Photo Finish, Pines, Radio Shack, Realty Centre, Red Cross Shoes, Regal Shoes, Richman Brothers, Schradzki's, Security Savings, Seno Formal Wear, Service Optical, Singer, So Fro Fabrics, Stride Rite Shoes, Stuart's, Suns of Britches, Susie's Casuals, Swiss Colony, Talman Home Federal Savings, Tandy Brass, Things Remembered, Thom McAn Shoes, Tiffany Bakery, Tinder Box, Tobin Hughes Jewelry, Ups & Downs, Wedding Boutique, Wicks 'N' Sticks, Worth's, and Zondervan Bookstore unlocked their doors and propped them open or unlocked their gates and pushed them open. That's what happened at Richmond Brothers, but Jan-Paul Peavler wasn't there. That did not happen at Skewer Inn.

4. A botulism patient is transferred.

At 10:30 a.m. on Monday, October 17, 1983, Laurie Fryman, 24, of Pekin, Illinois, showing symptoms of botulism, was transferred to Saint Francis Medical Center in Peoria from Pekin Memorial Hospital.

5. Public health acts.

At 10:36 a.m. on Monday, October 17, 1983, at the Peoria International Airport on Everett McKinley Dirksen Parkway off of Airport Road, a package containing antitoxin arrived from the Centers for Disease Control facility in New York.

At 11:27 a.m. at the Peoria International Airport, a package containing antitoxin arrived from the Centers for Disease Control facility in New Orleans.

At 1:16 p.m., in a Centers for Disease Control laboratory in Cincinnati, Ohio, pickle juice from the Skewer Inn flown in from Peoria was injected into mice.

At 3:12 p.m., at the Peoria International Airport, a package containing antitoxin arrived from the Centers for Disease Control facility in Seattle.

Everette McKinley Dirksen, native of Pekin, Illinois, former short-story writer, former investor in electric washing machine production, Republican Senate Minority Leader for ten years, loved the calendula officinalis, or common marigold, and regularly suggested that it be named the national flower of the United States of America.

6. A *Journal Star* copyeditor prepares for a long night.

At 11:00 a.m. on Monday, October 17, 1983, at the Peoria *Journal Star*'s copy desk, which is a room with three heavy oak desks separated from the printing plant by seven-foot walls far short of the ceiling with large glass windows that always seemed on the verge of bringing down the shakily braced wood that framed them, Mike

Major, knowing he would have a long night copyediting the various stories in process about the botulism outbreak, stories that would replace some of the wire stories that didn't require more than a glance from the copyeditor, decided to clear out his in-basket of what little was there, which turned out to be one piece of the next day's editorial. When he finished his editing—which had to be light or his editor would hear about it from the publisher and Mike would hear about it from his editor, whose favorite piece of direction was, "Don't do anything that makes my phone ring"—the editorial read as follows:

Neutering the Bible

You probably never thought about it, but there are people who believe it is sexist of the Bible to say, "Man does not live by bread alone."

Their reasoning, of course, is that woman does not live by bread alone either, and therefore she must be put out not to be included in this warning.

So the National Council of Churches has put out a new version of Bible readings, neuterizing them by expunging all the thoughtless masculine references handed down through the ages.

Thus, It is now: "One shall not live by bread alone."

We used to be told to let our light "shine before men," but now we must let our light shine before "others." Forget about God the Father; it is now God the Father and Mother. That will certainly make it more difficult to sing "The Our Father."

Jesus—how thoughtless of God to make him male—is no longer the Son of God but the Child of God. A child even at age 33.

"King" and "Lord" are out; "God the Sovereign One" or "Sovereign God" are in.

The value of pronouns in language becomes obvious when the writer is denied their use. "For God so loved the world that he gave us his only Son" has been depronouned to say, "For God so loved the world that God gave God's only Child."

As if this isn't bad news enough, we see where Bell Laboratories has developed a computer program for word processors that would remove all references to "man" and "mankind" from the Declaration of Independence, substituting "humanity," "men and women" and "we all." This from Ma and Pa Bell.

The whole movement is what you might call manslaughter.

7. Interest in the pickle continues.

At 12:05 p.m. on Monday, October 17, 1983, Cliff Caldwell, reporter at WQRX radio, walked through the newsroom and said to no one in particular, "Authorities continue to suspect the pickle," and Cat Kouns laughed again, this time taking less care to stifle it.

8. And another admission.

At 1:00 p.m. on Monday, October 17, 1983, Randall Brown, age 36, of Peoria, was admitted to Methodist Medical Center with symptoms of botulism.

9. The acting director of the Peoria health department is a bit of a wit.

At 2:00 p.m. on Monday, October 17, 1983, in the board room on the first floor of the Saint Francis Medical Center in Peoria, Illinois, Thomas F. Jackamore, acting director of the Peoria City and County Health Department, called to order a press conference. At the press conference, Jackamore said, "We pretty much have it nailed down to either the meat, the cheese, the condiments, or the pickles. We may have a completely innocent pickle, but it was the only thing we had on hand to test." (He neglected to mention the scrapings from the foil that contained Sande Spore's leftover portion of patty melt.)

When asked about whether he might have revealed the name of the restaurant sooner, and thus saved many people from exposure, Jackamore responded, "Once we got into Sunday, yeah. What we were primarily concerned with was not the release of the names but whether the restaurant should be closed. At the time the decision was made, all the food that was involved and suspected was consumed. It's beautiful to look at something seventy-two hours later and say 'Why? Why? Why?' But all of this information that currently is available did not exist Saturday night at seven o'clock."

10. Hospitals get busier and one welcomes a dancer.

At 3:47 p.m. on Monday, October 17, 1983, James Walser, age 39, of Peoria, was admitted to Saint Francis Medical Center with symptoms of botulism.

At 6:00 p.m. on Monday, October 17, 1983, Addie Fisher, age 40, of Pekin, was transferred to Saint Francis Medical Center in Peoria from Pekin Memorial Hospital with symptoms of botulism.

At 6:37 p.m. on Monday, October 17, 1983, Doris Hawksworth, age 51, of Peoria, was admitted to Methodist Medical Center with symptoms of botulism.

At 8:32 p.m. on Monday, October 17, Monique Gruter was admitted to Saint Francis Medical Center in Peoria with symptoms of botulism. Nine days earlier, at 8:00 p.m. on Saturday, October 8, 1983, Monique Gruter, age 22, representing the Peoria Civic Ballet Company, had danced in support of a guest flute recital by Nancy Gillette at Kaeuper Hall in Millikin University of Decatur, Illinois.

11. John Mason's family gathers at his bedside.

At 8:50 p.m. on Monday, October 17, 1983, shortly before the end of visiting hours at Saint Francis Medical Center, John Mason's brother, father, wife, and son took turns kissing John's forehead and telling John that they loved him.

John, aware of what was happening around him but unable to respond, wondered at the extreme nature of their reaction. It was almost as if they thought he was dying.

As they left John's room and looked for the elevator to take them to the lobby, the family discussed whether they wanted to stop somewhere for a bite to eat.

12. More people enter Peoria's hospitals.

At 8:56 p.m. on Monday, October 17, 1983, Norman Porter, age 38, of Washington, Illinois, was admitted to Methodist Medical center with symptoms of botulism.

Also at 8:56 p.m., Geraldine Roedell, age 31, of Peoria, was admitted to Methodist Medical Center with symptoms of botulism.

At 9:19 p.m., Mary K. Schonberger, age 25, of Sparland, Illinois, was admitted to Saint Francis Medical Center with symptoms of botulism.

At 9:22 p.m., Cathy Lynn Doughtery, age 27, of Woodridge, Illinois, was admitted to Saint Francis Medical Center with symptoms of botulism.

13. Thomas Jackamore gets a bit of a promotion.

At 9:30 p.m. on Monday, October 17, 1983, after an executive session of the Peoria/Peoria County Department of Health board meeting at 2116 N. Sheridan Road, a mile and a half north of Bradley University and almost four miles southeast of the Northwoods Mall, Sidney Newirth, MD, chairman of the board, announced that the "acting" had been removed from the title of Thomas Jackamore, and he was now officially the director of health for the city and county of Peoria. Dr. Newirth said that the board had not come to an agreement about Dr. Jackamore's salary, however, and that a three-member subcommittee of the board would make that decision.

The board next voted to pay sixty-two dollars as its share of the cost of appraising the former Pabst Brewing Co. property in in Peoria

Heights. Next, the board heard from Mr. Jackamore with an update on the local botulism outbreak.

14. Even more people enter Peoria's hospitals.

At 10:04 p.m. on Monday, October 17, 1983, Andrew Albee, age 12 months, of Peoria, was admitted to Saint Francis Medical Center with symptoms that suggested the possibility of botulism.

At 10:12 p.m., Michael Albee, age 12, of Peoria, was admitted to Saint Francis Medical Center with symptoms that suggested the possibility of botulism.

At 10:27 p.m., Theresa Albee, age 17, of Peoria, was admitted to Saint Francis Medical Center with symptoms that suggested the possibility of botulism.

At 11:29 p.m., Wallace Phillips, age 41, of Peoria, was admitted to Methodist Medical Center with symptoms that suggested the possibility of botulism.

Tuesday, October 18, 1983

New York City

1. A person falls from the sky.

At 3:00 a.m. on Tuesday, October 18, 1983, on Webster Avenue near the winding walk that led to the Butler Houses in the Bronx, New York, Sidney Cleveland, walking home from the 167th Street subway station, where he had departed the train that brought him from work at the Howard Johnson's Restaurant on 46th and Broadway near Times Square, saw a girl, well, he thought it was a girl, about 13 or 14 years old, walking toward him, then away from him, then toward him, then stopping. She was maybe six inches shorter than him, and he was five foot seven, and she wore a light-blue rain jacket unzipped over a hoodie. As Sidney passed her, the girl seemed to be talking, but no one else was around, and the sounds didn't make words, at least not that he could tell.

At 7:00 a.m., a group of people stood surrounding the girl in a grassy area that, in turn, was surrounded by three twenty-one-story apartment buildings. One person said the girl had jumped off a roof, although no one was sure that she would have been able to travel from the roof as far as this spot. Another person said she fell straight down from the sky. Another person said she looked like Tanya Boyd, but later the police were not able to link the body with anyone by that name. A housing detective said she might have "taken some drug."

2. A district attorney in Nashville asks a district attorney in the Bronx for the name of a sexual behavior clinic in Manhattan.
At 9:20 a.m. on Tuesday, October 18, 1983, in the Bronx District Attorney's Office on 198 East 161st Street, one mile south of the location of the body that seemed to drop from the sky, an assistant district attorney named Johanna Resnick, who was head of the office's domestic violence unit, had a call transferred to her from Harold Twombly, an assistant district attorney from Nashville, Tennessee, who was full of pleasantries.

Eventually, Harold asked Johanna if she could recommend what he called a clinic for "people with sexual troubles that could lead to legal problems."

Johanna told Harold that she was sure he had explained the background for this request but that perhaps she had forgotten amid all his pleasant talk about the weather in New York compared with the weather in Nashville.

With no apparent reaction to this sarcasm, Harold supplied the background. A former District Attorney of Brooklyn who, Harold said to Johanna, he would rather not mention by name but whose name he was sure she knew...

"Eugene Gold," Johanna interrupted.

Harold continued, explaining that this unnamed individual, the former District Attorney of Brooklyn—and by the way, what a great job he had done prosecuting the Son of Sam—anyway, this person's attorneys were in the middle—well, actually, nearing the conclusion—of some negotiations with Harold's boss, Nashville District Attorney Thomas Shriver. A condition of the deal was that the individual...

"Eugene Gold," Johanna interrupted.

That this individual, Harold repeated, would issue a statement confirming that, in contradiction to his previous denial, he had fondled the 10-year-old daughter of an Alabama prosecutor in the room of her father, an Alabama prosecutor, at the Opryland Hotel during a convention of the National District Attorneys Association, which was probably more information than he should reveal, but since Johanna seemed familiar with the case…

"Would he do time?"

Harold continued, saying that this individual would commit to going to a clinic for treatment of his, well, his problem…

"Would he do time?"

Harold demurred, saying details were still being worked out, but that he was sure the deal would be consistent with the usual ways such matters are handled down here and up there as well. He was not the one making the decision, he just needed the name of a few clinics to give his boss, a man who did not consider patience a virtue.

"The Sexual Behavior Clinic at Columbia Presbyterian Medical Center in Manhattan," Johanna said, "the Belt Clinic in Long Island City, and Fairfield Oaks Clinic in Brookline."

Harold, noting that New Yorkers tend to speak a whole lot faster than Southerners, asked Johanna if she would mind terribly repeating those names, but Johanna had already hung up.

3. A wide-eyed police lieutenant explains old bones.

At 11:10 a.m. on Tuesday, October 18, 1983, Lieutenant Nicholas Delmonico was at his desk on the second-floor front of the long, squat charcoal-colored brick 83rd Precinct building on 480 Knickerbocker Avenue in the Bushwick neighborhood of Brooklyn. Two months ago, he would have been at his desk on the fourth floor of the high-ceilinged Romanesque Revival 83rd Precinct building on 179 Wilson Avenue in the Bushwick neighborhood of Brooklyn. That building, designed by William Bunker Tubby, built in 1894, named a historic landmark five months ago, was referred to by police and public alike as, variously but not mutually exclusively, a castle, a fortress, a stable (because it included one), and because of its single flagged turret, a raised middle finger to the shambles that surrounded it.

The new building took the middle name of the previous building's architect, Bunker, and ran with it, looking like a facility that took security from the crazed and angry masses seriously, resembling a modern prison or perhaps a high school.

Working in one building or another, or for that matter performing one task or another, seemed to make no difference to Lieutenant Delmonico's facial expression, his manner, or his view of the world, all of which were defined by his eyes, which were so peculiar that they held the attention of anyone the lieutenant encountered, no matter how many times previously that person may have seen them. At all times, Lieutenant Delmonico's eyes were so wide open that he seemed to have just received shocking news, or perhaps more aptly, an electrical shock. His eyes did not communicate alarm, however. Quite the opposite. Lieutenant Delmonico's wide-open eyes seemed equal parts comic surprise and true delight so intense he may at any moment emit a belly laugh or give those around him bear hugs.

A person meeting this affect for the first time would be forgiven for feeling the subject of a put-on. And the people who knew Lieutenant Delmonico, with the possible exception of his wife, never quite rid themselves of the feeling that Lieutenant Delmonico was putting on an act—a consistent one, to be sure, but still an act. However, no one had ever caught Lieutenant Delmonico breaking character, and the consensus was that he really found delight in every damn thing.

This afternoon, Lieutenant Delmonico was carrying out the usual tripartite mission of a head of detectives. First, he was reading paperwork others had completed, which he withdrew from his in tray. Second, he was completing paperwork, which he dropped in his out tray. These two tasks he likened to spring cleaning, if it were to be carried out every day. Third, he was answering phone calls from people who wanted answers to questions for which answers didn't exist, and the callers knew it, but they called anyway because they knew that Lieutenant Delmonico would take their requests seriously and find whichever scrap of information constituted the best available response.

At the moment, Lieutenant Delmonico's wide-open eyes threatened to acquire a glassiness. He was completing his own report on a matter that had been both received and resolved yesterday afternoon by the Civilian Complaint Review Board. Amazing, Lieutenant Delmonico thought, how many complaints the CCRB was able to review and deliver a conclusion on within the same day. Pretty much every one he had ever seen. In this case, a 24-year-old male resident of Bushwick had accused Officer Edward Santiago, badge number 645, of using unnecessary force. After a CCRB representative spoke with the man, he withdrew his complaint. Filed and resolved the same day. This was the second complaint against Officer Santiago in thirteen months—the previous accusation was force and disrespect, also resolved by the CCRB in one day because "complainant uncooperative." Alas, Officer Santiago had been on the force only since January 1981, and Lieutenant Delmonico resisted doing the calculation to estimate the number of complaints that Officer Santiago would amass at this rate over twenty-year career that would undoubtedly see him rise to the rank of Detective Specialist before retiring, and then spending a satisfying and, Lieutenant Delmonico hoped, less confrontational thirty or more years drawing a police pension.

Before he had finished writing the report, the phone rang, and Lieutenant Delmonico took a moment to cleanse Officer Santiago from his mind before lifting the receiver.

On the other end was the desk sergeant, who as usual sounded as sad as Lieutenant Delmonico sounded delighted, informing the

Lieutenant that a reporter from "the picture book," the department's name for the *Daily News*, was asking whether they'd learned anything about those bones the kids found yesterday.

Holding the receiver to his ear with his shoulder, Lieutenant Delmonico began flipping through the papers in his in tray.

"Well, hell's bells"—unironic use of dated slang was another of Lieutenant Delmonico's specialties—"here it is. That was fast. Must have caught the lab's fancy."

While the call connected, and the reporter, who had that meek voice Lieutenant Delmonico noticed so many reporters had, was making his request, the lieutenant skimmed the report and registered its conclusions, which he recited to the reporter as if each were a fresh delight.

"Seven skulls," he said into the telephone. "Fourteen leg bones. From eleven people. Two were infants. More than one hundred years old. No signs of violence. No signs of any injury. Covered in dirt, so probably not lab specimens. Further tests being done."

The reporter next asked several questions woven into one another within the same sentence, something else Lieutenant Delmonico noticed most reporters did, which seemed counter to the goal of getting clear information from officials to share with the public. Unwoven, the questions were: How did the bones get into the boxes? How did the boxes get into the lot? What did the sender on the label have to say? What did the addressee on the label have to say?

When the reporter paused, Lieutenant Delmonico said, "Well. How about we think about this together? Just thinking out loud. Nothing concrete. Nothing for the record. But I'll bet you and I can solve this right here on the phone."

The reporter made a sound that Lieutenant Delmonico inferred to be affirmative.

"Okay, let's see," Lieutenant Delmonico said, his tone suggesting that he was taking the reporter into his confidence. "Say that someone somewhere was working a construction project. Maybe excavating for some new building. And let's say that an excavator, or a backhoe, or even a bulldozer dug up those bones. And maybe one of the workers hollered out to the excavator to stop, and maybe the foreman looked over and asked what the hell? And maybe the guy who saw the bones went to take a closer look and the foreman came over to look too. And maybe, just maybe, the foreman's sense of curiosity was a little underdeveloped, or at least it was outweighed by the thought of how much shit he would encounter from his boss if they paused the job long enough to deal with bones. And now I'm really speculating, but why not? Do you have time? Yes? Okay, let's say that the foreman slipped the worker a ten and said something along the lines of, 'You pass some vacant lots on the way home, don't you? How about you make these bones disappear?' What do you think? How are we doing here? I think we're making some real headway."

After he hung up with the reporter, he consulted his pocket notebook for a telephone number he had written down when he had chatted with the kids yesterday by the front desk. Might as well let them know what we found out, he thought. He knew the information would be in the newspaper tomorrow, but maybe, he thought, they didn't read the newspaper.

4. Councilwoman Mary Pinkett compares two autopsies.

At 12:20 p.m. on Tuesday, October 18, 1983, Brooklyn Councilwoman Mary Pinkett sat in the district office on Hanson Place in the Clinton Hill neighborhood, an office that she helped pay for out of her own pocket to replace the basement office she had occupied when she first became a councilwoman almost ten years ago.

She was eating a tuna sandwich and comparing two autopsies. The first was issued on September 29 by Brooklyn Medical Examiner Elliot Gross, and the second was issued that morning by Robert Wolf, a physician from Mount Sinai Hospital. Dr. Wolf had witnessed the autopsy, hired by the family of the dead man, Michael Stewart.

Michael, a 25-year-old student at Parsons School of Design, a Black man, had been arrested by Transit Police at 3:00 a.m. on September 15 for drawing graffiti with a marker on the wall of the Union Square–14th Street subway station. Michael was taken from the station and struggled with police. Michael was taken by police to Bellevue Hospital for psychiatric treatment. Michael fell into a coma in transit and died on September 28.

The first report, that of Dr. Gross, said that Michael died of heart failure two days after suffering a heart attack and falling into a coma while in police custody. Michael's facial bruises, this report said, were consistent with a fall, and his wrist abrasions were consistent with the effects of manacles.

Dr. Gross concluded, "There is no evidence of physical injury resulting in or contributing to death."

The report from Dr. Wolf said that Michael's blood flow and breathing were constricted by a force consistent with a choke hold and that Michael had died of asphyxia.

Councilwoman Pinkett also reviewed a statement by Rebecca Reiss, a student whose apartment faced Union Square Park. Rebecca said that she saw the police kick and hit Michael with a billy club and heard Michael say, "Oh, my God, someone help me, someone help me."

5. Mayor Koch explains the genesis of graffiti's popularity.

At 1:20 p.m. Eastern Standard Time, 2:20 p.m. Atlantic Standard Time, on Tuesday, October 18, 1983, in San Juan, Puerto Rico, New York City Mayor Ed Koch told reporters he could pinpoint the cause of the popularity of the graffiti that had become a scourge of the city's subways. That "main culprit," Ed said, was the editorial page of the *New York Times*.

Being told of this remark by a colleague, a *Times* editor searched the archives. That editor found a guest opinion piece published in

1981 that said graffiti "trumpets the indestructible survival of the individual in an inhuman environment."

Well, the editor thought, that must be it. Not exactly an editorial, but still, there you go, we gave rise to the popularity of graffiti. Sorry and damn sorry.

6. Osborn Elliott makes a date but sends a proxy to keep it.

At 2:50 p.m. on Tuesday, October 18, 1983, at his 72nd Street townhouse, Osborn Elliott, dean of the Columbia University Graduate School of Journalism, received a phone call from David Hampton, although the caller did not initially identify himself with that name. Rather, the caller said he was "the guy from the other day, you know, the guy who came to your house, the guy you were so nice to. I said I was your daughter's friend. Well, I'm not."

His real name, the caller said, was David Hampton. He told Elliott he was sorry for tricking him. He said his behavior was inexcusable. He said he wanted to apologize "to you, Mr. Osborn, er, Mr. Elliott," in person.

More to stall for time than because he knew whether he wanted to meet this young man again and hear his apology and, doubtless, his tale of woe, Elliott asked where and when. David replied, too quickly, Elliott thought, remembering how deft this young man's patter had been this past Sunday and wondering whether Elliott was being set up for another scam of some sort. Elliott agreed to David's proposed meeting at 7:00 p.m. outside the phone booth on the corner of Fourth Street and Sixth Avenue in the Village.

Only two minutes were necessary for Elliott to work though whether he truly wanted to hear this young man's story as an equanimous presence or whether he wanted this young man to be held accountable. Having resolved that issue, Elliott called the member of the police department fraud squad with whom he had spoken on Sunday.

On 7:15 p.m. that evening, police arrested David outside the phone booth and charged him with petty larceny, criminal impersonation, and fraudulent accosting.

Washington, DC

1. The Senate prays for grace.

At 8:45 a.m. on Tuesday, October 18, 1983, in the Senate Chamber of the U.S. Capitol, Senate President Pro Tempore Senator Strom Thurmond of South Carolina called the body to order. Senate Chaplain Halverson then offered the day's prayer:

> Gracious God, infinite and impartial in love, who has "made of one blood all nations of men for to dwell on all the face of the Earth," the issue before the Senate today is fraught with strong conviction, deep emotion, and sensitive political implications. We invoke Thy presence in this Chamber this morning. As the Senate struggles with this potentially divisive issue, let Thy grace and peace overwhelm us. Grant cool heads and warm hearts to the Senators, let Thy love and wisdom fill this place, let reason prevail, and Thy will be done here, as it is in Heaven. We pray this in the name of Him whose sacrificial love embraced all peoples. Amen.

2. The Senate apportions time.

At 9:00 a.m. on Tuesday, October 18, 1983, in the Senate Chamber of the U.S. Capitol, Senate President Pro Tempore Thurmond said,

"Under the previous order, the hour of nine a.m. having arrived, the Senate will now proceed to the consideration of H.R. 3706, which will be stated by title."

And the legislative clerk said, "A bill, H.R. 3706, to amend title 5, United States Code, to make the birthday of Martin Luther King, Jr., a legal public holiday."

After which, Senator Thurmond said, "Under the previous order, the Senator from North Carolina is recognized."

Upon which Senator Jesse Helms said, "Mr. President, I move to commit H.R. 3706 to the Committee on the Judiciary, and I ask for the yeas and nays."

President Pro Tempore Thurmond, determining that there was a "sufficient second," spoke on the issue of the time for debate of this motion.

"There are twenty minutes," Senator Thurmond said, "equally divided, on this motion."

"Mr. President," Senator Helms replied, "I understand that the distinguished majority leader may seek a unanimous-consent agreement to extend the debate. He will address that question."

And Majority Leader Senator Baker said, "Mr. President, if the Senator will yield to me, that is correct. I may do that. We are involved in the cloakroom process to try to make it forty minutes equally divided, so that there will be twenty minutes on a side, rather than ten minutes on a side. I will not make that request at this time, but I hope to be able to clear it shortly."

And after a pause, Senator Baker continued, "Mr. President, I ask unanimous consent that the time for debate on this motion be extended until 9:40 a.m., which is forty minutes in total, to be equally divided. The vote on the motion will occur at 9:40 a.m."

"Without objection," said Senator Thurmond, "it is so ordered."

Senator Helms, then, asked for a clarification. "Will the majority leader agree with me, for the record, that I did not request the extension of time?"

"Yes," replied Senator Baker, "I say for the Record that the Senator from North Carolina did not request the extension. He very graciously acceded to it."

Mr. Helms said, "I thank the Senator."

3. Senator Helms speaks about dead brothers and straight sticks. At 9:30 a.m. on Tuesday, October 18, 1983, Senator Helms spoke in favor of the Senate moving to the Judiciary Committee for further review the bill to make Martin Luther King, Jr.'s birthday a federal holiday.

> Mr. President, the creation of a legal public holiday is a matter of no small moment. We have nine public holidays now, and of those nine, only three honor individuals: Christmas Day for Jesus Christ, Washington's birthday for George Washington, and Columbus Day for Christopher Columbus. The proposal now before the Senate seeks to add Martin Luther King, Jr., to this list.
>
> Mr. President, I have moved that this bill be committed to the Judiciary Committee for a very simple reason. The Senate, to be blunt about it, has not done its homework on this matter. Despite the rarity of holidays for individuals in our country, we are obviously on the verge of passing this bill without one minute of consideration by a committee, let alone hearings, in the Senate.
>
> When the Senate received this bill in August, the bill did not go to committee, as is normal procedure, but it went straight onto the Senate calendar. I find no fault with the majority leader having exercised his right in this regard. I do wish he had checked with me and perhaps some others before he implemented that

judgment. But that responsibility is uniquely his, and I do not criticize him in the slightest.

At the same time, while this may be acceptable practice on bills of little importance, it is not acceptable for measures as serious and as far reaching as a new national holiday which will shut down this country for another day each year.

Moreover, Dr. King, to say the least, was a highly controversial figure during his lifetime and remains so today. Given these facts, it is only reasonable and prudent that the Senate slow down a bit, give this matter the full and careful consideration it deserves, and send it to the Judiciary Committee for hearings and a comprehensive report before the Senate finalizes its judgment on the issue.

Mr. President, on October 3, when the debate on this matter began, I put into the record a comprehensive report detailing the political activities and associations of Dr. King and Dr. King's associates over a long period of time. The record is clear about his association with far left elements and elements in the Communist Party U.S.A. Some of the proponents of this measure may not like the truth, but that is the truth. On the other hand, if they contend that it is not the truth, why do they object to hearings?

My father told me many, many times that the best way to prove that a stick is crooked is to lay a straight one beside it. No, Mr. President, the Senate is ducking this issue.

I recognize the political pressures involved in this issue. I cannot begin to say how many Senators have come to me in the cloakroom and have said, "Jesse, you are exactly right about this thing; but if I stand with you, the newspapers back home will eat me alive." I said, "What do you think they do to me?"

Mr. President, the report that I placed in the record on October 3 recited Dr. King's efforts to hide his associations with far left elements and Communist Party U.S.A. elements.

But very clear throughout the record, Mr. President, is the fact that Dr. King's speeches and remarks contained insults to his own country and the institutions of this country, and I also mentioned in that report the unsuccessful efforts of President John F. Kennedy and Attorney General Robert F. Kennedy to persuade Dr. King to break off his associations.

I shall wait until the distinguished Senator from Massachusetts makes his remarks, but following my comments on October 3, Senator Kennedy, according to the congressional record, made certain observations about canards and that sort of thing, but Senator Kennedy's argument is not with the Senator from North Carolina. His argument is with his dead brother who was president and his dead brother who was Attorney General and not with the Senator from North Carolina.

I reiterate, Mr. President, the report that I inserted in the record on October 3 was not based on assertion, rumors, or so-called segregationist propaganda. It was based on the most recent scholarship of academic liberals, on the findings of official investigative bodies, and on the speeches and writings of Dr. King himself. My sources for the report are contained in the sixty-two footnotes printed at the end. And no one, no one, Mr. President, has refuted the evidence that I presented, and accordingly I assume that it deserves the close consideration of the Senate.

In addition, Mr. President, since October 3, the FBI has released under a Freedom of Information Act request some sixty-five thousand documents relating to Dr. King. Needless to say, neither the Senate nor I have had an adequate opportunity to digest this volume of material, much of which has been heavily censored. Samples, however, have been made available to my colleagues and they, like the other evidence I have presented, raise questions which deserve close consideration by the Senate, and such consideration can best be given by sending the bill to the Judiciary Committee for independent evaluation.

I say again that if after hearings, if during hearings it can be proved that there is not cause for concern, fine; I repeat what my father said, "If the stick is crooked, lay a straight one beside it; don't hide it, don't ignore it; confront it."

In addition to my evidence and the FBI materials, considerable evidence on Dr. King is being kept secret under a court order at the National Archives. At this very moment, the court is hearing a motion to which I am a party that the records be provided to the Senate, in confidence if the court sees the necessity of it, but the Senate....

I think the public's right to know and certainly the Senate's responsibility to know are paramount. I do not recall that there was a great deal of privacy accorded some other people who ran into difficulty during their lifetime.

So, Mr. President, we now have before us a strange situation. On the one hand, Congress is on the verge of enacting a national holiday for Martin Luther King, Jr., shutting down the country for a tenth day each year, with not one minute of Senate hearings on the matter, and by that I mean this Senate, not some Senate in the past—I am talking about the Senate of today, constituted by the members of today and a total lack of normal Senate investigation of a major bill. On the other hand, extensive evidence on Dr. King is now, this day, in possession of federal agencies in the executive branch.

And that is why I am urging, no doubt unsuccessfully, that my colleagues move to correct this glaring anomaly and at least send the bill to the Senate Judiciary Committee for consideration.

4. Senators discuss the meaning of the word "false."

At 9:55 a.m. on Tuesday, October 18, 1983, Senator Edward Kennedy of Massachusetts having asserted that Senator Helms' contention that the Senate had not deliberated on the issue of making Martin Luther King, Jr.'s birthday a holiday was "inaccurate and false," the following conversation ensued.

Senator Helms: "Mr. President, a point of order."

Senator Kennedy: "Mr. President."

Senator Thurmond, in his role as Presiding Officer: "Will the Senator yield for a point of order?"

Senator Kennedy: "I do not yield the floor. Mr. President, I have in my hand the sets of hearings held jointly by the Senate Judiciary Committee and the House Post Office and Civil Service Committee on March 27, 1979, on June 21, 1979. These joint hearings were held on the issue of establishing a national holiday to honor Martin Luther King."

Senator Helms: "Point of order."

Senator Thurmond: "Point of order is called for. Under rule XIX, no senator during debate shall directly or indirectly by any form of words impute to another senator or to other Senators any conduct or motive unworthy or unbecoming a senator."

Senator Kennedy: "Mr. President, the statement of the senator from North Carolina is inaccurate. I do not impute any motive to the senator. I simply say that his statement is inaccurate and false. If the chair wants to make a ruling, I have the hearings right here in my hand. If the chair would like to examine the hearings, the chair is prepared to do so."

Senator Thurmond: "Under rule XIX when a senator is called to order, he shall take a seat and may not proceed without leave of the senate, which if granted shall be upon motion that he be allowed to proceed in order, which motion shall be determined without debate."

Senator Kennedy: "Mr. President, may I continue?"

Senator Thurmond: "Is there a motion to that effect?"

Senator Kennedy: "Mr. President, these hearings were held with—"

Senator Helms: "Mr. President, regular order."

Senator Thurmond: "The senator will withhold."

Senator Helms: "The senator needs to learn the rules."

Senator Thurmond: "Is there a motion?"

Senator Mathias (of Maryland): "Mr. President, is it in order for me to move that the senator from Massachusetts may proceed with his statement?"

Senator Thurmond: "It is in order."

Senator Mathias: "I so move."

Senator Thurmond: "The question is on the motion."

Senator Helms: "Just a minute. Will the chair state the motion? I was in a conference."

Senator Thurmond: "The motion is that the senator from Massachusetts may proceed. It is not debatable."

Senator Helms: "I ask for the yeas and nays."

Senator Thurmond: "Is there a sufficient second?"

Senator Mathias: "Mr. President, I make a point of order that a quorum is not present."

Senator Thurmond: "The clerk will call the roll."

The legislative clerk called the roll.

Senator Baker: "Mr. President, I ask unanimous consent that I might proceed without the time being charged against the time allocated for debate on the motion of the senator from North Carolina at this point."

Senator Thurmond: "Without objection, it is so ordered."

Senator Baker: "Mr. President, I was away from the chamber at the time that the rule XIX controversy arose. But I have now asked the official reporters of the proceedings of the senate to read to me the transcript. I believe I understand how the problem arose, and even though I was not here, I can feel and appreciate the emotions that go with an issue of this sensitivity. As I recall the record as it was read to me, the point of order was made by the senator from North Carolina that the senator from Massachusetts had infringed the provisions of rule XIX of the Senate by saying that there had been false and inaccurate statements made by the senator from North Carolina."

Senator Helms: "Correct."

Senator Baker: "I think, frankly, that the hooker in this comes because we in the Senate, and I guess most other places these days, tend to join words together that do not have the same or equivalent meaning. There is a difference between false and inaccurate. 'False' perhaps would imply a violation of rule XIX, and 'inaccurate' certainly would not. However, the usage is so common in the Senate that I can fully understand how it is done. I use it myself. I do it that way sometimes in written statements and speeches I have on the floor of the Senate. But I really would not want an issue as important as the King holiday resolution or the motion to commit, which is contemplated by the unanimous-consent order, to be diverted by a questionable situation under the provisions of rule XIX. Therefore, may I make a suggestion, and it will require the acquiescence of both the senator from Massachusetts and the senator from North Carolina. I hope both of them will consider this in the interest of proceeding on this important matter and doing so in a timely way. I would suggest, Mr. President, that by unanimous consent the word "false" be stricken from the transcript and the word "inaccurate" be left in, and that the senator from North Carolina, who made the point of order, and I believe got the yeas and nays on the point of order—"

Senator Helms: "I did not."

Senator Baker (continuing): "That the senator from North Carolina as a matter of right may withdraw his point of order on the basis of that correction. The motion of the senator from Maryland that the senator from Massachusetts may proceed under the provisions of rule XIX is perfectly in order and fully contemplated in the rule. As I understand the chair, the yeas and nays were not ordered. Therefore, if the senator from Maryland would wish to do so, he could withdraw his motion and we would be back where we started from. The record would then reflect by order of the Senate that the statement of the senator from Massachusetts was that the statement of the senator from North Carolina in respect of hearings was inaccurate. Mr. President, may I first ask the senator from Massachusetts—I will ask either senator, whichever chooses—I will create another flap here if I am not careful. Let me ask either senator if they are inclined to agree to that effort."

Senator Helms: "Reserving the right to object, Mr. President, I would be perfectly willing to let this matter drop if the record is made clear that the distinguished senator from Massachusetts was clearly in error when he said that I made a false and inaccurate statement about this Senate never having conducted hearings. I took great pains at the time I made the statement, Mr. President, to say this Senate as presently constituted, and I submit that is an absolutely correct statement. If the record will be made clear in that regard, we could go right ahead and I would not object to the unanimous-consent request by the majority leader."

Senator Baker: "Mr. President, my unanimous-consent request is simply that the word 'false' be expunged from the record and that the point of order be withdrawn and that the motion be withdrawn. That is my unanimous-consent request. Of course, senators will wish to interpret that as they please, but I believe that we have here an inadvertence that can blow up in our face and it is not worth that."

Senator Byrd: "Will the majority leader yield?"

Senator Baker: "I yield without losing my right to the floor."

Senator Byrd: "Mr. President, I think the majority leader's recommendation is the best that can be made under the circumstances.

I would hope there would be no objection and that we can proceed with the debate and put this matter behind us. I hope there will be no objection."

Senator Baker: "Mr. President, once again, what I am asking is that the word 'false' be expunged from the record and that the point of order be withdrawn and the motion withdrawn."

5. The Senate votes on Senator Helms' motion to refer H.R. 3706 to the Judiciary Committee.

At 11:10 a.m. on Tuesday, October 18, 1983, after a roll call vote, Senator Helms' motion to refer H.R. 3706 to the Judiciary Committee was defeated, with 12 Senators voting yea, 76 voting nay, and 12 not voting.

6. Senator Rudman offers an amendment cosponsored by Senator Helms.

At 11:20 a.m. on Tuesday, October 18, 1983, the clerk of the United States Senate read the following for the record:

> Rudman (and Helms) amendment number 2328. Mr. Rudman, for himself and Mr. Helms, proposed an amendment to the bill, H.R. 3706, to amend title 5, United States Code, to make the birthday of Martin Luther King, Jr., a legal public holiday; as follows: On page 1, strike out lines 6 and 7, and insert in lieu thereof: "National Equality Day, February 12." On page 2, add after line 4 the following new section: Sec. 3. The provisions of section 6103(b) of title 5, United States Code shall not apply to National Equality Day established pursuant to the first section of this Act.

Section 6103(b) of title 5 identifies the days that are designated a national holiday with a paid day off for federal workers. Thus, the amendment would establish February 12 as National Day, but not as a federal holiday.

At 10:24 a.m. on Tuesday, October 18, 1983, after a roll call vote, the Rudman and Helms amendment number 2328 was defeated, with 22 Senators voting yea, 68 voting nay, and 10 not voting.

7. Senator East offers an amendment.

At 11:45 a.m. on Tuesday, October 18, 1983, the clerk of the United States Senate said, "The senator from North Carolina, Mr. East, proposes an amendment numbered 2329." He did not, however, read the amendment, Senator East having asked that reading of the amendment be dispensed with. The amendment was as follows:

> Strike out all after the enacting clause and insert in lieu thereof the following: That this Act may be cited as the "National Civil Rights Day Act of 1983."
>
> Sec. 2. The Congress finds that:
>
> (1) the birthday of President James Madison is March 16;
> (2) James Madison played a significant role in the drafting and adoption of the Constitution of the United States;
> (3) James Madison played a significant role in the drafting and adoption of the "Bill of Rights" contained in the first ten Amendments of the Constitution of the United States;
> (4) the Constitution of the United States is the source of and authority for the laws of the United States and the civil rights and liberties of the citizen; and
> (5) the laws of the United States and the civil rights of the citizen guarantee the right of protection of the laws without regard to race, color, creed, national origin, sex, or disability.

Sec. 3. March 16 of each year is designated as "National Civil Rights Day," and the President is authorized and requested to issue a proclamation each year calling upon the people of the United States to observe the day with appropriate programs, ceremonies, and activities.

At 12:00 p.m., the Senate recessed prior to voting on the amendment.

8. A disturbance takes place in the U.S. House of Representatives. At 1:25 p.m. on Tuesday, October 18, 1983, in U.S. House of Representatives Gallery 10 in the left corner of the chamber, Israel Rubinowits adjusted the two two-liter plastic Pepsi bottles taped to his belt. Sitting still with these things attached to him was proving impossible. Equally impossible was keeping from talking to himself. At the moment, he was talking to himself about the ceiling directly over his head. Not the central skylight he saw by tilting his head back an inch and lifting his eyes, but the ceiling he saw when tilting his head and upper body as far back as he could, which revealed, and which he described aloud to himself, something far less majestic: a drop ceiling with acoustic tile that looked as cheap and undistinguished as the ceiling in any third-rate office or largely ignored basement.

He stood so he could lean further back, which not only allowed him to better study and more accurately comment on the ceiling, but also relieved some of the pressure of the bottles strapped to his belt pressing into his abdomen and also loosened the pressure of his belt and jacket on the wires protruding from the bottles and the detonation cap at the wires' destination. But, standing, he was still constrained by others in the tour group, seated, their knees protruding into the aisle.

At 1:30 p.m., as Israel stood, staring up at the ceiling and narrating the experience, and as two members of the U.S. Capitol Police maneuvered past the knees of the others in the tour group and approached Israel, a roll call vote was underway on the Vietnam Veterans National Medal Act, which would direct the Secretary of the Treasury to coin and sell a medal in honor of the members and former members of the Armed Forces who served in Vietnam and would declare that the secretary shall offer such medals for sale to the public at a price sufficient to cover the cost of minting and distributing of such medals. The House passed the bill with 410 yeas and 0 nays.

Previously, on March 3, 1983, the bill had been referred to House Committee on Banking, Finance and Urban Affairs.

On September 27, 1983, the House Committee on Banking, Finance, and Urban Affairs referred the bill to the Subcommittee on Consumer Affairs and Coinage, and that subcommittee held hearings.

On October 17, 1983, the bill was discharged by the House Committee on Banking, Finance, and Urban Affairs by Suspension of Rules, called up by the House under suspension of rules, and considered by the House as unfinished business, with a vote on the measure postponed until the next day.

After the House passed the measure, the House clerk was directed to transmit the bill to the U.S. Senate for its consideration.

9. The Senate reconvenes.

At 2:00 p.m. on Tuesday, October 18, 1983, the Senate reconvened. At 2:03 a.m. on a roll call vote, the Rudman and Helms amendment number 2329, seeking to replace a legal public holiday for Martin Luther King, Jr.'s birthday with a National Equity Day that is not a public holiday was defeated, with 18 Senators voting yea, 76 voting nay, and 6 not voting.

10. The United States District Court suggests that Senator Helms take his quest for records on Martin Luther King, Jr., to "the legislative arena."

At 2:10 p.m., Judge John Lewis Smith, Jr., of the United States District Court in the District of Columbia issued his ruling in the matter of Lee v. Kelley, 99 F.R.D. 340. Judge Smith wrote, in part:

> Senator Jesse Helms seeks leave to intervene pursuant to Fed.R.Civ.P.24(a)(2) in two cases decided by this Court in 1977. In *Lee v. Kelley,* No. 76-1185, and *Southern Christian Leadership Conference v. Kelley,* No. 76-1186 (D.D.C. Jan. 31, 1977), this Court ordered that tapes and transcripts generated by Federal Bureau of Investigation electronic surveillance of Dr. Martin Luther King be held under seal in the National Archives for a period of fifty years, and that the tapes or their contents not be disclosed except under specific court order. The case is currently before the Court on Senator Helms' motion to intervene and his motion, under ed.R.Civ.P.60(b)(5), to vacate or modify the Court's 1977 order.
>
> Senator Helms requests access to the sealed materials before the Senate considers, on October 19, 1983, legislation establishing a national holiday honoring Dr. King. Such legislation has been introduced numerous times in prior sessions of Congress. On August 2, 1983, the House of Representatives passed a King holiday bill and sent it to the Senate for consideration. More than two months later, on October 11, 1983, and barely one week before the Senate is scheduled to vote on the bill, Senator Helms filed this motion for intervention….
>
> Senator Helms' attempt to intervene in effect represents a "dispute with his fellow legislators." In his supporting papers, Senator Helms emphasizes what he views as an inadequate factfinding process in the Senate: because the "*Senate leadership*

waived the normal rules," "*no hearings* have been conducted concerning the proposed legislation in order to inform the Senators of facts either to justify or to defeat the passage of this legislation." Helms Memorandum of Points and Authorities at 5 (emphasis supplied). "No Senate committees have been charged with the responsibility to investigate Dr. King." Helms Supplemental Memorandum of Points and Authorities at 6. By intervening in this case to obtain the King surveillance materials, Senator Helms seeks to perform the investigative function of the committee hearings the Senate leadership decided to forego. It is not for this Court to review the adequacy of the deliberative process in the Senate or to question decisions of the Senate or question decisions of the Senate leadership. *Cf. Vander Jagt v. O'Neill, supra,* 699 F.2d at 1176; *Metcalf v. National Petroleum Council,* 553 F.2d 176, 188 (D.C.Cir.1977). To conclude otherwise would represent an "obvious intrusion by the judiciary into the legislative arena." *Riegle, supra,* 656 F.2d at 882. Senator Helms, of course, is not prevented from entering the "legislative arena"; he can argue to the Senate that the sealed materials should be obtained and considered by a committee before a vote. In any event, the proper forum for this contention is the Senate, for "[i]t would be unwise to permit the federal courts to become a higher legislature where a Congressman who has failed to persuade his colleagues can always renew the battle." *Id.*

11. Senator Helms does what the court suggests.

At 2:20 p.m. on Tuesday, October 18, 1983, on the Senate floor, Senator Kennedy said, "Mr. President, I have just been notified that the court has ruled that the request that was made by the senator from North Carolina for certain papers has been rejected, and I shall include in the record the findings of the court and a more detailed explanation of the action. I understand it was made only a few minutes ago."

At 3:15 p.m., Senator Helms was granted the floor and said, "Madam President [Senator Nancy Kassebaum having assumed the role of president pro tempore], I send an amendment to the desk." The Amendment, number 2332, follows:

At the end of the bill, add the following:

> Sec. Notwithstanding any other provision of this Act, the amendment made by the first section of this Act shall not take effect unless and until the Senate adopts and carries out the following resolution:
>
> Resolved, That the Senate Legal Counsel, on behalf of the United States Senate, in conjunction with such agencies of the United States as may be advisable, is directed to seek access, by all available legal means, including but not limited to subpoena, to the following:
>
> (a) Any and all records, tapes, documents, files, materials, and other evidence relating in any way to Martin Luther King, Jr. in the possession of the Department of Justice, the Federal Bureau of Investigation, the Central Intelligence Agency, the National Security Agency, and the Defense Intelligence Agency; and
>
> (b) Any and all records, tapes, documents, files, material, and other evidence relating in any way to Martin Luther King, Jr. and sealed by order of the United States District Court for the District of Columbia, dated January 31, 1977, in the cases of *Lee v. Kelley*, et al., Civil Action No. 76-1185, and *Southern Christian Leadership Conference v. Kelley, et al*, Civil Action No. 76-1186; for the confidential examination of the United States Senate;

> Resolved, further, That if the above items and materials are too voluminous for confidential examination by the United States Senate in a reasonable time, in the determination of the Senate Majority and Minority Leaders, a Select Committee on Martin Luther King, Jr. shall be established to summarize and present the salient portion of the material for confidential examination by the United States Senate.
>
> Resolved, further, That after examination of and debate on the above materials, the Senate shall affirm by majority vote that it is appropriate to approve a legal public holiday in honor of Martin Luther King, Jr.

At 3:45 p.m. on Tuesday, the Helms amendment number 2332 was defeated, with 3 Senators voting yea, 90 voting nay, and 7 not voting.

At 6:00 p.m., the Senate adjourned for the day.

12. Ronald Reagan has a good day.

At 10:40 p.m. on Tuesday, October 18, 1983, in the second floor residence of the White House, President Ronald Reagan wrote his daily diary entry:

> An easy day—1st day with Bud MacFarlane in charge of N.S.C. The 9:30 A.M. Brf. dealt with coming Japan trip. Question is do we press them to extend their voluntary limit on autos to U.S. or not & if we do, should we hold figure to 1.68 mil. as it is now or increase? Our auto prod. increase is such that percentage wise holding the fig. would reduce Japan from more than 22% of our mkt. to about 17%. N.S.P.G. meeting on Lebanon. All the options on how to keep trying for peace, avoid murder of our Marines, not suffer a disastrous pol. defeat etc. No decisions, but option papers being drawn up for my decision. Lunch with about 90 editors & publishers of ethnic papers of all descriptions.

It was pleasant—their Q's were mainly on subjects having to do with their own ethnic or racial source. Haircut & then 2 hours in Family Theatre prepping for tomorrow nights press conf.

At 10:55 p.m., President Reagan went to bed.

Peoria, Illinois

1. Just after midnight, another possible botulism case arrives at a hospital.

At 12:38 a.m. on Tuesday, October 18, 1983, Kim VanTine's parents, Dicky and Garnet, drove Kim, who was 20 and still living at home in a two-bedroom clapboard house across from the Madison Park Golf Course and the Elks Lodge to Methodist Medical Center, where she was admitted and listed in good condition.

2. Coach D recalls a line of poetry.

At 5:00 a.m. on Tuesday, October 18, 1983, Lou Dobrydnia lay in bed at Methodist Medical Center in Peoria, Illinois. She could not move. She could not speak. But she felt when people touched her—when the nurses put the tube down her throat and when the doctor jiggled the tube for no reason Lou could understand. And she could think. Just now she was thinking about Dr. Dwyer's class on classic literature at Bradley. Well, not about the class, but about Dr. Dwyer's weird habit of standing pushed into the far corner of the room while he spoke, as though he was about to be attacked, and also about a line Dr. Dwyer pointed out from one of the works they read, the *Aeneid* by Virgil. Not that Lou read it all, and probably none of the other students had. That book was a slog. She had read less than half of it, even though she usually finished what she started, no matter how unpleasant, and she usually liked to read about heroes, although mostly in magazines and the sports pages of the newspaper.

The passage in the *Aeneid* she thought about now, forming and reforming words to try to get the line the way it was in the book, came fairly early in the story, if she was remembering correctly. The scene took place in the evening, she thought, or anyway during a moment between battles. Aeneas and his troops had been savaged, if Lou was remembering correctly, and he was trying to keep up the troops' spirits. He said, this is the line she was trying to remember, something like, "Someday it will please us to remember even this." Or maybe it was "one day." And maybe "may" instead of "will." Or maybe the word "perhaps" was stuck in there somewhere.

She knew she didn't have the exact words, and it was a translation, and Lou may not have known Latin—or was it Greek?—but she felt confident that she was in as good a position as anyone to find the right way to express that particular thought if she could keep the words from falling out of her grasp.

In one way, the line was a promise. You'll look back at being exhausted and hungry and bloodied, at seeing your friends eviscerated, at expecting more of the same tomorrow, and the feeling you have will be pleasure. And what might that pleasure be? A good laugh? A story that keeps listeners on the edge of their seats? Gratitude at being alive? Commiseration among fellow sufferers?

To Lou, lying here in bed, breathing through a tube, feeling as if she were in a full body cast, Aeneas' promise seemed mighty thin, close to insulting her intelligence. Yes, if she survived, she would have quite a story to tell. "Once I ate a patty melt sandwich at a restaurant in a mall in Peoria, Illinois, and I ended up in the hospital unable to speak or breath or move for—" fill in the duration, the doctors clearly didn't know and weren't as free as Aeneas with their promises.

She might even look back and feel a sense of relief. Or she might feel a sense of gratitude. Or she might feel safe, thinking she had experienced one freak catastrophe and therefore likely would not run into another one, although as a coach and a driver's ed teacher, she knew enough about probability to know that the likelihood of, say, getting into a car accident was the same whether you had an accident yesterday or hadn't had one for twenty years.

So, yes, memory would dull the pain, would play up the entertaining or dramatic or silly aspects of a hideous event. Memory would highlight the positive contrast between the memory's vantage point and the memory itself.

However, even Aeneas didn't believe those suds.

First, he left himself an out: "may" please us, "perhaps" will please us. A politician could do no better, and as a leader of men in battle, Aeneas was, Lou thought, a kind of politician.

Second, as soon as his speech to the troops was over, Lou recalled, Aeneas went off by himself and said something about keeping up the appearance of hope while burying anguish in his heart.

The kicker, of course, was that if you're dead, you have no memory. Which didn't make what Aeneas said wrong, exactly, but limited its application.

Present pain was present pain. You can't reason your way around it. What you can do, what Lou did, was put her faith in God, not to allay her pain, not to ensure she would live, not to provide her with a funny story, but simply to do whatever God, in His infinite and unknowable wisdom, would do.

Still, she might try that "one day it may please us to remember even this" line on her team when they were getting throttled. The players would probably just shake their heads. "Coach D is losing it," they would say. Perhaps she was.

3. Sam Somers folds today's newspaper.

At 6:35 a.m. on Tuesday, October 18, 1983, in a parking lot on Airport Road in Limestone Township, Sam Somers folded in perfect thirds today's edition of the Peoria *Journal Star*. On one visible third was the middle portion of a headline: "ys crowded superma" and below that enough text to discern that an employee had lit a cigarette inside a supermarket causing an explosion in Charleston, South Carolina.

Visible below that was a more generous portion of a slightly larger headline, its first line "21 people trea" and its second line "for food poiso".

Below the headline, visible in this center third was "By Ray Long of the *Journal Star*," several short paragraphs of type, and a portion of a photograph showing a balding man in a white shirt and tie but no jacket who seemed to be lecturing an expressionless white-haired man in a hospital bed.

When Sam stacked the papers, he placed this third face down. The third that remained face up showed a photograph of a long, narrow painting of what appeared to be a hooded Mary holding a hooded baby Jesus. Beneath the photograph were these words: "Peoria's August H. Schmitz Co. specializes in designing church interiors. The firm does original work for newer churches and restoration work for older ones. This artwork at St. Mary's Cathedral was done by the firm's founder in 1952. Details, Business/Tuesday." Visible beneath that was a box containing three small headlines: "Packers win 48–47," "Illinois No. 11," and "Another Guilty Plea for Vida Blue."

4. The bassist gives a stool sample.

At 10:10 a.m. on Tuesday, October 15, 1983, in a sterile-looking room that was not quite an examination room and not quite an office at the Peoria/Peoria County Department of Health on Sheridan Road, Jason Cook, bassist for a band called, for now, anyway, Samson and cook at the Skewer Inn, perhaps, he thought, former cook, as he had no idea when the restaurant would reopen, was receiving instructions from a nurse with the thinnest lips he had ever seen forming a gentle smile suitable for the topic of conversation.

The instructions were how Jason was to collect a stool sample, which would be examined as part of the investigation into the apparent, that was the qualifying word she used, botulism outbreak.

The nurse handed Jason a plastic container with an opening about the size of a half dollar and another plastic container that looked like what the fussy families used to pack sandwiches for their kids' lunches. Inside of that was a tiny spatula, a plastic miniature of the ones hanging from pegs in the Skewer Inn kitchen, and a small white garbage bag.

The nurse told Jason to take all the equipment from the larger plastic container and set it on the shelf next to the toilet. Then he should set the container inside the toilet bowl. It would stay steady, she assured him. If he needed to pee, she said, be sure to do that before he put the plastic container into the toilet. He should poo—that was the word she used, "poo"—into the larger plastic container. Then he should use the tiny spatula to scoop about a teaspoonful of the poo. She began to illustrate with her fingers how much a teaspoonful would be but stopped herself. "Oh, you're a cook. You know about teaspoons."

He was to put the poo—that word again—into the smaller plastic container, and put on its plastic lid. He was to dump the remaining poo into the toilet and flush. He was to place everything except the specimen jar into the garbage bag, tie it closed, and put it in the bin. Then wash his hands thoroughly with soap and warm water. They would have the results in a few days. In the meantime, he was not contagious, but if he felt dizzy or had trouble breathing or moving, he should go to the hospital.

Jason thought about asking if it was okay to play a gig that night, but figured he already had enough information to answer that question on his own.

The nurse led him out of the room and around a corner, gesturing with a fully outstretched arm and pointing with her full flattened hand—like a game show model—toward the men's room.

Another question Jason decided not to ask what to do if he didn't need to poo.

5. The CDC and the State Health Department converge, but not in Peoria.

At 10:40 a.m. on Tuesday, October 18, 1983, Robert Spencer, PhD, chief epidemiologist of the Illinois State Department of Health, was waiting in the gate area of the Abraham Lincoln Capital Airport, just three miles north on J. David Jones Parkway, named after the largely forgotten Republican Illinois U.S. Representative, from his office in Springfield.

An American Airlines flight (the only civil airline that served the airport, although it had a military purpose as well) from Washington, DC, was due to land in ten minutes, at which time a terminal door would open and in would come a burst of fifty-degree air and a line of passengers with the slightly confused look even seasoned travelers had when they deplaned into a terminal. The Capital Airport, as it was called—sorry, Lincoln, Dr. Spencer thought, for not being part of the shorthand airport name, but your name is on practically every building in Springfield, so your reputation is secure—did not have the fancy tubes that fed people from airplane to airport; you had to walk down the steps and on the runway, which Dr. Spencer rather appreciated and he was sure was familiar to Dr. Kristine McDonald, an epidemiologist from the Centers for Disease Control in Washington, DC, the person he was meeting, who spent a good amount of her work traveling to hot spots that didn't necessarily sync up with the spots having the most modern airports.

Dr. Spencer had met Dr. McDonald once at a conference in Washington. His memory of her was vague, and he had no reason to think her memory of him would be any better; probably she didn't remember him at all.

The fact that Dr. McDonald was basically a stranger to Dr. Spencer was one reason, one of two, that he was annoyed, although not surprised, at the way the CDC or the IDH or someone somewhere in the state or federal government made the travel arrangements in the way they had.

Dr. McDonald was to fly from Washington to Springfield, where Dr. Spencer was to meet her. From there, Dr. Spencer would drive Dr. McDonald in one of the rattletrap state vehicles the hour and a half—not including the inevitable stop for lunch, given the timing—to Peoria. Dr. Spencer did not consider himself shy. Perhaps, he thought, a shade introverted, but he could make conversation when required at the odd cocktail or dinner party. But driving a stranger for an hour and a half, plus at least another half hour for lunch, plus the same on the return trip, was a larger demand for conversation than he wanted to face. What in the hell would they talk about? Doubtless, he and she had read the same reports about the botulism cases, so what was the point of reviewing them? The tracking steps were pretty obvious and were, as far as he could tell, underway. The visit was mostly a gesture of oversight by the state and federal governments. That said, the case was unusual, both in the size of the outbreak and the mystery of its source. Still, that didn't for Dr. Spencer translate into hours-long conversation with a stranger.

The second reason the travel plans were annoying is that they didn't make any sense. If it was so important for state and federal public health experts to be on site in Peoria, why on earth didn't the logistics whizzes have Dr. McDonald fly from Washington directly to Peoria and have him drive from Springfield and meet her in Peoria. They could get to the site hours earlier, and Dr. Spencer would make the drive accompanied by the radio rather than someone to whom he wasn't entirely sure what to say.

He strolled toward the window and was pretty sure he saw the American Airlines plane approaching. Maybe Dr. McDonald would be talkative, and Dr. Spencer could just say "yes" and "mmhm."

Unknown to both Dr. Spencer and Dr. McDonald, as well as to whoever in the federal or state government made these travel plans, by meeting at the Abraham Lincoln Capital Airport in Springfield rather than the Peoria International Airport, the travelers were missing a remarkable sight. Across the broad, open lobby of the Peoria International Airport was a breathtaking display of tile in small, tight, black-and-white squares, looking like a thousand chessboards for mice, and very popular among the Peorians and visitors who traveled by air.

4. John Mason figures something out.

At 11:20 a.m. on Tuesday, October 18, 1983, in a bed at St. Francis Hospital in Peoria, Illinois, John Mason worked out a puzzle in his mind, which was the only part of him he was able to make perform, and even that not well, not well at all.

He was attempting to work out something off kilter about what had happened in the hospital last night, when his brother, father, wife, and son all had visited him. His wife and son, that made sense. They were close by. His father lived a little further away and typically didn't drive at night. Why hadn't he waited until today to visit? And his brother lived even farther away and was less likely to believe that John being in the hospital was an occasion for prompt action. His brother, well, John would have expected to see him late on the second day in the hospital, or maybe the third, if John was going to be here that long.

Beyond their presence was the strange way they had behaved. Everyone kissing him on the head? Again, his wife, okay, but his son was 13, and at that age kissing Dad was pretty low on his list of things he wanted to do. Someone must have told him to do it. Same with his brother. Same with saying, "I love you." Someone had told his son and brother to say that. As for his dad, he would only kiss John and say "I love you" if he thought John was about to die.

At which point John understood why what had happened in his room last night had happened.

5. People make pickle jokes.

At 12:30 p.m. on Tuesday, October 18, 1983, at Lum's Restaurant on Knoxville Avenue, a long block north of Peoria Stadium, where John Mason and his son had attended a game on Saturday morning before John started vomiting, a server named Willa Tinley, who had worked at Lum's for 12 years, placed two platters on a booth table. In the booth were the two men she thought of as the twins: both wore white shirts, striped ties, and beige sport jackets. Both apparently didn't realize that putting Brylcreem in your hair had gone out of style even before she had started working at Lum's. On most visits, they found some way to, speaking in grand tones, remind her that they worked up the street at an insurance company the name of which she assiduously avoided remembering. Anyway, she was unsure why they wanted to impart this information. Did they believe their being gainfully employed was impressive? She, too, was gainfully employed. Did they think she would visit them at the office when she got off work?

In front of one of the twins, she set a platter with Lum's Famous Hot Dog Steamed in Beer with Sherry-Flavored Sauerkraut with chips and a dill pickle sliced lengthwise. In front of the other she set a platter of Lum's World Famous (she often wondered why one item was "famous" and the other "world famous") Submarine made with imported Holland ham, Genoa salami, provolone cheese, and spicy Italian salami on a large crisp Italian roll and chips and a dill pickle sliced lengthwise.

The submarine eater, in addition to having the largest appetite, also talked the most, but this time he just stared at his platter as though something were wrong.

Finally he said, "Are these pickles safe?" and turned toward Willa with over-acted consternation.

"Yes," Willa said. "I'm sure of it."

"Good," he said, "then you eat one."

The man laughed at his own joke. His companion laughed too, but had the decency to stop when he saw Willa wasn't laughing or for that matter smiling, just looking blandly.

It wasn't that Willa was offended or even bothered. It was just that the joke wasn't funny, and that's what you did when a joke wasn't funny: look bland.

6. More admissions.

At 3:30 p.m. on Tuesday, October 18, 1983, Jean Parker, 55, of East Peoria was admitted to Methodist Medical Center in Peoria with symptoms of botulism.

At 4:36 p.m., Margaret Riley, 72, was transferred from St. Elizabeth Hospital in Ottawa Illinois, a half hour north of Peoria, to Saint Francis Medical Center in Peoria with symptoms of botulism.

7. The bassist plays a show.

At 9:30 p.m. on Tuesday, October 18, 1983, at a barn-like structure called the Second Chance Nightclub on Willow Knolls Drive way the hell and gone north of Peoria just south of the Kellogg Golf Course, Jason Cook was stepping onto the foot-high stage, thinking that Tuesday shows were for the birds, and he didn't mean girls. But the band needed any exposure they could get, and the Second Chance was the best rock club in the city—practically the only one, but still the best—and maybe if they did well and some of their friends showed up, the band, Samson, would be asked back to headline a Thursday, or even to open for another band on a Friday or Saturday.

Late last week, the same night as the first botulism cases at the restaurant, which Justin was growing more suspicious that he had caused, the lead singer had called Justin with the depressing news that there was another band called Samson—a heavy metal band in England. It figured. Samson was too good a name not to be already taken. The question was what to do about it. He and the lead singer discussed the situation. They could stick with the name and hope that the English Samson didn't get popular or that they broke up soon. More likely, the Peoria Samson would never get big enough to come to the attention of the English Samson or anyone else outside Peoria. But that was no way to think. The name would have to go. Neither Jason nor the lead singer had any band names in waiting, and at the next band practice, the ideas from the guitarist and drummer were so bad they weren't even funny.

From the stage of the Second Chance, as the band started their first song, a cover of "Jumpin' Jack Flash"—might as well get the audience on your side from the start—Jason thought, how about Stool Sample for a band name. Or, if he let the public health nurse name the band, it would be Poo Sample.

Or he could go solo: Jason Cook, the Cook Who Kills.

The doctors said the restaurant did nothing wrong, and of course the Skewer Inn owners said the same thing, but Jason had no idea how they could make that assertion with such confidence when no one had any idea what the hell had actually happened except that two dozen people who ate patty melts he had made were in the hospital and some of them seemed sick enough to die.

Jason was glad he had played "Jumpin' Jack Flash" a thousand times, because clearly he wasn't giving the song his full attention tonight.

The health department people had questioned him—grilled him, one might say in this case, terrible pun—about every step of the preparation. He hadn't done anything different. Well, he thought he hadn't. But maybe he had. It seemed like they were losing interest in the pickles. It must have been the meat. It must have arrived already contaminated. It was nothing he had done.

Soon-to-not-be-Samson's next song, Jason was fully aware, took pandering to a new level: a cover of the 1980 hit "Take It on the Run" by local (Peoria and Champaign, Illinois) heroes REO Speedwagon. Maybe Samson should change its name to Pander Bear.

The crowd was spotty but not quite embarrassingly so. Some people were even dancing, except that a squint against the meager stage lights revealed the dancers were actually three mohawked skate kids, a breed that had only recently shown up in Peoria. Jason saw them hanging out at Coop Tapes & Records on Main Street as if they lived there. He knew some of them were in bands that played in vacant lots and church basements. These three were dancing, but they were dancing ironically or angrily or ironically angrily because everything these kids did seemed either ironic or angry or ironically angry.

When the song ended, the kids clapped and hooted—ironically, he was pretty sure, rather than angrily or ironically angrily—and hollered for songs Jason couldn't quite make out. As soon-to-not-be-Samson's lead singer was drinking water, and the skate kids were reasonably still, Jason studied the t-shirt of the one on the right. He was only a few feet away, but the lettering and picture, obviously homemade, were hard to make out. Was that a drawing of a burger? Maybe. And those words were, yes they were:

"Peoria" then a heart, then "Botulism."

After the first set, one of the skate kids, not the one with the botulism shirt, came up to Jason and said, "You're better than those songs, and you're better than those other guys. You should join our band."

Jason asked, "Does your band have a name?"

The kid said, "Not really."

Jason said, “What do you think of Stool Sample?”

“See?” the kid said. “I knew you were better than that band you’re in.”

8. Admissions and symptoms.

At 10:29 p.m. on Tuesday, October 18, 1983, at Saint Francis Medical Center in Peoria, 19-month-old Angela Ansili of Washington, Illinois, was, out of caution, admitted with symptoms that doctors doubted were those of botulism. She was discharged later that night.

At 11:29 p.m. on Tuesday, October 18, 1983, at Saint Francis Medical Center in Peoria, 60-year-old Oiliaden McCammon of Peoria was, out of caution, admitted with symptoms that doctors doubted were those of botulism.

Wednesday, October 19, 1983

New York City

1. A citizen weighs what level of detail, if any, to share with police. At 7:15 a.m. on Wednesday, October 19, 1983, near the corner of Avenue D and East 59th Street in the East Flatbush neighborhood of Brooklyn, near the entrance to the Harry Maze Playground, Joshua Leonard, walking to work at a nearby warehouse, passed a new-looking Dodge station wagon with a sign saying, "BMW Printing, Smithtown, Long Island" and a telephone number mounted on its side. Glancing through the car's windows, Joshua saw a figure in the driver's seat leaning in an awkward position, as though he were sleeping, except that the figure was bloody, and its head and chest seemed to have been blown open. Taking a step or two back, Joshua looked through the side window of the rear portion of the station wagon and saw another figure, this one lying on its back, also with a bloody face and chest, and covered with small boxes and metal objects that Joshua couldn't identify.

"Why," Joshua imagined the police saying if he called to report what he had seen, "did you notice the car?"

"Why," Joshua imagined himself replying, "does anyone notice anything?"

"Why," Joshua imagined the police asking, "were you so curious you had to you look through the window?"

"Why," Joshua imagined himself replying, "is anyone curious about anything?"

"Why," Joshua imagined the police saying, "are you such a smartass son of a bitch?"

Alternatively, Joshua imagined, if he did not report what he saw and was questioned later, he could hear the police asking, "Why didn't you notice the car when you passed? It had two dead bodies in it, for Christ's sake."

Best to split the difference, Joshua thought, and he stopped at a payphone, dialed 911, told the attendant that he saw a man sleeping in a car, and hung up without identifying himself.

At 7:45 a.m., less than one mile away on Foster Avenue at the front entrance of a full-block building that once housed a bowling alley, billiard hall, lounge, and hotel, since 1973 was occupied by the Jersey Lynne Farm Dairy, a wholesale food distributor, several employees stepped over or on empty shell casings and blood-stained cardboard before opening the front door and reporting for work.

2. A small protest takes place.

At 10:00 a.m. on Wednesday, October 19, 1983, at 100 Centre Street in lower Manhattan, outside the main entrance of the seventeen-story granite-and-limestone art deco building that housed the Manhattan Criminal Courthouse in four towers in front and a jail in back, City Councilwoman Mary Pinkett of Brooklyn and nineteen other of what the three reporters who had been invited to accompany the group tomorrow would inevitably call "Black leaders" gathered under the huge granite archway that defined the building's entrance. The archway, Councilwoman Pinkett thought, was doing its job. The councilwoman knew that she, that twenty people, that two hundred people, would always seem tiny, maybe even ridiculous, in contrast to that archway and the massive slab of a building on which it was mounted.

That was fine. she didn't mind looking ridiculous to others. Because she certainly didn't feel ridiculous.

Even when the group entered the building, their mass was only a modest presence in comparison with the size of the square atrium and the swarming people making their way in twenty different directions to carry out justice or to have justice be carried out on them.

Some of the councilwoman's group took the stairs, and some the elevator. They converged again on the sixth floor outside the frosted glass door on which painted black letters proclaimed, "Office of the District Attorney of Manhattan Robert M. Morgenthau." Councilwoman Pinkett tried the doorknob and found it locked, although she could see people inside. She knocked on the glass, and after some shuffling of bodies visible through the frosted glass, the door opened just wide enough for a thin young woman to pop out and stand in front of the opening, one hand kept on the knob behind her. The woman let her eyes graze the people in front of her and settle on Councilwoman Pinkett, who said, "Good morning. We are here to see Mr. Morgenthau on the matter of Michael Stewart."

"Michael Stewart," repeated the young woman, not as a question but just an echo.

"About justice for Michael Stewart, who died at the hands of the New York City Transit Police."

"Just a moment," the woman answered and, without turning her back to the group, opened the door and backed through the doorway.

Now, in this hallway, Councilwoman Pinkett's group of twenty—and three reporters—was a more striking presence, as people either edged past them with their backs to the wall or turned in search of a route that would not take them past the group.

After three minutes of silence, the councilwoman knocked on the glass harder, three sharp raps, one, she thought, for every minute they had waited.

"Mr. Morgenthau," the councilwoman said in a voice that seemed to bounce against the hallway walls like a handball, "we demand to speak with you. And we demand justice for Michael Stewart. We will not have young African Americans killed by the police. There will be accountability."

As she was knocking again, the door opened the same thin amount and the same thin woman emerged, who took in the group once more, as if hoping it had decreased in size since she had gone back into the office, or as if fearing it would have grown. She inhaled and then spoke.

"Mr. Morgenthau says," she paused, "he says in view that the matter will go before a grand jury next month, he has no comment at this time." She paused again. Then in a voice just barely above a whisper, she said, "I'm really very, very sorry," as she withdrew back into the office and closed the door.

Various others in the group knocked on the door glass or frame and shouted sentences that included the words "Michael Stewart," "death," and "justice."

The young woman did not appear again. Nor did District Attorney Morgenthau.

Councilwoman Pinkett knew that ending these things right was important. Their declarations should not dwindle to nothing, as if the group had drifted away in disappointment. She looked toward the group, held up a palm, and achieved the desired silence. She knocked again, her original three decisive knocks on the glass, which at this point rattled a bit in its frame, and said, "Mr. Morgenthau, you can be very sure this is not the last word you will hear on this matter," swept her hand toward the group, and they left, their exit returning them to their original spot, specks beneath the two granite columns.

3. The New York State Supreme Court hears testimony about the medical condition of Baby Jane Doe.

At 10:30 a.m. on Wednesday, October 19, 1983, in the New York State Supreme Court of Suffolk County, on the first day of a two-day evidentiary hearing, Judge Melvyn Tanenbaum heard testimony from George Newman, MD, the lead physician for Baby Jane Doe. Dr. Newman, a neurosurgeon, testified that the surgery encouraged by the baby's court-appointed guardian ad litem, as opposed to the nonsurgical regimen favored by the parents, was not within "medically accepted standards." The surgery, Dr. Newman acknowledged, would possibly extend Baby Jane Doe's life from two to as many as twenty years. However, Dr. Newman continued, "to perform this surgery would increase the total pain that the child would experience." Dr. Newman said that Baby Jane Doe was "not likely to ever achieve any meaningful interaction with her environment, nor ever achieve any interpersonal relationships."

4. The head of Maintenance for Waste Collection in Cleveland, Ohio, gets an angry call from New York City.

At 11:04 a.m. on Wednesday, October 19, 1983, at the Cleveland Department of Public Works headquarters, a block and a half from City Hall and three blocks from North Harbor to Lake Erie, in the office of the superintendent of maintenance for Waste Collection, Janet Marshall buzzed the office of her boss, John Griffen, and told him he had a phone call from "someone in the New York City Comptroller's office."

Griffen rolled his eyes and waited for the call to be connected.

"Mr. Griffen, this is Daniel Bulston, the Deputy Comptroller for New York City. I am looking at a piece of paper, well, several pieces of paper, pieces of paper with your name on them. And these pieces of paper are causing some concern for the Comptroller's Office, the Board of Estimates, and the thirty thousand citizens of a city called

Elmira, New York, which is about four hours to the west and north of the office from which I am speaking to you now, and which now stands to lose forty-one million dollars and one hundred three jobs."

The accent and tone, Griffen thought, were pure New York City, but the circumlocution was straight from the Carolinas. The caller seemed to have paused for encouragement to continue. Griffen did not want him to continue, but figured just saying "goodbye," as attractive an option as it was, likely would not make the pugnacious Mr. Bulston evaporate.

So Mr. Griffen said, "Okay."

Apparently that was sufficient for Mr. Bulston's needs, for he continued. "These papers, Mr. Griffen, they are titled a report, but to my mind, reports have charts and numbers and, in this case, comparative bids. That's what a report is. This report, this so-called report, which is from the New York City Department of Sanitation, which I admit is not known for its analytical or verbal skills, reads more like something a high school freshman might write late the night before an essay is due."

Mr. Griffen knew that curiosity was his enemy in this situation, but he also accepted that most of humanity's actions contradict its best interests, and who was he to oppose such a universal impulse?

So he said, "You say my name is on this, uh, this document?"

"In fact, sir, the conclusion of this carefully constructed, exhaustively researched, and tightly reasoned analysis seems to rest on one piece of evidence and one piece alone, and that isn't evidence at all, but only an opinion. And that opinion is yours, Mr. Griffen."

By this time, Mr. Griffen's memory had fought its way through this man's trowel-applied oratory.

So Mr. Griffen said, "The letter?"

"The letter," Mr. Bulston agreed, with stunning brevity.

What had happened was this. Mr. Griffen had received a call from some deputy commissioner of the Department of Sanitation in New York City. The caller said that they—Mr. Griffen did not know who, exactly—were considering buying new garbage trucks, and a company called LaFrance trucks had listed Mr. Griffen, the superintendent of maintenance for waste collection in Cleveland, Ohio, as a reference. To which Mr. Griffen had replied, yes, they had some LaFrance trucks.

And what did he think of the LaFrance trucks?

Mr. Griffen said that they were fine, they were good trucks. No problems.

The caller asked whether Mr. Griffen would be willing to write a letter to that effect.

Mr. Griffen, with that same feeling that he was not acting in his own best interest, said, sure, and asked which model they were considering buying, just to be sure the letter would be relevant.

It turned out that New York City was looking at a different model of LaFrance truck, and Mr. Griffen noted that in his letter, but said Cleveland's LaFrance trucks had caused no problems, and he would recommend them favorably to New York City.

Now, according to the voluble Mr. Bulston, the New York City Sanitation Commissioner, a man named Norman Steisel, was saying in this report, and here Mr. Bulston seemed to be quoting, "We have surveyed the field, and we found that the Crane truck from Oklahoma is simply the better truck," and that the assessment of the inferior alternative LaFrance trucks was based on information from a letter written by Mr. Griffen.

Mr. Griffen had rarely been interviewed by the media, but he had certainly heard of being misquoted by reporters. He had never, however, heard of being misquoted by the New York City Commissioner of Sanitation. Yet here it was.

And so Mr. Griffen said, again, "The LaFrance trucks are good trucks. The ones we have are a little different from the ones you wanted to buy, but we've had good success with them."

"Would you," said Mr. Bulston, "be willing to write a letter to that effect?"

And so Mr. Griffen, who probably could have restrained himself if he had really wanted to, sighed—plenty loud enough for Mr. Bulston to hear.

5. A man is sentenced to prison because no one could think of any other place to send him.

At 1:25 p.m. on Wednesday, October 19, 1983, in another courthouse, this one the New York State Supreme Court in Queens, Judge James F. O'Donoghue sentenced Dwayne L. Gosso to one and a half to four years in prison for burglary. Judge O'Donoghue said, "If anyone is responsible for his antisocial traits, other than himself, it is obviously the system that weaned him, supported him with material benefits and nothing else. Unfortunately, with the limited resources we have available to us, we have not been able to solve your problem. I hope that prison will offer you the vocational training and discipline you need."

On November 7, 1961, Dwayne L. Gosso was born at Bedford Hills, New York, Correctional Facility for Women, where his mother had been incarcerated eight months before for offering sex for money.

On April 10, 1962, Dwayne was sent to the New York Foundling Hospital on Third Avenue at 68th Street in Manhattan.

On April 11, 1962, Dwayne's mother was released from prison.

From 1962 to 1971, Dwayne lived in various foster homes, where he was neglected, malnourished, and physically abused.

From 1972 to 1980, Dwayne lived in twelve different group homes and rehabilitation centers in New York and, at one point, in Florida when New York lacked necessary facilities. He was diagnosed as "mildly retarded."

In 1980, Dwayne was transferred to the MacDougal Diagnostic Center in Brooklyn, New York, where staff said he was bullied and abused by other residents, and then to the Crystal Run Village rehabilitation center in Middleton, New York, where staff said he bullied other residents, and then to the Boerum Hill rehabilitation facility in Brooklyn, where staff said they were unable to provide the direct supervision necessary for Dwayne.

In 1981, Dwayne entered the New York State South Beach Psychiatric Center on Staten Island.

On November 7, 1982, Dwayne turned 21, thus ending the state of New York's legal responsibility for him.

On November 17, 1982, Dwayne left the South Beach Psychiatric Center.

In 1982, Dwayne lived in parks, in streets, and in a men's shelter, and at an apartment rented for him by his girlfriend.

On January 17, 1983, Dwayne was arrested in Brooklyn for trespassing at a psychiatric facility where he previously had lived.

On January 25, 1983, Dwayne was arrested for trespassing in his girlfriend's sister's apartment building.

On January 26, 1983, Dwayne was arrested for jumping an elevated train station turnstile.

On February 3, 1983, Dwayne was arrested for burglary of a house in Queens. At Bellevue Hospital in Manhattan, staff said he had "borderline intellectual functioning."

On June 14, 1983, Dwayne was released pending sentencing.

On June 15, 1983, Two social workers arranged for Dwayne to move into the Hotel Barbour on 36th Street between 8th and 9th Avenues in Manhattan for forty-eight dollars per week, to receive two hundred sixty dollars per month in living expenses, and to be screened for possible vocational training.

On June 30, 1983, Dwayne's sentencing was postponed to assess how well he might function if the sentence were to be parole rather than incarceration.

On July 5, 1983, near a New Jersey facility where he had once stayed, Dwayne was arrested with nine hundred ninety-three dollars, jewelry, and a bottle of cologne, charged with theft, and put in the Bergen County Jail.

On September 5, 1983, Dwayne was sentenced to time served for the New Jersey theft and sent to the Queens, New York, House of Detention to await sentencing on the February burglary charge.

On September 15, 1983, Queens State Supreme Court Judge James F. O'Donoghue sent Dwayne to Samaritan Village, a residential facility for drug behavioral health treatment. Judge O'Donoghue said to Dwayne, "Bouncing around from foster home to foster home certainly didn't do you any good." Judge O'Donoghue also said, "The ball is in your court for the last time."

On September 17, 1983, staff at Samaritan Village reported that Dwayne was found in the women's section of the facility.

On September 19, 1983, Dwayne was sent to Rikers Island, a ten-jail facility in the Bronx that holds up to fifteen thousand prisoners awaiting sentencing or serving sentences of less than one year.

On October 11, 1983, Judge O'Donoghue postponed sentencing as the New York Office of Mental Health, Mental Retardation, and Alcoholism Services looked for suitable placement for Dwayne.

Sara L. Kellermann, PhD, Commissioner of that office, said, "It may be that the only place where he would be tolerated is in jail."

6. Mayor Koch admits a mistake.

At 4:10 p.m. on Wednesday, October 19, 1983, back from his Caribbean trip and in his City Hall office, New York City Mayor Ed Koch, having been informed by his press secretary, Evan Cornog, that the *New York Times* had never published an editorial praising graffiti as Mayor Koch had said in his San Juan remarks the day before and having heard Cornog's suggestion that some form of retraction might be warranted, said, "Details, details."

Washington, DC

1. The Department of Health and Human Services gets a new telephone.

At 8:30 a.m. on Wednesday, October 19, 1983, at the reception desk of the seven-year-old, eight-floor, Marcel Breuer-designed, brutalist-style Hubert H. Humphrey Federal Building on Southwest Independence Avenue at the foot of Capitol Hill, which housed the U.S. Department of Health and Human Services and which on this foggy morning seemed to disappear into the fog, or perhaps the fog became its own piece of brutalist architecture, Selma Jefferson, the receptionist, having woken at 5:30 and traveled via bus and train from her apartment in Oxon Hill, Maryland, now stared at the beige Nortel Norstar M7310 telephone that yesterday morning had made its first appearance as the main tool of her job.

Yesterday had been a bit like a fever dream of survival during wartime as she tried to make this thing do what she needed it to do. This morning, having arrived a half hour before the start of business, she was determined to conquer the thing before it started ringing, or at least before she was required to answer it.

First, she counted the buttons, which she recognized was more a gesture of outrage than an honest attempt to master operating the thing. Still: Forty buttons! Speaking of fever dreams, whose fever dream gave rise to the notion that a telephone needed forty buttons to do what a telephone needs to do, even a receptionist's telephone, much less that any human could master forty buttons and use them with the speed and alacrity needed to do the job of a receptionist? Did anyone ask a lowly receptionist before designing this thing? But perhaps she was being unfair; after all, ten of those buttons were the digits one pressed to enter a phone number and so not exactly unfamiliar.

Having allowed herself momentary and fully justified outrage on grounds of morality, pragmatism, and class, Selma opened the reception desk's shallow top middle drawer, removed the operating manual for the thing, and turned to page one, which was headed in a friendly fashion: "Your Norstar M7310 Phone." Well, Selma thought, technically it's the government's phone, not my phone, but okay, I'll make believe it's my phone, that it's a friend to be cherished.

This page featured a diagrammatic image of the thing, with lines extending from each button and each of several other features. The lines led to the name in bold type and function in smaller, lighter type—all of which made for a crowded page.

She thought the best approach, to start, was to simply read the name of each button and panel. She presumed this would give her a sense of comfort, a sense of place, a map of the terrain, so to speak. And so she did. The names were: shift button, dual-memory buttons, display, display buttons, release button, feature button, dial pad, volume control, memory buttons, outside live buttons, indicators, intercom line buttons.

Only a very few of these names being familiar to her, and as a result discouraged but not cowed, Selma began reading what each of these things did in the telephone-operating universe.

The first, at the top left of the page, just under the headline words "Your Norstar" (remember, she told herself, your Norstar is your friend), was, "Shift button for using the top function of a dual-memory button."

Not entirely sure why she would need to use the top or the bottom (presumably if there was a top there was a bottom) function of a dual-memory button, she proceeded, happy to see that the next definition was for dual-memory buttons, which she hoped would solve the mystery of the concept of top (and bottom?) functions: "Dual-memory buttons can store any combination of two features and/or autodial numbers. Use the triangular shift button to program and access the top feature or autodial numbers."

Should she, Selma wondered, attempt to understand—and perhaps, somehow, test—each button based on its definition before proceeding to the next? Or should she read through all the descriptions and try to retain them, and then use the combined information to study the remaining pages of the manual?

Before deciding her approach, she decided to read one more definition, which turned out to be "display," which wasn't inherently mysterious, but yesterday in addition to showing the number of the caller, the display had displayed other information that was not intuitive and not even clear enough to be counterintuitive. "Display shows the time, date, call information and prompts you while using Norstar features. The lower line of the display is reversed for display button instructions."

Selma was proud but not too proud to admit that this last sentence almost broke her, because which person would these words not break, except for the person who wrote it, and even that person may have simply written it because that person had to write something, and this was the best the writer could come up with.

Selma thought that perhaps she should skip this definitional page, that the actual operating instructions that she prayed existed on the subsequent pages would make clear how to do the basic things she needed to do.

Turning the page, she saw the headline "Making Calls," which was promisingly practical. However, she rarely made calls, being employed here mostly to receive and route calls. Nonetheless, she was hopeful. If there was a "Making Calls" page, assuredly there would be a "Receiving Calls" page and even, hoping even harder, a "Transferring Calls" page. Flipping forward in the manual, the page headings brought her close to tears: Programming Memory Buttons, Using Speed Dial, and a series of perforated pages each labeled M7310 Tear-Off Feature List.

She looked up. The flip-number clock at the back of her desk, tucked under the ledge visitors leaned against, read 8:40. Selma took a deep breath, because what else could she do? And she settled in to poke around at the phone, because what else could she do?

Just as the flip-number clock on the reception desk of the Department of Health and Human Services flipped to 9:00 a.m., the phone rang. Not a ring, exactly. The previous phone had rung the way phones ring. This one emitted more of a protracted, warbling beep, like a sickly, distant police siren.

Selma had been practicing on the phone for a few minutes, and so was fortified against not only the technical challenges of operating the new phone, but also the tactile challenges of the lightweight handset that felt so fragile Selma hesitated to hold it too tightly lest it crack, with a surface so smooth that the too-short and too-tightly coiled cord had the tendency to pull the handset out of Selma's hand before she could greet the caller. This morning, better prepared for battle with the new phone, she gripped the handset tightly and, now understanding that lifting the receiver did nothing toward connecting the call, pushed one of the buttons, and hearing the faint white noise that was the universal signal of a connected call, said, "Good morning, Department of Health and Human Services. How may I direct your call?"

A man's voice—not particularly high or low, particularly raspy or smooth, just a normal man's voice—said, "I would like to report a baby who may die because she is not receiving necessary care at University Hospital in Stony Brook, New York City."

Selma gave her head a sharp shake, as though to jostle her brain into place, but did not lose her grip on the phone's handset. She replied, "Just a moment" and put the call on hold, something she had learned how to do this morning. While considering whether to send the call to the Office of the Assistant Secretary for Public Affairs or the Office of Civil Rights, another line rang. Wishing that this modern new phone system would make calls bounce to another extension when she was already on the line, Selma left the man on hold and pushed the button to receive the new call on its new line, something else she had practiced this morning, having two friends call her, and she listened to a woman's voice—not particularly high or low, not particularly raspy or smooth—say, "I would like to report a baby who may die because she is not receiving necessary care at University Hospital in Stony Brook, New York City."

2. The Senate Chaplain offers another prayer.

At 9:30 a.m. on Wednesday, October 19, 1983, in the Senate Chamber of the U.S. Capitol, Senate President Pro Tempore Senator Strom Thurmond of South Carolina called the body to order. The Senate Chaplain, Reverend Halverson, offered the day's prayer:

> Search me, O God, and know my heart; try me, and know my thoughts, and see if there be any wicked way in me, and lead me in the way everlasting. —Psalm 139: 23, 24
>
> God of truth and justice and righteousness, may this ancient prayer of the Israeli psalmist be taken seriously by each senator as the moment of decision approaches. We know we have no secrets from Thee, O Lord, our lives are like an open book to

> Thee. Thou dost judge us not only for what we do but why we do it. Examine our motives, Lord, and give us grace to do what we believe is right for the right reasons.
>
> Dear God, overrule every thought in our hearts that is contrary to Thy sovereign love and when this day is over may there be no regrets and may the Senate pursue its duty to the crucial issues which confront it. In Jesus' name. Amen.

3. Senator Helms offers an amendment about Thomas Jefferson. At 10:15 a.m. on Wednesday, October 19, 1983, in the Senate Chamber of the U.S. Capitol, Senator Jesse Helms addressed Senator Thurmond, president pro tempore of the Senate that day, saying, "Mr. President, I have an unprinted amendment at the desk. I ask for its immediate consideration."

Directed by Senator Thurmond to do so, the legislative clerk read as follows:

> The senator from North Carolina, Mr. Helms, proposes an amendment numbered 2338. At the end of the bill, add the following:
>
> Notwithstanding any other provision of this Act, this Act shall not take effect unless and until a legal public holiday is established under federal law in honor of Thomas Jefferson on or about April 13 each year.
>
> Notwithstanding any other provision of this Act, this Act shall only take effect provided that the total number of legal public holidays under federal law does not exceed nine.

The amendment having been read, Senator Helms proceeded to explain its significance.

> Mr. President, now we are talking about my number one hero in American history, Thomas Jefferson. The sage of Monticello needs no introduction by Jesse Helms or anybody else. Nor does he really need a national holiday to keep alive his memory because his memory is vibrant in our total political discourse, our architecture, our commitment to the right to life, the right to liberty and the right to the pursuit of happiness free of government control.
>
> But even so, the national observance of April 13, the birthday of Thomas Jefferson, our third president, would be salutary in an important way. It would provide a focal point for the American people to assess the extent to which their leaders are living up to the ideals of Jeffersonian government.
>
> We all hear so many of the brethren and the sisters in the political world pay homage to Jeffersonian principles and yet we see the anomaly of some of the votes cast in the Congress of the United States.
>
> One can imagine the consternation in many congressional offices as hundreds of thousands of constituents remind public officials that whenever any form of government becomes destructive of their rights, "[I]t is the Right of the People to alter or to abolish it." Some may call that rabblerousing, Mr. President. If so, it was Thomas Jefferson's rabble-rousing, not mine. I wish I could claim credit for it, but he said it first.
>
> Mr. President, the pending amendment conditions the Martin Luther King holiday on two events: one, the establishment of a legal public holiday for Thomas Jefferson; and, two, assuring the taxpayers of this country that the total number of federal holidays will not be more than nine.

A roll call vote resulted in the Helms amendment number 2338 being defeated, with 10 Senators voting yea, 82 voting nay, 3 voting present, and 5 not voting.

4. President Reagan sees a movie in IMAX.

At 12:35 p.m. on Wednesday, October 19, 1983, in the Samuel P. Langley Theater of the National Air and Space Museum on Independence Avenue SW near 7th Street SW, two miles southeast of the White House, as part of a celebration of the twenty-fifth anniversary of the U.S. National Aeronautics and Space Administration, Ronald Reagan watched a thirty-five-minute documentary movie titled *Hail Columbia,* about the U.S. space shuttle program.

The movie was filmed in the revolutionary IMAX format and directed by IMAX co-founder Graeme Ferguson. The film was narrated by the actor James Whitmore, who starred with Nancy Davis Reagan in the movies *The Next Voice You Hear* (1950), *It's a Big Country: An American Anthology* (1951), and *Shadow in the Sky* (1952). Whitmore supported Adlai Stevenson in his 1952 presidential campaign against Dwight Eisenhower, who, after he left the White House, was a political mentor to Ronald Reagan.

In his diary that evening, Ronald Reagan wrote that IMAX "is the most spectacular thing of its kind I've ever seen."

5. Senator Byrd repeats himself.

At 1:55 p.m., on Wednesday, October 20, 1983, Senator Robert Byrd, majority leader from West Virginia, a member of the Senate since 1959 and a member of the U.S. House of Representative from West Virginia's 6th District from 1953 to 1959, walked through the underground passageway of the U.S. Capitol from his office toward the Senate floor. Senator Byrd's chief of staff, Morris Townsend, walked a bit behind the senator and to his left, not out of deference but because he knew the senator liked a sense of solitude before an important vote. Morris had a quarter-profile view of the set of Senator Byrd's eagle-like jaw. When the senator spoke, he did not slow his pace or turn his head, leaving Morris free to interpret the comment as being directed toward him, being voiced internal monologue, or for that matter, Morris thought, being directed toward the people of the State of West Virginia or perhaps toward the senator's future legacy. What the senator said was something he had said before, to Morris and others:

"I'm the only one in the Senate who MUST vote for this bill."

Senator Byrd never explained why he was the only one in the Senate who must vote for this bill, but everyone to whom the comment was addressed—even if it was addressed to something as amorphous as the senator's legacy—understood. The reason was that forty years ago, the man who was now Senator Byrd had been an Exalted Cyclops in the Sophia, West Virginia, Chapter, which Byrd had formed, of the Ku Klux Klan, and that then-twenty-seven-year-old Byrd in 1944 had written a letter to Mississippi Senator Theodore Bilbo in which Byrd said, "I shall never fight in the armed forces with a Negro by my side. Rather I should die a thousand times and see Old Glory trampled in the dirt never to rise again than to see this beloved land of ours become degraded by race mongrels, a throwback to the blackest specimen from the wilds," and that Byrd in 1946 had written to the KKK's Grand Wizard, "The Klan is needed today more than ever before," and that Byrd had led the filibuster against the Voting Rights Act of 1964, and that in 1967 he had voted against the confirmation of Thurgood Marshall as a Supreme Court Justice because Senator Byrd believed that Marshall had communist ties.

As they approached the elevator to the ground floor of the Capitol and Morris stepped forward to push the button, he thought he heard the senator say, "Time to get rid of the albatross," something else he had heard the senator say before.

6. Senator Helms offers an amendment about Marcus Garvey. At 2:10 p.m. on Wednesday, October 19, 1983, Senator Majority Leader asked what amendments remained to be proposed regarding the bill making Martin Luther King, Jr.'s birthday a national holiday.

Senator Helms: "The one that I have at the desk now relates to Marcus Garvey."

Senator Baker: "Marcus Garvey."

Senator Helms: "Yes."

Having been directed to do so by the president pro tempore, the assistant legislative clerk read as follows:

> The senator from North Carolina, Mr. Helms, proposes an amendment numbered 2339. At the end of the bill, add the following:
>
> Since Marcus Garvey is known universally throughout the world as the Father of Black Nationalism; and
>
> Since Marcus Garvey was a major leader in the development in the United States of Black consciousness; and
>
> Since the writings of Marcus Garvey have served as an inspiration to all those who favor opportunity for all, and the doctrine of self-help; and
>
> Since the conviction of Marcus Garvey in 1923 occurred in an atmosphere charged with emotionalism and publicity; and
>
> Since the excessiveness of the sentence was recognized by President Coolidge in 1927 in commuting that sentence;
>
> Therefore, let it be stated that it is the sense of Congress that the president should remove this cloud over the reputation of Marcus Garvey by granting a full pardon of any crimes of which he may have been convicted.

A roll call vote resulted in the Helms amendment number 2339 being defeated, with 5 Senators voting yea, 92 voting nay, 1 voting present, and 2 not voting.

7. Senator Helms offers an amendment about Hispanic Americans.

At 2:32 p.m. on Wednesday, October 19, 1983, Senator Jesse Helms said to the president pro tempore, "Mr. President, I have an unprinted amendment at the desk and I ask that it be stated."

Having been so ordered by the president pro tempore, the assistant legislative clerk read as follows:

> The senator from North Carolina, Mr. Helms, proposes an amendment numbered 2341. At the end of the bill, add the following:
>
> Notwithstanding any other provision of this Act, this Act shall not take effect unless and until a specific legal public holiday is established under federal law in honor of Hispanic Americans for one day each year.
>
> Notwithstanding any other provision of this Act. this Act shall only take effect provided that the total number of legal public holidays under federal law does not exceed nine.

A roll call vote resulted in the Helms amendment number 2341 being defeated, with 4 Senators voting yea, 93 voting nay, 1 voting present, and 2 not voting.

8. The Senate votes on making Martin Luther King, Jr.'s birthday a national holiday, and the majority leader apologizes to the minority leader for a breach of decorum.

At 3:45 p.m. on Wednesday, October 19, 1983, Vice President of the United States George H.W. Bush entered the Senate chamber and assumed the role of presiding officer.

At 4:00 p.m., the assistant legislative clerk for the third time read H.R. 3706, the bill to amend title 5, United States Code, to make the birthday of Martin Luther King, Jr., a legal public holiday.

The vice president directed the assistant legislative clerk to call the roll.

Seventy-eight senators voted yea: Senators Andrews, Armstrong, Baker, Baucus, Bentsen, Biden, Bingaman, Boren, Boschwitz, Bradley, Bumpers, Burdick, Byrd, Chafee, Chiles, Cochran, Cohen, Cranston, D'Amato, Danforth, DeConcini, Denton, Dixon, Dodd, Dole, Domenici, Durenberger, Eagleton, Evans, Ford, Glenn, Gorton, Hart, Hatfield, Hawkins, Heflin, Heinz, Hollings, Huddleston, Inouye, Johnston, Kassebaum, Kasten, Kennedy, Lautenberg, Laxalt, Leahy, Levin, Long, Lugar, Mathias, Matsunaga, Mattingly, Melcher, Metzenbaum, Mitchell, Moynihan, Nunn, Packwood, Pell, Percy, Proxmire, Pryor, Quayle, Riegle, Roth, Sarbanes, Sasser, Simpson, Specter, Stafford, Stevens, Thurmond, Trible, Tsongas, Warner, Weicker, and Wilson.

Twenty-two Senators voted nay: Senators Abdnor, East, Exon, Garn, Goldwater, Grassley, Hatch, Hecht, Helms, Humphrey, Jepsen, McClure, Murkowski, Nickles, Pressler, Randolph, Rudman, Stennis, Symms, Tower, Wallop, and Zorinsky.

Amid duly recognized celebratory and congratulatory remarks and requests by the presiding officer for the gallery to remain quiet, Senator Baker said, "Mr. President, if I could have the attention of the Senate for a moment…I want to express an apology to the minority leader. When I suggested the absence of a quorum a moment ago, I did not notice that the minority leader was on his feet."

Minority Leader Byrd put in, "I had the floor."

Senator Baker continued, "And I believe may have had the floor, and perhaps my quorum call was out of order. But regardless of the technicalities, I want to acknowledge that it was an oversight on my part and that I wish to apologize to the minority leader for that."

Senator Byrd, having been recognized by the presiding officer, replied, "Mr. President, I thank the majority leader. He is very kind and always accommodating to me. He owes me no apology.

I understand how those things can happen with all the hustle and bustle, so I thank him."

Senator Baker replied, "I thank the minority leader."

9. At an evening press conference, President Reagan demonstrates recursive mentalizing for the purpose of coordination.

At 8:01 p.m. on Wednesday, October 19, 1983, in the East Room of the White House, President Ronald Reagan held a press conference at which he was asked, "Mr. President, Senator Helms has been saying on the Senate floor that Martin Luther King, Jr., had communist associations, was a communist sympathizer. Do you agree?"

In their article "Common knowledge, coordination, and strategic mentalizing in human social life" in Volume 116, Number 28 (June 28, 2019), of the *Proceedings of the National Academy of Sciences*, researchers Julian De Freitas, Kyle Thomas, Peter DeScioli, and Steven Pinker "review experiments that test the hypothesis that the human mind is acutely sensitive to common knowledge as an adaptation to successfully coordinate with others." The authors define "common knowledge" as "a kind of recursive metalizing: holding beliefs about other people's beliefs about other people's beliefs, and so on." The authors suggest that common knowledge can be captured by a recursive formula such as "Y: Everyone knows X, and everyone knows Y," although they acknowledge that another way to define common knowledge is the sense that something is "out there."

The authors posit that we are most sensitive to common knowledge in social situations, and that common knowledge is a way for us to coordinate our social relationships. The authors illustrate this concept with the story of the emperor's new clothes, in which the crowd's common knowledge that the emperor is naked translates into the strength in numbers that allows them to laugh.

In response to the reporter's question about Senator Helms, Martin Luther King, Jr., and communism, President Reagan said,

"I don't fault Senator Helms' sincerity with regard to wanting the records opened up. I think that he's motivated by a feeling that if we're going to have a national holiday named for any American, when it's only been named for one American in all our history up until this time, that he feels we should know everything there is to know about an individual."

The president's statement demonstrates the nesting of several propositions that, recognized by the president, his staff, and the reporters, in the aggregate, constitute common knowledge: Senator Helms said that his sole purpose in seeking to learn everything there was to know about Dr. King was simply due diligence prior to creating a national holiday; President Reagan and every other person in the room, watching on television, or listening on the radio, or who would read accounts in newspapers, believed that Senator Helms' statements about his motives were disingenuous; President Reagan was stating his own disingenuous belief that he took Senator Helms at his word because Senator Helms had lost his struggle to see FBI records about Dr. King, the Senate has passed the bill establishing the holiday, and the president planned to sign the bill; the president would prefer some other form of recognition for Dr. King, but his veto would be overridden and would needlessly anger the majority of legislators that supported the holiday; the president did not need to state any of these beliefs because they were already commonly known.

This instance of recursive mentalizing establishes a foundation of common knowledge that maintains coordination by fortifying political party loyalties, political decorum, and the established roles of polite adversarialism between the president and the press.

The press conference lasted thirty-six minutes, concluding at 8:37 p.m., after which the president retired to the second-floor residence of the White House and wrote in his diary about the event: "It went well—no grenades or torpedoes."

10. An unauthorized vehicle breeches security at the Central Intelligence Agency.

At 10:04 p.m. on Wednesday, October 19, 1983, William Halley, on his first solo run as a Washington Metropolitan Area Transit bus driver, piloted his bus, occupied by only six passengers at this late hour, along the 5-W route from Washington, DC, into the suburbs of Virginia, in the course of which entering unincorporated Langley, Virginia, where, cruising north on Colonial Farm Road with Langley Fox Park on his left, William guided his bus toward the next stop indicated on his route sheet: the headquarters of the Central Intelligence Agency.

William noticed that Colonial Farm Road did not actually pass the entrance to CIA headquarters. In fact, anyone wanting to catch his bus from the building would have quite a hike, as best he could tell in the dark based on the pattern of lights. Although his printed route indicated no turns from Colonial Farm Road until he has passed the CIA complex, he applied common sense to the situation. He knew he was the last bus of the night. He saw no one waiting alongside the road across from the complex. He did not want to leave anyone stranded overnight. So, at the unmarked drive that led into the CIA complex, William turned.

Seated in the sixth row, right of the aisle, in a window seat, Marilyn Wilkerson was smiling more broadly than she had all day. Not that it had been such a bad day or that she was especially averse to smiling, in fact, she was known to find many things funny that her co-workers in the Department of Veterans' Affairs found not at all amusing, but it was just that what was happening now was the funniest thing that she had witnessed that day.

A regular customer on this route, she knew this bus was not supposed to enter the CIA complex. That was the 5-K bus, not the 5-W bus. She also knew, from riding the 5-K bus, what this driver she had never seen before would encounter when it reached the gate:

men—and perhaps women as well, Marilyn certainly hoped so—in uniform holding firearms. And maybe even pointing them at the bus.

Marilyn's smile got even wider when the gate opened without incident and the bus continued beyond, fifty yards, one hundred yards, three hundred yards, during which time Marilyn was rapidly constructing the plot of a novel in which terrorists or protesters or perhaps high-IQ but maladjusted high school students stole a city bus and used it to infiltrate the CIA, until the bus pulled up to the curb and, air brakes exhaling as if they had been holding their breath, stopped with its front doors precisely aligned with the front doors of the building through which thousands who supported undercover activities in foreign countries passed each day.

Marilyn was contemplating the next move for her terrorists, protesters, or maladjusted teenagers when sirens sounded from behind, and Marilyn twisted around in her seat to see Tootsie Roll lights on roofs of official cars seeming to envelop the bus on all sides at once, followed by shouted but unintelligible voices.

Like Marilyn, William turned around this way and that in his seat. His eyes happened to meet Marilyn's, and the need for comradeship in a time of personal and community stress overriding the usual embarrassment of being caught looking into the eyes of another, William held his head for a moment, as did Marilyn, although she was not in the habit of looking away when her eyes and another's met.

Momentarily succored and seizing an opportunity to transform his embarrassment into sardonicism, William said to Marilyn, "They must think we're KGB agents."

To which Marilyn raised both brows, which she hoped William would interpret as something like, "Ah, one never knows; perhaps we are."

After William understood that he was being asked to open his front bus door and probably would not be shot for doing so, he conversed with four or five officials simultaneously, who despite their conversational ricochets seemed to agree soon and simultaneously that the thing to do was send the bus on its way. With much backing and adjusting, William finally executed what Marilyn calculated to be an eight-point turn and sent the bus, with official escort, back the way it had come. Marilyn was sorry the adventure was over, and she was too weary from a long day to take her nascent novel plot much further.

A block from a street corner in Salona Village, Marilyn pulled the cord, generating the soft bong requesting a stop, and as the bus slowed, she made her way to the front door. When the bus had come to rest and the doors hissed open, Marilyn descended two steps before turning, extending her torso so that her head was visible to William and to her five fellow passengers, and said, "Goodnight, comrades!"

Peoria, Illinois

1. The copyeditor kicks himself.

At 7:15 a.m. on Wednesday, October 19, 1983, at the kitchen table of his apartment in the West Bluff neighborhood of Peoria, *Journal Star* copyeditor Mike Majors, reading the paper's lead story, the one by Ray Long about the botulism outbreak—finally, he thought, the powers that be decided that botulism would be the lead story—winced. Goddammit, and Ray is a good guy. In the ninth paragraph, Dr. Richard O'Connor is quoted as saying, "Those who are incubated and have an airway in the trachea...are still alert and are medically stable." Ugh ugh ugh. "Incubated" should have been "intubated." How did he let that get by? He hoped that Dr. O'Connor wouldn't call Ray about it. Mike put down the paper, picked up a piece of by-now cold and soggy buttered toast, and formulated the wording of his apology for the next time he saw Ray.

2. A Bradley University student is still angry about a game during Parents Weekend.

At 9:50 a.m. on Wednesday, October 19, 1983, while walking from his fraternity house on Bradley Avenue toward a biology lecture in Olin Hall, Stan Marshall was still fuming about the previous weekend.

He had always prided himself on being an open-minded individual. However, in this case, he was being forced to be narrow-minded and maybe even a bit prejudiced. But, dammit, not without cause.

Saturday afternoon. Parent's Weekend. Haussler Hall. Volleyball game. Court one. Students (then again, maybe not!) from Lebanon and the like were playing against some other students from campus with many parents watching.

He really did, he thought to himself as he crossed Bradley Avenue, try to keep an open mind about things and people and their actions, but never before in his lifetime had he seen such unruliness, inconsiderateness, thoughtlessness, and ill-will as what he saw personified by these students. And he had never witnessed such a poor display of sportsmanship and general misconduct throughout a sporting event.

It was a good thing, he thought, the other team let those vagabonds win; who knows what they might have done if they had lost. They couldn't even win gracefully.

Maybe, he thought, their blood runs hot through their veins, but they'd better learn to cool out. Their hot tempers coupled with their ruthless playing must have made one hell of an impression on those parents casually passing through Haussler with their sons or daughters.

It was about time, he thought, shifting his backpack from his right shoulder to his left, somebody did something about these guys running roughshod over everyone.

To be fair, he recalled, some foreign students present went out of their way to make sure no trouble arose. They were the reason a riot didn't occur. Thanks to whoever they were, he thought, and let's hope their concerned attitude spills over into the minds of their foreign companions.

Okay, enough of that, he thought, pulling open the heavy door to Olin Hall and calming his mood somewhat by the gentlemanly act of holding the door open for a heavyset girl to enter before he did.

3. Linda Peavler cannot hold her baby.

At 9:50 a.m. on Wednesday, October 20, 1983, in her room at Saint Francis Medical Center in Peoria, Illinois, Linda Peavler wondered if her baby, Tiffany, a bundle of squirming pink fabric from which intermittent screams emerged, inexpertly held in the arms of Jan-Paul, was bothering the doctor.

The doctor, who was wearing the same bow tie the second day in a row, his expression earnest, had entered the room a few minutes before and extended a hand for Jan-Paul to shake and left his hand mid-air while Jan-Paul did the best he could to disengage a hand without dropping Tiffany. He proceeded to speak in that doctor tone of light-hearted, over-confident gravity, shifting his gaze from Linda to Jan-Paul as if unsure to whom he should be speaking.

As Tiffany's screams became more continuous and her squirms more productive, Linda diagnosed the doctor's pivoting gaze as trying to figure out what to do about Tiffany so he could be heard. Linda could see the doctor calculating wither Jan-Paul should hand Tiffany to Linda—no, of course not, Linda couldn't raise her arms—or whether Jan-Paul should leave the room with Tiffany—no, of course not, the husband needed to hear what the doctor had to say especially because the doctor wasn't sure how much Linda was understanding, and she certainly couldn't ask questions—or whether there was someone else around who could take the baby—not likely because any other family member would probably be in the room if they were nearby—or whether he should suggest some method of quieting the baby. His interior baby-quieting machinations thwarted, the doctor, whose name Linda could not remember, plunged forward.

Linda was already exhausted by the doctor's presence, but gave him as much attention as she could, resulting in her noticing the doctor was emphasizing through repetition two phrases: "stable" and "every hope for a recovery." Both seemed thin gruel to Linda, but the phrase that particularly grated was "stable." She was lying on a lumpy hospital bed unable to breathe on her own, unable to speak, unable to hold her six-month-old baby. Stable was not the word she would use. She suspected that Jan-Paul wanted to express a similar sentiment and would have if he weren't trying so hard to keep Tiffany from getting on the nerves of the person in charge of keeping Linda alive.

4. Confusion lingers over Parents Weekend at Bradley University. At 9:50 a.m. on Wednesday, October 19, 1983, while walking from his dorm in Geisert Hall toward the Cullom Davis library, his path forming an X when overlaid on that of Stan Marshall on his way to Olin Hall, Carl Helmut found himself still thinking about this past weekend, Parents' Weekend at the University. Not that he was upset, just thinking.

His parents had come down, and they had purchased tickets for a couple of events, including the Glen Miller Orchestra at the Robertson Memorial Fieldhouse. When Carl's dad, his mom, and Carl were in their seats, when the lights went down, and when a spotlight shone on a single figure holding in each hand what looked like a bowling pin, which he started to juggle, Carl's mom turned to him and said, "Who is that?" Carl started to answer, but his mom had already turned to his dad and asked, again, "Who is that?"

"I don't know," Carl's dad said, "I thought we were seeing Glen Miller."

"So did I," Carl's mom said.

Carl found this sort of amusing, because he knew about the juggler, but was, himself, confused about whether the Glen Miller Orchestra was going to play. His dorm had been plastered with posters of Michael Davis, the juggler, but his parents said after the show as they were all walking toward the car that the only information they had received was about the Glen Miller Orchestra. On Monday, Carl asked some of his friends, and they reported the identical situation: the students knew about Michael Davis the juggler, but their parents did not.

At this point in his ruminations, Carl and Stan crossed paths.

Approaching the library, Carl wondered why the university would promote one act to the students and another to the parents, without making clear to either that another act was on the bill. Was this some sort of advertising technique? If so, he thought, as he opened the front door of the library, he wasn't sure he approved. After all, was parents' weekend for fun or to turn a profit?

5. A husband joins his wife.

At 12:00 p.m. on Wednesday, October 19, 1983, at Saint Francis Medical Center in Peoria, Gale Hiter, husband of Anna Hiter, who had been admitted to the same hospital on Sunday night and was now attached to a respirator in the intensive care unit, was also admitted with symptoms of botulism.

6. They are grave sellers, not gravediggers.

At 1:40 p.m. on Wednesday, October 19, 1983, in his office at the back of Tillitson Funeral Home, Gary Tillitson, not having anything else to do at the moment, was going over expenses, something he did occasionally and that he found oddly soothing. Perhaps, he thought, he should have been an accountant. Or perhaps, he thought, he should have been a jazz musician, because although the process was analytical, to him it sometimes felt subjective, intuitive, as though he were playing clarinet in an improvisational jazz combo and listening to his fellow musicians and his own consciousness for that subtle tug that hinted at what he should play.

Life was full of such tugs; the artist paid attention to them. Today, his finger dragging along the figures in a spreadsheet, Gary became aware of such a tug. It was one he had felt before, he knew now, but had ignored. This time, however, for whatever reason—the quality of light coming through the windows behind him, a smell in the air, the song on the piped-in music—he had that feeling of combined calm and alertness that made him receptive to the tug and ready to attend to whatever signals it was sending.

The expense line was for the company's workers' compensation insurance premium, an item paid every six months. What was it about that figure? It seemed wrong. It seemed high. After all, what sort of workers' compensation could occur in the office of a funeral home? It was basically a sales office. The only injury he could imagine was a paper cut or perhaps a finger being smashed in the lid of a coffin being shown a customer.

Yet every six months, they were paying this not-insubstantial sum. Well, he wasn't an insurance person; he didn't really know that it was high. It was just his intuition talking. But Gary was listening.

He pushed his chair back from his desk, swiveled it to his right, stood, and headed for one of the five filing cabinets, some putty-color, some olive green. He always thought that one day he would get them all in matching colors, but couldn't quite decide whether to replace the putty ones with olive or the olive ones with putty.

Gary withdrew the folder with the company's insurance policies and returned to his desk. Soon enough—he did not know how soon; he did not pay attention to time when he was answering the call of intuition—Gary explained, "Well, I will be goddammed. I will be GODdammed."

What Gary had discovered was this: Alfred Moore of the National Insurance Company, his pal Al Moore, the recipient of years and years of his business, had written Tillitson Funeral Home a policy not for grave SALESPEOPLE but for grave DIGGERS. As if Alfred didn't know that no one in his business touched a shovel except to clear snow off the sidewalk in front of the front door.

How long had this policy been in force? Good lord, twelve years. Gary was surprised at the rage he felt. It was as though every wrong ever done to him, every frustration he had ever felt, everything that was wrong with the world had coalesced into the unfairness of his having overpaid for twelve years because Alfred Moore wrote him a workers' compensation policy for grave DIGGERS instead of grave SALESPEOPLE.

Already seeing ahead of him years of battle, complex litigation, and legal fees, but with the bracing winds of righteousness behind him, Carl picked the telephone receiver out of its cradle, held it against his shoulder with his cheek, looked up in his Rolodex Alfred Moore's telephone number at National Insurance Company, and dialed it, hoping he could keep his voice from trembling.

7. Some Caterpillar employees get a new boss.

At 3:00 p.m. on Wednesday, October 19, 1983, in the Caterpillar Tractor Company administrative building on Southwest Jefferson Street across from the County Courthouse in Peoria, Illinois, Katherine Milstein sat next to her favorite co-worker, Justine White, in a small conference room on the third floor, listening to their boss' boss, Jeffrey Steinmetz, speaking.

So far this week, Katherine and Justine had been without a boss, theirs being in the hospital and suspected of having botulism. Which, Katherine had to admit, was bad for their boss but good for her. She wasn't exactly in love with her boss, who tended to be cranky and to criticize her—and Justine—for things he didn't really understand.

Jeffrey was saying that he knew they were all concerned about Katherine's boss, that he was still in the hospital, that he seemed to be doing okay, but that he likely would not be back at work anytime soon.

As a result, Jeffrey went on, taking the place of Katherine's boss would be Frieda Umstead. Frieda, sitting in the front row, turned around and shot the group a little wave.

Katherine turned to Justine and poked her in the ribs, which they both knew meant *Jackpot! Frieda is SO nice! What an upgrade!*

8. A visitor misses seeing movie stars.

At 11:00 p.m. on Wednesday, October 19, at Methodist Medical Center in Peoria, Illinois, Faye Leach, 35 years old, of Pontiac, Illinois, sixty miles east of Peoria on old Route 66, was admitted with symptoms of botulism. Earlier that day, Faye had hoped to watch filming of the movie Grandview U.S.A., which was taking place in Pontiac and maybe catch a glimpse of Patrick Swayze or Jamie Lee Curtis, who were rumored to be in town, but she hadn't felt well enough.

Thursday, October 20, 1983

New York City

1. Columbia students hone their assassination skills.

At 7:30 a.m. on Thursday, October 20, 1983, on the steps leading from John Jay Hall on West 117th Street near Amsterdam Avenue, a dormitory of Columbia University in New York City, Richard Clew, a freshman, emerged from the doors of the building, hoping that he had timed his first outside appearance of the day early enough to avoid being assassinated.

He had not.

As Richard appeared on the steps, Gerhard Holt, a sophomore, who had been sitting on the steps for the past 20 minutes, looked up from a copy of Aeschylus' *The Oresteia* he had been pretending to read, brought a plastic gun up from behind the book, pointed it at Richard's torso, and pulled the trigger. A dart with a suction cup on its tip flew from the gun and hit Richard's chest. The dart did not stick; they never did.

Richard yelled, "God DAMN it."

Gerhard took a sheet of paper from inside the book, unfolded it to show that it was a form headed "DEATH CERTIFICATE," withdrew a pen from his hip pocket, and began filling in the blanks.

Richard took his own plastic gun from a jacket pocket and looked at it morosely, wondering if actually dying might be preferable to the sensation of feeling like such a fucking failure.

The previous week, he had explained to his mother that the Assassination Game was sponsored by the university's Game Club and that a couple hundred students took part. His mother asked him how participating in the game made him feel. He said, "Like shit."

His mother called Robert Krauss, PhD, head of Columbia's psychology department, and was surprised to reach him. She asked his opinion of the game. Dr. Krauss said, "Every decade students find something to do, whether it's eating goldfish or running naked across campus. This strikes me as no more or less meaningful."

Realizing that she hadn't been all that interested in this man's opinion after all, Richard's mother said, "Okay," and hung up.

2. In a courthouse, part 1: Nashville, Tennessee.

At 9:04 a.m. on Wednesday, October 20, 1983, in the eight-story Davidson County Courthouse, in downtown Nashville, Tennessee, past the entryway flanked by etched images of Moses, Justinian, and King John, down a grand corridor, inside an uncrowded courtroom of only six rows of seats, at the defendant's table, former District Attorney of Brooklyn, New York, Eugene Gold rose. Nashville District Attorney Thomas Shriver was already standing.

In the hands of the judge, the district attorney, and the former district attorney were identical two-page documents. The judge invited former district attorney Gold to read the document.

Gold said that he had met a 10-year-old girl, the daughter of a follow prosecutor at an association convention, on a bus trip. At that time, Gold said, he "engaged in unlawful sexual conduct" with the girl. Later, he invited the girl to take him to the room she was sharing with her father at the Opryland Hotel. In the room, Gold said, he "engaged in unlawful sexual fondling" of the girl.

After Gold completed his statement and was invited to sit, District Attorney Shriver remained standing. He told the judge that the Nashville District Attorney's office proposed to handle this case in a "routine manner" with an arrangement agreed to by the Davidson County Department of Justice, the family of the child in question, and Mr. Gold and his attorneys. In return for Mr. Gold's signing a statement admitting his guilt and agreeing to undergo psychiatric care during his probationary period, Mr. Gold would be placed on probation for two years, during which time he would reside in either his home in Brooklyn, New York, or his home in Israel. This agreement, said Shriver, had the benefit of avoiding the "additional trauma" of a trial for "a child who already has been subjected to trauma."

The judge accepted the plea agreement.

Gold's wife, Ronnie, took his arm as they made their way down the aisle dividing the rows of long-backed benches. As they moved forward, a reporter asked Gold how he felt. Gold said, "Very, very glad to have this behind me."

Another reporter asked Mrs. Gold how she felt. "I've been with my husband since I'm 16 years old and he was 17, and we have had thirty-six fantastic years together. We plan to continue."

3. In a courthouse, part 2: Manhattan.

At 10:04 a.m. on Thursday, October 20, 1983, in a courtroom of the Manhattan Criminal Courthouse, 19-year-old David Hampton of Buffalo, New York, a slim teenager with a thin face, even thinner at this moment, twisted around in his seat at the defendant's table to look at the spectators. David half-expected to see Mr. and Mrs. Elliott, perhaps showing empathy toward him, or perhaps gloating that he was being held accountable, or more likely, considering the cerebral prowess testified to by his lofty positions at *Newsweek* and the Columbia Law School, something more complicated. But Mr. and Mrs. Elliott were not there.

Once the judge entered and the room was called to order, David listened to his attorney plead not guilty on his behalf to charges of burglary and criminal impersonation. David then listened to the judge order him held on $10,000 bail and his attorney reply that his client did not have the resources to make bail.

4. In a courthouse, part 3: Riverhead, New York.

At 2:00 p.m. on Thursday, October 20, 1983, the second and final day of the evidentiary hearing into the matter of Baby Jane Doe, in the New York State Supreme Court of Suffolk County, Long Island, in Riverhead, New York, Justice Frank DeLuca, sitting in the next-to-the-last row of long-back benches in a courtroom, studied the back of the head of another member of the audience, Larry Washburn, seated two rows in front of him, and what he saw made him grumpy.

Frank did not think of himself as fastidious, nor had he ever heard himself described that way. He dressed neatly, but didn't think much about it. He got haircuts every three weeks, but it was just something on his calendar, not something he craved or particularly cared about. But the back of Larry's head bothered Frank. His hair was clean, but it lay in clumps that had no particular pattern. His hair wasn't what anyone would call long, but some tufts poked down behind his shirt collar and others poked just over his shirt collar, and some even hid behind the collar of his suit jacket, which gapped from his shirt collar. Gray hair—fine, everyone went gray. Baldness—fine, not something you can control. But this was just sloppy. Maybe it only happened when Larry was away from his home in Vermont, away from his wife, Sona, although Frank felt himself wincing at the thought of anyone other than Larry having the duty of dragging a comb through the back of his hair or straightening his suit collar. Maybe this was a small act of rebellion left over from Larry having grown up with five sisters.

Frank wondered why he cared. He decided that it was the incongruity of Larry's quest and the unkemptness at the back of his head. Larry was a warrior for the vulnerable—unborn children and now disabled children. Warriors didn't need to worry about their appearance. However, Larry's war and the instances of vulnerability Larry sought to protect required battle against forces intent on harm. The specific form of that battle entailed proving in court that those forces, the people causing harm, were behaving in a manner that was morally wrong. Larry's war, then, was a war for right behavior, right-mindedness, high principle, proper behavior. To Frank, the visual equivalent of those words was a decent haircut and hair decently combed on the back of one's head.

What the back of Larry's head made Frank think of, as well as the way Larry's shoulders twitched when his attorney said things like "these parents are denying their child life-preserving surgery," was not a warrior for principle, but of someone who went around picking at people's scabs, which Frank had to admit was not the first time this notion had come to him. Frank was on Larry's side, he believed in what Larry believed in, but there was such thing as decorum.

When Judge Melvyn Tanenbaum said, "The court concludes that "Baby Jane Doe is in need of immediate surgical procedures to preserve her life and hereby orders that the surgery be performed," Frank, satisfied with the outcome, but not any less grumpy, stood and turned to leave before he had to see Larry's face.

5. A critic seeks continuity.

At 9:00 p.m. on Thursday, October 20, 1983, at the Public Access Synthesizer Studio of the Harvestworks organization in a second-floor loft on Broadway between Houston and Prince Streets in the Soho neighborhood of Manhattan, Tim Page, music critic for the *New York Times* sat in a metal folding chair listening to a piece titled

"Enigma of a Lovely/Loveless Existence" written and performed by Elodie Lauten. The piece included sounds burbling and wailing sounds from circuit-bent children's toys, chord organs, amplified heartbeats, an electric fan, and vocals that Tim thought of as "droning."

At the end of the performance, Tim turned to his companion and said, "Some interesting sounds, but not the sense of formal continuity one would have liked."

Washington, DC

1. The U.S. House of Representatives receives a message from the U.S. Senate.

At 9:35 a.m. on Thursday, October 20, 1983, on the floor of the U.S. House of Representatives in the U.S. Capitol, a message was received from Mr. Sparrow, assistant clerk of the U.S. Senate, announcing:

> The Senate has passed without amendment bills of the House of the following title:
>
> H.R. 3044. An act to grant the consent of the Congress to an interstate agreement or compact relating to the restoration of Atlantic Salmon in the Connecticut River Basin, and to allow the Secretary of Commerce and the Secretary of the Interior to participate as members in a Connecticut River Atlantic Salmon Commission; and
>
> H.R. 3706. An act to amend title 5, United States Code, to make the birthday of Martin Luther King, Jr., a legal public holiday.

2. Senator Byrd sees an opportunity for a comment on eternity and an anecdote.

At 9:45 a.m. on Thursday, October 20, 1983, on the Senate floor of the U.S. Capitol in Washington, DC, after a surprisingly thin prayer from Richard L. Cosnotti, minister of the First United Presbyterian Church, Cedar Falls, Iowa, sponsored by Iowa Senator Charles Grassley, and after Senator Ted Stevens of Alaska called to the attention of the Senate the decision by the Alaska Department of Fish and Game to terminate the king crab harvest in the Kodiak and Bristol Bay areas of Alaska, Senator Robert Byrd found himself feeling sorry for Reverend Cosnotti.

The reverend had seemed nervous and painfully aware that this was a big opportunity for visibility that he was blowing with a lame prayer. "Forgive us that in the demands that lie before us this day we may not always remember Thee." Seriously, that's all the insight you have for your one shot at addressing the U.S. Senate? Senator Byrd could almost see the flop sweat threatening to breach the underarms of the reverend's suit jacket.

Senator Byrd wasn't prone to feeling sorry for others. He did feel sorry for himself over the way people harped on the mistakes he had made in his youth. He had apologized a thousand times. He admitted he had tunnel vision, that he had been jejune (a wonderful word that he always hoped would stun his critics into at least momentary silence as they dove for their dictionaries) and immature. He had only sought out the KKK because he thought it could provide a venue for his talent as a leader. He now realized that the United States Congress was a far more promising venue.

He was less public about admitting his self-pity when a certain John William Warner III of neighboring Virginia entered the Senate. Senator Byrd had come from poverty in coal-mining country, his mother dying when he was 10 and little Bob being raised by relatives and later working as a gas station attendant and a butcher before being elected to the West Virginia House of Delegates, and then rising through the ranks based on sheer grit and charisma.

This John William Warner III, on the other hand, screamed elite. Born in DC. Attended St. Albans. Veteran of both the Navy and the Marines. Served in both World War II and Korean—that was just gaudy. Then a rich lawyer who donated his way to an appointment by that venal Nixon as Under Secretary of the Navy. And now a full-fledged senator of a state larger than Byrd's West Virginia.

But what really burned Byrd was that Warner's jaw was even stronger and sharper than Byrd's famously sharp jaw, and Warner had a patrician forehead to match topped by a shock of thick hair, the full package that allowed Warner to instantly surpass Byrd as the senator who looked most like an eagle. Worse still, Warner was three inches taller than Byrd. And even worse than that, Warner had been married to Elizabeth Taylor, for the love of God. They had divorced last year, but still, talk about gaudy good fortune.

In Reverend Cosnotti, Senator Byrd did not see any evidence of his own gift for fiery oratory, surely a close-to-fatal shortcoming for a minister, even one from Cedar Falls, Iowa. However, he did see in the reverend's slumped shoulders some part of Senator Byrd's own rough beginnings, his own daily struggle to stand tall among silver-spoon-fed colleagues like Senator John Warner of Virginia and answer to reporters looking for a carcass to peck.

Senator Byrd saw an opportunity to lift up poor Reverend Cosnotti. The senator also saw an opportunity to raise the level of discourse, to see the biggest of big pictures, one of his specialties. And the senator saw an opportunity—triggered by the word "chaplain"—to tell one of his favorite anecdotes.

Thus, when the Senate president pro tempore, recognized the Senate minority leader (and that was another annoyance—he was stuck as minority leader when that sanctimonious, bespectacled shrimp Howard Baker, always wanting to compromise instead of standing up for what was right, was majority leader), Senator Robert Byrd addressed the Senate, well, the handful of senators milling about, on the subject of eternity.

> Mr. President, I thank the visiting minister from Iowa for his prayer and I thank our senate chaplain for his daily prayers for guidance.
>
> As I was saying to my friend, my good friend, Senator Stevens, a moment ago, the day will finally come when that is all that really will matter. We will find ourselves, if we are still members of the Senate, perhaps over in Bethesda hospital surrounded by four walls, with intravenous feeding, strapped to the bed, and the great and overriding issues of today, tomorrow, or months from now, will no longer be very important. In the hospital, we will be very popular for a few days. We will get some flowers and some nice letters and cards.
>
> And then, after a couple of weeks, pretty much will be forgotten, with nobody to comfort us but our immediate families, and perhaps a loyal friend or so, and when time comes to pass on to another world, and we go out to meet God, we will even sooner be forgotten.
>
> So it should be kind of sobering to us, as we listen to these prayers every morning, to know that when we have finished our work here, and venture into the great unknown from which no mortal has ever returned, the Senate will go on, the world will go on, the traffic congestion will be the same as always, the rushes to the airport and back therefrom will be just like always, they will continue to hold the rollcall votes open for more than fifteen minutes for Senators who are a little late getting here, the sun will shine, the moon will rise, the stars will be in their places, seasons will come and go, and the only thing that really, really will matter will be the eternal and the spiritual side of life.

So I compliment our visiting minister and our own chaplain.

Our chaplain was very close to me and my family in an hour of great need and there will come a time when the same will be true of most others of us.

I remember visiting the cell of a man in West Virginia who was scheduled to be executed in the electric chair. I went down to his cell just a few minutes before I witnessed the execution and talked with him. I said, "What would you have me say to the young people, the Boy Scouts, the boys' clubs and so on, that I speak to from time to time?" He said, "Tell them to go to Sunday school and church." He said, "If I had gone, I probably wouldn't be here tonight."

I was told by the warden at the penitentiary that over the long period of time in which the prisoner had been incarcerated, he had scoffed at religion and did not want a chaplain in his cell.

He had been sentenced to die in the electric chair because he employed a taxi driver on the way from Huntington over to Logan, West Virigina, shot the cabdriver in the back, robbed him, threw him out on the side of the road and left him there to die, and was later apprehended in a theater in Montgomery, West Virginia.

But when it finally came down to the last week and it was evident that the governor was not going to commute the sentence, the man wanted a chaplain. So a chaplain was called.

Last year in the campaign, I stopped to visit with a priest in a village in the northern panhandle of West Virginia. I have to relate this part of the story concerning witnessing the execution thirty years ago last year.

I told the story of visiting the young man and a priest in that cell. The priest listened very carefully to what I said. He did not interrupt me. After I finished, he asked, "Do you know who that priest was?" I said, "No, I do not remember his name." He said, "It was I."

Senator Byrd had intended to end his remarks there. That was, he believed, the powerful spot to end. The place to, as they said in gymnastics, "stick the landing." However, judging from their faces, his audience was not exactly in his hip pocket, or even listening very closely. So the senator rushed forward to tie his remarks into a bow for a group of people obviously unwilling to do a little thinking for themselves.

"The point is that these things we view with such enormity from day to day may not be that important when we come down to the end of the way."

Still not much in the way of nodding or smiles or contemplatively furrowed brows. Senator Byrd had to admit that he had had difficulty with that anecdote in the past. After all, it was essentially just coincidence rather than illustration for some intellectual insight. Perhaps it was time for that story to be retired.

3. Surgeon General Koop drafts a memo.

At 11:45 a.m. on Thursday, October 20, 1983, Sarah Epstein, executive assistant to United States Surgeon General C. Everett Koop, MD, entered her boss' office to see him standing beside his desk, a sheet of paper from a yellow legal pad in his hand.

Today, Dr. Koop wore a charcoal pinstripe three-piece suit and one of his many bow ties. Yesterday, he had worn the full-dress military uniform that came with the position. Why the country's chief doctor required a military title, Sarah couldn't say, and Dr. Koop kept her too busy to have time to inquire. Not that she would have asked Dr. Koop a question like that. Sarah had discovered in the past month that Dr. Koop had earned the reputation as a grump that her coworkers had warned her about when she had started the job.

Dr. Koop's height, his suits and uniform, his broad, upright soldiers, the grim expression on his face, and especially the affectation of his mustache-less curtain beard all suggested a martinet. Sarah had to admit, however, that Dr. Koop was no figurehead. One look at the papers strewn across his desk and piled on his chairs, and the folding luggage cart ready with the suitcase and briefcase that would accompany him on the next of his trips, indicated that this was an office whose occupant did actual work.

Today, Sarah knew the subject of at least some of the papers on Dr. Koop's desk. She had placed them there at 8:00 a.m. They were documents from a trial in New York, and they included medical information about a baby, and Sarah knew Dr. Koop had been studying them this morning and that other top people from HHS had been in the office looking at them and drafting something with Dr. Koop. Sarah had read about this case in the *Post*, and she thought it was disgusting that someone who wasn't this baby's parents and wasn't related to the baby and had never even seen the baby was trying to tell the parents and the doctors what to do for the baby. She also thought it was disgusting that Dr. Koop, even though he was obviously a caring man, despite his grumpiness and general air of being in some kind of costume, was able to get this baby's medical information without asking the parents. She was, therefore, interested in what this piece of paper with Dr. Koop's handwriting on it would say.

"Type it, please," was all Dr. Koop said, but then that was frequently all he said.

Back in the outer office, Sarah seated herself, swung her chair so she faced her machine, and clipped the paper to the typing tray. Seeing the document was intended to be a memorandum, she inserted a piece of letterhead and began to type a memo to the Secretary of the Department of Health and Human Services that said, in part:

> An appropriate determination concerning whether the current care of Infant Jane Doe is within the bounds of legitimate medical judgment, rather than based solely on a handicapping condition

which is not a medical contraindication to surgical treatment, cannot be made without immediate access to, and careful review of, current medical records and other sources of information within the possession or control of the hospital.

Authority of the Department of Health and Human Services to conduct such an investigation can be based on section 504 of the Rehabilitation Act, which provides in pertinent part that "[n]o otherwise qualified handicapped individual...shall, solely by reason of his handicap...be subjected to discrimination under any program or activity receiving Federal financial assistance." The Department further basis its direction on 45 C.F.R. § 80.6(c), as incorporated by 45 C.F.R. § 84.61, which states: "(c) Access to sources of information. Each recipient [of Federal financial assistance] shall permit access by the responsible Department official or his designee during normal business hours to such of its books, records, accounts, and other sources of information, and its facilities as may be pertinent to ascertain compliance with this part.... Asserted considerations of privacy or confidentiality may not operate to bar the Department from evaluating or seeking to enforce compliance with this part."

With these as rationale, please request immediately that University Hospital make available to the U.S. Department of Health and Human Services for inspection all of Baby Jane Doe's medical records since October 19, 1983. Notify the hospital that Federal investigators will be at the facility at 9:00 AM on Friday, October 21, 1983, and mobilize the appropriate individuals from HHS to carry out this investigation.

4. Morton Blackwell adds content to a file folder.

At 11:50 a.m. on Thursday, October 20, 1983, in his Old Executive Office Building office, Morton Blackwell's secretary buzzed him and announced a call from Richard Tarlinson, vice president, Division of Government Services, of the Catholic Health Association of the United States. After instructing his secretary to send the call through and hearing a click on the line, Morton greeted the caller as "Dick."

Fifteen minutes later, Morton had written a page of notes from the call, including "like HHS, we would like to see the medical records." He sent the call back to his secretary with the instructions to set up an in-person meeting. On the page of handwritten notes, Morton stapled a small, square note on which he wrote, "Baby Jane Doe file," and put the result into his out tray for his secretary.

Already in that file were two items. One was a photocopy of a five-page letter with a two-page attachment to Betty Lou Dotson, the HHS director of the Office of Civil Rights, from John E. Curley, Jr., president of the Catholic Health Association of the U.S.A. responding an invitation for public comment to a proposed July 5, 1983, government rule titled "Nondiscrimination on the Basis of Handicap Relating to Health Care for Handicapped Infants." In the letter and attachment, the Mr. Curley asserted that "the government should not become involved in treatment decisions unless it has clear evidence that the rights of persons are being violated and that a significant potential exists for such violations to continue."

The other item in the folder was a letter to Morton received on September 7, 1983, from Denise F. Cocciolone, national executive director of Birthright Inc., thanking Morton for keeping Birthright Inc. apprised (which the letter spelled "apprized") "of human life issues and in particular the recent and in particular the recent mailings regarding Indiana's Baby Doe and the president's letters on behalf of the Hatch/Eagleton Amendment." Preceding the signature was, "Sincerely for the Preborn."

5. The Senate puts a stop to additional holidays.

At 6:37 p.m. on Thursday, October 20, 1983, on the Senate floor of the U.S. Capitol, Senator Pete Wilson of California rose to introduce Senate bill 1970, cosponsored by Senators Nickles, Cochran, Levin, Cranston, Mattingly, Trimble, Rudman, and Simpson, to amend Title 5 of the U.S. Code to limit the number of national holidays to the present number of ten.

Senator Thurmond, today not acting as president pro tempore but solely as a senator from South Carolina, asked Senator Wilson to yield the floor, and Senator Thurmond said, "Mr. President, I rise in support of the bill introduced by the able senator from California. I have talked to many people in my state and other states, too, and they feel that we have too many holidays already."

S. 1970 passed with 86 senators voting yea, 2 voting nay, 1 voting present, and 11 not voting.

6. The Speaker of the House signs two bills.

At 8:08 p.m. on Thursday, October 20, 1983, on the floor of the U.S. House of Representatives, California Representative Augustus Hawkins, Chair of the Committee on House Administration, reported:

> The committee has examined and found truly enrolled bills of the House of the following titles, which were thereupon signed by the Speaker:
>
> H.R. 3044. An act to grant the consent of the Congress to an interstate agreement or compact relating to the restoration of Atlantic Salmon in the Connecticut River Basin, and to allow the Secretary of Commerce and the Secretary of the Interior to participate as members in as Connecticut River Atlantic Salmon Commission; and
>
> H.R. 3706. An act to amend title 5, United States Code, to make the birthday of Martin Luther King, Jr., a legal public holiday.

7. For the U.S. House, tomorrow will be another day.
At 8:08 p.m., Henry (born Enrique) Barbosa González, U.S. Representative from the 20th district in Texas, swiveled his head not quite one hundred eighty degrees, took a deep breath, rose, and said, "Mr. Speaker, I move that the House do now adjourn."

The motion was agreed to; accordingly at 8:09 p.m., the House adjourned until tomorrow, Friday, October 21, 1983, at 10 a.m.

8. For the U.S. Senate, tomorrow will be another day.
At 9:33 p.m. on Thursday, October 20, 1983, Majority Leader Senator Howard Baker of Tennessee swiveled his head slightly less than one hundred eighty degrees, removed his heavy-framed eyeglasses, took a deep breath, and rose.

"Mr. President," he said, "I see no other senator seeking recognition, and I move, in accordance with the previous order, that the Senate stand in recess."

The motion was agreed to, and at 9:34 p.m., the Senate recessed until Friday, October 21, 1983, at 9:30 a.m.

9. For the president, tomorrow will be another day.
At 10:25 p.m. on Thursday, October 20, 1983, in the Lincoln Bedroom on the second floor of the White House, after the last official event of the day, a reception for the 1984 U.S. Olympic Ski Team, who the president referred to later as "a really great bunch of young people," with members of the press in attendance, and after dinner with First Lady Nancy Reagan and the president's daughter from his first marriage, Maureen Reagan Revel, President Ronald Reagan retired for the day, with plans to rise at 7:00 a.m. on Friday, October 21, 1983.

Peoria, Illinois

1. Linda Peavler considers the process of pain.

Linda Peavler was not aware that the time was 9:50 a.m. nor that the day was Thursday, October 20, 1983, nor the time elapsed—six days—since she had visited the Northwoods Mall and eaten a patty melt sandwich at the Skewer Inn, but in a more general sense, she was very much attuned to passing time.

Linda's point of reference for physical pain was childbirth, this experience entailing pain intense enough to be absurd to expect anyone to endure, pain unbearable enough to have made her sense of the present moment not a passing thing but a perpetual thing, an endless, timeless state, an explosion that never actually progressed from one stage to another, and an event so ridiculous to expect the human body to endure that it was beyond reason that it was happening. At the same time, during her four experiences of childbirth, stuck in that perpetual present of unreal suffering, always somewhere in her consciousness was at least the whisp of a realization that the pain was part of a process. During labor, she didn't give a damn about the conception or gestation parts of the process, but she did have an awareness, although as faint as an awareness of a single drop of rain or a single flake of snow, that something would result from this pain. A baby, probably healthy, and either her own death or her motherhood of that baby. She was also aware, even less palpably but still aware, that as absurd and unthinkable and inhumane as childbirth was, it did happen, it had happened before, after her first it had happened before to her, and it would happen again, although God grant not to her.

Not that any of that did anything to relieve her pain, but it gave the pain at least a barely perceptible bed of reason and a barely perceptible trajectory of process.

Her pain at this moment, not that some designation of this moment was any longer relevant, was not even close to as intense as her pain during childbirth, and it bore a completely different relationship to any kind of reason or context.

Aside from not being able to even express her sensations to Jan-Paul or her doctors—if not with words, then by shouting or screaming—she couldn't even explain them to herself, which felt necessary only in order to transform something without any reason into something that at least had the reason of words. And if her condition could be given even that much reason, perhaps it could also be given a process.

Her doctor had attempted to do that, an attempt Linda witnessed imperfectly through her visual and mental haze. He—what on earth was his name?—told Linda that the Centers for Disease Control in Washington, DC, had confirmed that she had botulism (sounding like the officialness of all that should make her feel proud and accomplished) and that previously, they had been working on a diagnosis of botulism based solely on her symptoms. He told Linda that her symptoms were not unusual. He told her that she was doing as well as could be expected. Which meant, she supposed, that she was no worse than others with botulism (whatever that meant—perhaps it meant she was not dead) and no better (whatever that meant—perhaps it meant she was unable to go ballroom dancing). He said that he "had every reason to hope she would make a good recovery." Linda could tell the doctor was saying that mostly to Jan-Paul while half-hoping Linda was too dopey to understand, given the equivocal nature of the prognosis.

That was the medical profession's attempt to give her something besides her perpetual present of suffering, but looked at closely, or as closely as Linda could look at anything, it was actually flimsy. First, it didn't tell her shit about what was actually happening to her. Why couldn't she breathe? Why couldn't she move? Why did she see everything double? Why did her brain feel like sludge?

As pressing as "why" was "when." When would it end? Would she wake up tomorrow and rise from her bed and pirouette to the bathroom for her morning pee? Next week? Next month? And what did "end" mean? Did it mean her vision would be clear but she couldn't raise her arm to point? Did it mean she could raise her arm to point but she couldn't stand? Did it mean she could breathe but would continue to feel like a refrigerator lying on her chest?

She was giving birth to nothing. The process she was on may not be the opposite of childbirth, it may not be death rather than birth. It was less tidy than that. It was like two dozen cars driving into the path of her car, some hitting her, some grazing her, some forcing her into a ditch, some just scaring her, but all reducing to fragments the process of her life—the intimacy of every day with her children as they got bigger and stronger and more aware and more sensitive and then, when they set off on their own, the birth of herself as a richer and more worldly and more satisfied person ready to live the rest of her life.

Now there was only the torment of a perpetual now that had no relationship to date or time or place. The fact that tomorrow would be Friday, October 21, 1983, in Peoria, Illinois, meant little, perhaps nothing.

2. John Mason likes the sound of work.

John Mason was not aware that the time was 11:11 a.m. nor that the day was Thursday, October 20, 1983, nor the time elapsed—six days—since he had had visited the Northwoods Mall and eaten a patty melt sandwich at the Skewer Inn, which undercut John's organized approach to life, an organization that was largely a function of work, and work was nothing to him now.

All his adult life, John had listened to colleagues gripe about work—physical demands, overtime demands, low pay, inane or cruel bosses, empty-suit executives. All entirely justifiable complaints. But John liked work. Mostly, although he wouldn't tell this to anyone except Leslie—and maybe he would tell his son one day, if John lived, and if he was ever able to speak again—what he liked about work was its sound.

Every one of his jobs had had beautiful sounds—regular thumps, irregular bells, expressive hisses, sparkling sizzles. The best sounding job of all, the best sounding job he could imagine anyone having, was his current job as press operator of the five-unit Goss Urbanite web press that produced the Peoria *Journal Star* and random other booklets and newsletters and books (although they had to outsource book binding to a company in Henry, Illinois).

The operators, if they had the brains god gave them, wore earplugs, and so did John, but the earplugs didn't wipe out the sounds of the press, just moderated the volume. The wiping out was done by the press sounds themselves, first with a low hum, which got higher as the press gained speed and then settled into a muscular whirr as the press hit its steady state, first with a throb slower than a heartbeat that became for only a minute consistent with a heartbeat, then became the heartbeat of a sprinter although only loud enough to be a reminder that the heart was still beating. When the press stopped, there were otherworldly metallic twangs as plates were changed. In some parts of the pressroom were slurping sounds, like a giant eating ice cream, of ink being applied. In other parts of the pressroom were *thwack thump, thwack thump* as papers folded in half hit the conveyor belt.

All of which wiped out thought, wiped out time, wiped out bad bosses. The sounds didn't exactly wipe out fatigue, but if you were clever, you could imagine yourself riding the sounds like a cross-country traveler in no particular hurry riding a train, the sound carrying you along, the sound providing all the energy and forward momentum needed.

The sounds wiped out all of life that was extraneous and replaced it with a calm sense of propulsion, a quiet sense of purpose. That faint throb was always there, unless the press shut down for adjustment, and then none of the operators felt right again until it was back, signaling order, regularity, forward movement.

The tangible output of these sounds and sensations—a daily newspaper with perfectly placed type and crisp images and advertisements that kept customers patronizing local businesses (including, he reflected now from his hospital bed, the Skewer Inn) and news that kept the people of Peoria informed and engaged and opinions that bound the people of Peoria into a community of ideas and beliefs, sometimes in glorious concert and sometimes in vicious opposition—was an important thing, but to John, the result, the personal result, was even more important and perhaps even more tangible, and that was a sense of rationality, a sense of order, a sense of life as something that was progressing positively.

On his drive to work on the day before his Friday meal at the Skewer Inn, John had passed a man standing on Glen Avenue where it met Bigelow Street. The man had a gym bag on the ground beside him, as though he had been standing there a while and was prepared to stand longer. The man had that expression that people waiting for a bus have, John assumed, in cities all over the world, but perhaps especially in Peoria, where buses came no more frequently than every half hour and on many routes only every hour. The man was staring as far into the distance as he could, his jaw slack as if he had given up any effort to keep his jaw closed for the sake of appearance, his face a blank of hope that he would see a speck in the distance that would emerge into the form of a bus, his face a blank of hopelessness knowing that the speck would either remain a speck or become something else and that his bus would only arrive when it was good and ready and that he had no power over its arrival and that its schedule likely was more a fantasy than a reality and that staring into the distance did no good, but after all, what else was he supposed to do? John had felt a little sorry for the man, but not very.

Now, John did not hear the sounds of the Goss Urbanite, did not feel serene with its hum, did not feel propelled by its throb. Now John was the man waiting for the bus that he had no control over and that may or may not ever come. He had no confidence his work would result in a newspaper. He had no confidence that a bus would take him to the next corner. He had no sense of moving in time toward Friday, October 21, 1983.

3. Lou Dobrydnia reflects on the intelligence of sports.

At 12:40 p.m. on Thursday, October 20, 1983, Lou Dobrydnia was aware that she was lying on her back in her bed in Saint Francis Medical Center in Peoria, Illinois, but not able to pinpoint the time—no clock in sight, and even if there was one right in front of her face, she doubted she would be able to bring it into focus—or the date or the number of days that had passed since she had eaten that damned patty melt—well, it was she and not the patty melt who had been damned—at the Skewer Inn. Although Lou didn't think of herself as especially fixated on time in her everyday life, during sporting events watching the clock and incorporating what it said into strategies and tactics was as natural as breathing to a player or coach of even moderate ability. It was one aspect of the specific type of intelligence that for Lou was the most thrilling part of sports.

How, she often wondered, did an attacking player in field hockey moving the ball forward view and assess thousands of possibilities—not just which player might be more open than another, but how every player, offensive and defensive, might react to a specific player receiving a pass, and whether to scoop or sweep or flick, and then the hundreds of possible subsequent actions and reactions, each calculation taking into account each player's strengths and propensities, who at that moment was hot and who was not, the score, the stage of the game, the look on each player's face—all in seconds, sometimes in one second, sometimes less.

To do all that without a piece of graph paper or a slide rule or the luxury of leaning back in a chair and rubbing your chin but rather while your entire body was not just employing the gross coordination of jogging forward, but the fine motor coordination of controlling a ball in such a way that it was protected from a grabby or a sneaky defender. Every aspect of being alive happening simultaneously.

If that was being alive, what was Lou now, with her brain, which today felt like a rotten slab of a bad cut of beef, incapable of tangible thought, her body incapable of movement, her lungs incapable of working on their own? She imagined herself an incapacitated coach, wheeled onto the sidelines of a softball game, but even at that reduced level, she would have been useless, unable to understand the game, formulate thoughts about the happenings on the field, or shout loud enough to be heard.

If she could have just one of these elements of life back, it was the ability to think rationally. With that, Lou felt herself slipping. What was slipping? Was she falling asleep? Perhaps not. Was she losing her sight? It seemed no different than it had a moment ago. Was she dying? Entirely possible. Slipping away, that's what people said when they talked about someone dying. If she had been able to formulate a metaphor to describe the sensation, it would be of the most beautiful silk scarf ever created sliding off the edge of a table and about to fall into molten lead.

If she would never be able to think clearly. If she would never again feel the joy of filling her lungs with cool spring air. If she would never be able to sprint or even walk. If she would never be able to touch someone she loved. If she were to die now. If all of that, she had faith that God had her back, that whatever state she entered would be another entwining of the aspects of existence, and perhaps nonexistence, that would be as exhilarating as a strike in a field hockey game, even if it did not lead her to living another day tomorrow, Friday, October 21, 1983.

Sequels

On October 21, 1983, at 1:50 p.m., Teresa Martin, 39, of Brimfield, Illinois, was admitted to the hospital in Peoria with symptoms of botulism. At 5:18 p.m. that day, Cindy Closen, 29, of Peoria was also admitted with symptoms of botulism.

That day, six of the botulism patients developed pneumonia.

*

The day after Judge Tanenbaum ruled that the surgery on Baby Jane Doe should proceed, the New York State Appellate Court reversed the decision and dismissed the case. The decision stated that the "concededly concerned and loving parents have made an informed, intelligent, and reasonable determination based upon and supported by responsible medical authority."

Attorney Lawrence Washburn continued to file lawsuits against the hospital, against all hospitals in a class action suit, and against anyone else he could think of. Most were thrown out. For example, in January of 1984, Judge Roger Minor of the Federal District Court in New York rejected Washburn's suit asking for appointment of a legal guardian for Baby Jane Doe. Judge Miner said, "There is no need for appointment of a guardian," based on the "assumption that parents are concerned about the welfare of their children." He fined Washburn five hundred dollars for bringing a frivolous lawsuit.

Washburn died on October 13, 2013. Being dead, he no longer sues anyone.

The Baby Jane Doe case, and a similar case from the previous year, led Congress to pass a 1984 amendment to the Child Abuse Prevention and Treatment Act of 1974. The amendment established criteria for the care of disabled infants regardless of the wishes of their parents that states must meet in order to receive federal funding for child abuse and neglect prevention and treatment programs. Those criteria are:

> [A]n assurance that the State has in place procedures for responding to the reporting of medical neglect (including instances of withholding of medically indicated treatment from disabled infants with life-threatening conditions), procedures or programs, or both (within the State child protective services system), to provide for—
>
> (i) coordination and consultation with individuals designated by and within appropriate health-care facilities;
> (ii) prompt notification by individuals designated by and within appropriate health-care facilities of cases of suspected medical neglect (including instances of withholding of medically indicated treatment from disabled infants with life-threatening conditions); and
> (iii) authority, under State law, for the State child protective services system to pursue any legal remedies, including the authority to initiate legal proceedings in a court of competent jurisdiction, as may be necessary to prevent the withholding of medically indicated treatment from disabled infants with life threatening conditions…

*

Elisabeth Beaugrand survived being stuck by the falling window air conditioner. On October 14, 2020, exactly thirty-seven years after its awning did not stop the downward momentum of the window air conditioner, Dangerfield's comedy club closed, citing COVID-caused financial problems.

*

In June of 2002, Justice Ira Gammerman, who issued the injunction against the eviction of Joseph Sonnabend's AIDS clinic, presided over a lawsuit in which movie director Woody Allen was suing his former friend and former manager Jean Doumanian.

At one point in the proceedings, Justice Gammerman asked Allen whether he was currently making a film.

Woody Allen: "Yes, and that's why I haven't been able to be here all the time, because..."

Justice Gammerman: "Yes is the answer."

Allen: "Because I have a film crew out now, shooting on the streets of New York, and I'm trying to..."

Gammerman: "Stop talking."

Allen: "Stop talking?"

Gammerman: "I'm the director here."

*

Volume 2 of *An Inclusive Language Lectionary* was published in 1984. Volume 3 was published in 1985. In 1995, Oxford University Press published a far broader effort to create a gender-neutral Bible: *New Testament and Psalms: An Inclusive Version*. Several people involved in the *Inclusive Language Lectionary* helped to create this work: Victor

Roland Gold, Thomas L. Hoyt, Jr, Sharon H. Ringe, Susan Brooks Thistlethwaite, Burton H. Throckmorton, Jr., and Barbara A. Withers.

*

Morton Blackwell, President Reagan's liaison to conservative religious groups, at this writing continues to be president of the Leadership Institute, which he founded in 1979. According to its website, the Leadership Institute "provides training in campaigns, fundraising, grassroots organizing, youth politics, and communications," and "teaches conservatives of all ages how to succeed in politics, government, and the media."

A former College Republican and Young Republican state chairman in Louisiana and national vice chairman at-large of the Young Republican National Federation, Blackwell developed at the Leadership Institute what the organization calls a "unique college campus network" that "has grown to more than 2,300 conservative campus groups and newspapers."

*

Ralph Westberg, executive vice president and chief engineer for Auto Meter Products, Inc., who lectured his Peoria audience about the "High Frontier" space missile defense system, lived until 1985 in the same town, Sycamore, Illinois, where Auto Meter had its headquarters. In 1985, Ralph and his family moved to Provo, Utah, because he liked the lifestyle there. He continued in his role at Auto Meter, commuting by airplane each week from Provo to Sycamore.

On Wednesday, March 15, 1989, in a press conference in the governor's mansion, Ralph and Utah and Governor Norm Bangerter announced that Auto Meter Products had established a division at 2227 S. Larsen Parkway in Provo and that Ralph would be the manager of that division, thus allowing Ralph to avoid his weekly flights from Utah to Illinois.

As of this writing, Ralph continues to work for Auto Meter.

*

Several months after sculptor Richard Serra had his model of two steel panels rejected by the Peoria, Illinois, Civic Center Authority, he was asked what he thought about Peoria. Serra replied, "I don't think of it at all." He paused and added, "Maybe they wanted a sculpture of Ronald Reagan on horseback."

*

After Ronald Reagan's death, General Electric gave Nancy Reagan DVDs containing two hundred eight episodes of General Electric Theater with the intent that she share them with the Ronald Reagan Presidential Library.

*

On Tuesday, November 6, 1984, Warner Communications announced it would not proceed with the proposed acquisition of Polygram Records—the proposed deal that had spurred open-shirted, hairy-chested Walter Yetnikoff of CBS Records to spread his acquisitive wings—due to Federal Trade Commission opposition.

On Tuesday, November 17, 1987, the board of Sony in Tokyo approved Sony's acquisition of CBS Records, a deal designed by Walter Yetnikoff and his long-time friends and Sony executives Akio Morita and Norio Ohga.

On Friday, September 7, 1990, Ohga said, "I'm sorry, Walter, but this hurts me more than it hurts you," as he fired Yetnikoff.

*

Philippe Petit, the juggler performing within the chalk circle on the South Street Seaport and who previously had been arrested after walking on a wire between the roofs of the Twin Towers in New York, continues to live in New York. He has performed officially sanctioned high-wire walking in New York and around the world. A film about Petit, *Man on a Wire,* won the 2009 Academy Award for Best Documentary Feature. A film titled *The Walk*, directed by Robert Zemeckis and starring Joseph Gordon-Levitt as Petit, was released in 2015.

*

As of 2002, the Dan-Dee Country Inn and Restaurant was put up for sale. Subsequently, on a website called Bible Outlines, a post titled "Pet Peeve #33: Passing Away of My Favorite Eateries" said, "It started with the closing of Dan-Dee restaurant. My family lived for a time in Frederick MD and I came to love the country style meals with the relish dish and the fritters. But it catered to an older clientele and eventually was shut down."

The Dan-Dee's owner, Mildred Myrtle Rice, died in 2006 at the age of 98. Her daughter, Thelma Shafer Pryor, died in 2020 at the age of 93.

*

Textbook analyst and Christian drive-inn theater creator Mel Gabler died in 2004 at the age of 89, and his wife and colleague, Norma Gabler, died in 2007 at the age of 84. As of 2019, their organization, Education Research Analysts, was still a going concern, announcing its intention to review eleventh-grade American literature textbooks up for Texas state approval for 2020:

> Our concern is the content of their reading selections. Texas' regs for this course run to three dense single-spaced pages with tiny margins. They detail what skills 11th graders should develop… but never set rules for the contents of their reading selections. Leaving editors to their own devices in this huge vacuum, sans Texas direction, is folly. Texas cannot counterpoise California if Christian conservatives do not effectively stand in this gap. We will objectively rank these submitted programs by our unique standard review criteria on the subject.

William Jay Jacobs, whose 1973 book *Search for Freedom: America and its People* so irked Mel and Norma Gabler with its references to Marilyn Monroe, wrote more than thirty books of history and biography for young people. He retired from teaching at New York's Hunter College in 1993. On his death in 2003, donations were invited to the American Civil Liberties Union.

*

The shape of Senator Jesse and Dot Helms' two-story colonial house with saltbox roof in Arlington, Virginia, made it especially amenable to seven young men, during the early morning of Thursday, September 9, 1991, a day when Jesse and Dot were in North Carolina, climbing onto the roof of the house and covering it with a giant replica of a condom, on which the words "a condom to stop unsafe politics—Helms is deadlier than a virus" were clearly visible from the street.

Dot Helms' book *Interesting Deaf Americans* was never published.

*

The band Stool Sample existed for only three weeks and played only one show, but it helped inspire Peoria punk bands Caustic Defiance, Constant Vomit, Bloody Mess and the Skabs, and many others.

*

David Hampton's masquerade as the son of Sidney Poitier and his hoax of Osborn and Inger McCabe Elliott became the subject of a long-running play and popular film titled *Six Degrees of Separation.* In 2003, David died while being treated for AIDS-related complications in New York City.

*

Reverend Richard Halverson, chaplain of the United States Senate from February 2, 1981, to March 11, 1995, once composed a blessing the first line of which read, "You go nowhere by accident."

*

On October 5, 1986, a plane carrying military arms was shot down in Nicaragua, leading to exposure of the so-called Iran-Contra operation carried out by the Reagan Administration, in which the U.S. sold arms to Iran—illegal—and funneled the profits to rebels in Nicaragua fighting against the country's Marxist government—even more illegal. Robert (Bud) McFarlane was involved in the operation, primarily the sales to Iran. Exposure of the operation was a major scandal. One evening in February 1987, Bud took an overdose of valium and got into bed beside his wife, Jonda, who was grading English papers. In the morning, she could not rouse Bud. An ambulance took him to Bethesda Naval Hospital, where he recovered. He later said he attempted suicide because "it was the honorable thing to do" because he had "so let down my country."

In 1988, Bud pleaded guilty to four misdemeanors. In 1992, President George H.W. Bush pardoned McFarlane and others convicted for offenses related to the Iran-Contra scandal.

*

Between Friday, December 7, and Thursday, December 13, 1984, over the strong protests of Baltimore Orioles General Manager Hank Peters, team owner Ed Williams signed three free agents, Fred Lynn, Lee Lacy, and Don Aase, to long-term contracts that were later reported to be worth $11.4 million, a record amount at that time. In Lynn's case, a five-year contract included a no-trade clause. These actions not only cost a significant amount of money, but also required the Orioles to forego their top three draft picks. Peters believed that using draft picks and players in the Orioles minor-league system held greater long-term promise for the team's success. Williams characterized himself as being forced to sign free agents because of the sorry state of the team's minor-league teams.

On Monday, October 5, 1987, saying he was tired of watching the Orioles "lose and lose and lose," Ed Williams fired Hank Peters, who had been general manager of the Orioles for twelve years.

"Williams can do what he wants," said Peters. "I didn't get smart overnight, and I didn't get dumb overnight, either. My peers understand the situation here very well. That gives me some comfort."

Twenty-eight days later, on Monday, November 2, 1987, Peters became the president and chief operating officer of the Cleveland Indians with a three-year contract that guaranteed him near autonomy. In that role, he oversaw the renaissance of that team.

At 10:30 a.m. on Friday, June 14, 1985, in the middle of his third season at Orioles manager, Joe Altobelli, in his stadium office, asked anyone who passed by, "Am I fired? Does anybody know if I'm fired?" At 3:00 p.m., administrative staff escorted Altobelli to the office of Hank Peters, who at the time was still general manager. At a news conference held shortly after, Ed Williams said that Altobelli, about whom Williams had said publicly, "This is a cement head. Forget it. He's got cement up there," announced the firing, saying Altobelli, "did not have the kind of leadership that we have traditionally become used to in the Oriole organization."

Williams also announced that he was reinstating Earl Weaver as manager.

Baseball Commissioner Bowie Kuhn, fired in 1982, remained in office until September of 1984. The baseball team owners elected Peter Ueberroth to succeed Kuhn, and Ueberroth took office on October 1, 1984.

On Monday, December 1, 1984, President Reagan presented to Ueberroth something called the C Flag. It was white with a red stripe at the top and bottom and a letter C in the middle. The C represented the motto "We can, we care," intended to praise volunteerism. Reagan gave Ueberroth the first such flag to recognize his work in generating support from private businesses for the 1984 Summer Olympics.

After record spending by the baseball owners on free agents in the winter of 1984, led by the Orioles' $11.4 million, Ueberroth encouraged the owners to practice "fiscal responsibility," saying, "It's not smart to sign long-term contracts. They force clubs to want to make similar signings. Don't be dumb." In 1985 and 1986, owners spent far less for free agents. Later, arbitrators ruled that the owners had engaged in collusion both those years.

*

In 2001, D. James Jumer, founder of the now-bankrupt five-hotel Jumer's Castle Lodge chain in central Illinois, announced the sale of the Peoria location to a group of investors with the name Torrey Park LLC. In 2004, the investors sold the property to the Radisson Hotel chain. In 2009, the hotel closed. In 2010, the property became the Courtyard Estates, a senior living center, which later changed its name to Grand Regency of Peoria.

In life, the nine-foot-tall stuffed grizzly bear in the Jumer's lobby weighed 1,027 pounds. Jim Jumer shot the bear on April 6, 1970, near Uelen, Russia. In life, the bear had been light brown, but when he had the bear stuffed, Jumer asked that it be dyed black. The bear, now sporting a pair of sunglasses with green plastic frames, currently stands in a Peoria coffee shop located in a portion of a flatiron building constructed in 1911 that also houses a dry cleaner.

*

Sylvia Marshaun, one of the three discoverers of two boxes of one-hundred-year-old bones in the Brooklyn vacant lot, parlayed her interest in manipulation of sound from electronic toys into a long and satisfying career as an experimental musician, occasionally receiving reviews requesting a greater "sense of formal continuity."

In retirement, wide-eyed Detective Delmonico found joy as a birdwatcher, a world traveler, and a person who sat on park benches.

*

On June 29, 1986, at age 55, Senator John East of North Carolina killed himself by inhaling carbon monoxide from his automobile in his closed garage.

East had become a paraplegic at age 24 due to polio. For three years before his death, East suffered from a debilitating thyroid condition that at one point left him in a coma and led to him announcing that he would not run for reelection. In his suicide note, East said his doctor and the hospital "failed to diagnose my hypothyroidism as they should have. They ruined my health." In 1987, Senator East's widow, Priscilla East, filed suit against three physicians for not diagnosing Senator East's condition for two years prior to his falling into a coma. In 1990, the suit was dismissed as groundless.

*

In 2008, Peoria opened the newly constructed General Wayne A. Downing Peoria International Airport, built beside the old terminal. In 2011, the old terminal was dismantled, with sections of the checkerboard tile floor available for purchase by those hoping to retain a tangible piece of their fond memories.

*

Officer Edward Santiago, badge number 645, served on the New York City Police Department for twenty years, from January 1981 to January 2001, ending his career as a detective specialist at the 83rd Precinct in Brooklyn. During that time, five complaints containing ten allegations were filed against him, all resolved by the Civilian Complaint Review Board on the same day they were received.

*

In 1983, six officers were charged in the death of graffiti artist Michael Stewart. After five months, the case was dismissed because of juror misconduct.

In 1985, at the end of a second trial, the officers were found not guilty.

In 1987, the Metropolitan Transit Authority suspended one of the officers involved for committing perjury.

In 1990, Michael Stewart's family agreed to settle a lawsuit against 11 officers and the MTA for $1.7 million. The family had sought $40 million.

Jean-Michel Basquiat and Keith Haring created paintings about Michael Stewart's death.

*

Nortel Networks Corporation, the maker of the Norstar M7310 telephone system that gave Selma Jefferson at the Department of Health and Human Services such fits, declared bankruptcy in 2009. It was one of the largest bankruptcies in Canadian history. Eight years later, the company's employees were still owed millions of dollars, while its senior executives continued to receive retention bonuses, which at that point amounted to $190 million.

*

At the time of this writing, Eugene Gold is 99 years old and lives in Woodstock, New York. His wife, Ronnie Gold, died at age 98 on October 30, 2023. They knew each other for eighty-two years and were married for seventy-seven years.

*

C. Everett Koop, in response to a question from *Christianity Today* editor-at-large Philip Yancey during a 1989 interview, explained the genesis of his curtain beard:

"...I grew the beard as a lark when I went with my son Norman to Israel for two weeks. The night before we came home he shaved off his beard and kept his moustache; I shaved off my moustache and kept my beard. We did it just to shock our families. A few days later, when I looked at a picture of myself taken...before I started growing a beard, I realized I had three chins! And I didn't have them with a beard."

Dr. Koop's efforts to contain the AIDS epidemic, for several years blocked by the Reagan Administration, have been well documented and both praised and criticized.

*

On June 17, 2021, President Joe Biden signed a law establishing Juneteenth National Independence Day as the eleventh federal holiday. The measure passed the Senate with a unanimous vote. It passed the House of Representatives with a vote of 415 yeas, 14 nays, and 2 not voting. However, the legislative path toward creating this new federal holiday was not as smooth as these vote totals suggest. The year before, on July 22, Senator Ron Johnson of Wisconsin managed to derail passage of the holiday with his objection based on the expense of adding an eleventh day off for federal workers. If a holiday to celebrate Juneteenth was desired, Johnson suggested that Columbus Day be removed from the list of federal holidays.

On the floor of the Senate, Johnson said:

> I agree with virtually everything my colleagues from both Massachusetts and Texas have said about celebrating the emancipation of the slaves. That was an important moment in U.S. history. It should be observed, and it should be celebrated. I have no disagreement whatsoever with that at all. The one area of disagreement is how the bill's sponsors have chosen to celebrate that holiday. As the Senator from Massachusetts pointed out, since 1865, it has been observed with celebrations and cookouts, which is the appropriate way of doing this. I object to the fact that, by naming it a national holiday—and what they are leaving out of

their argument and its main impact—it will give federal workers a paid day off that the rest of America will have to pay for.

*

Senator Robert Byrd was the longest-serving U.S. senator, dying halfway through his fifty-second year in office at the age of 92, compared with Senator John Warner's thirty years in office. Senator Warner died at age 94, two years older than Senator Byrd at the time of his death.

*

Sam Somers, newspaper folder extraordinaire, grew up to become an origami artist and a poet specializing in found verse.

*

On January 20, 1984, in its newsletter *Morbidity and Mortality Weekly Report,* the Centers for Disease Control published an article titled "Foodborne Botulism—Illinois," that read in part:

> From October 15 to October 21, 1983, 28 cases of foodborne botulism occurred in Peoria, Illinois. All 28 persons had eaten at the same restaurant from October 14 to October 16; all were hospitalized. Twelve patients required ventilatory support. Botulinal type A toxin was detected in serum and/or stool specimens in 13 patients. The epidemiologic investigation implicated sauteed onions served on a patty-melt sandwich as the source of the botulinal toxin.

The patients were 20–72 years of age, and twenty were female. Detailed food histories were obtained from the patients and from groups of well persons who had consumed food at the restaurant during the same three-day period. Each of these comparisons showed a highly significant association between eating a patty-melt sandwich and developing botulism (p 0.001). Of the 28 patients, 24 recalled eating the patty-melt, which consisted of toasted rye bread, sliced American cheese, one-half or one-third pound hamburger patty, and sauteed onions. The remaining four patients recalled eating a variety of food items, none of which were implicated by epidemiologic data. Review of the serving practices in the restaurant indicated that the same utensils were used in serving multiple food items, including the patty-melt.

An additional case-control study was conducted to determine which items on the patty-melt were associated with illness. Eighteen persons who had eaten the patty-melt during the 3-day period and remained well were identified through repeated news media announcements. These 18 controls, plus the 24 patients who ate patty-melts, represented 42 of the estimated maximum of 45 patty-melts served over the 3-day period. All 24 patients, but only 10 of 18 controls, reported eating the sauteed onions ($p = 0.0004$). The onions were said to have been prepared daily with fresh whole onions, margarine, paprika, garlic salt, and a chicken-base powder; they were held uncovered in a pan with a large volume of melted margarine on a warm stove (below 60 C (140 F)) and were not reheated before serving.

The original batch of sauteed onions was not available for culture or toxin testing, but type A botulinal toxin was detected in an extract made from washings of a discarded foil wrapper used by one of the patients to take a patty-melt home. Type A botulinal spores were cultured from five of 75 skins of whole onions taken from the restaurant. No other ingredients of the sauteed onions contained botulinal toxin or spores. Additional laboratory tests are pending.

Editorial Note: This is the third largest foodborne botulism outbreak reported in the United States since 1899. The two larger outbreaks occurred in 1977 in Michigan, when 58 people became ill after eating home-canned peppers at a restaurant, and in 1978 in New Mexico, when 34 people became ill after eating potato salad or bean salad at a restaurant. Botulism outbreaks are usually isolated incidents involving small numbers of people who have consumed improperly preserved home-canned or home-processed foods.

Epidemiologic evidence implicated the sauteed onions as the source of this outbreak. Recent investigations of pot pies and baked potatoes have demonstrated the ability of C. botulinum to grow and produce toxin in cooked foods held at temperatures below 60 C (140 F). Sauteed onions have never before been associated with botulism.

*

Ray Long, who wrote many of the stories about the botulism outbreak for the Peoria *Journal Star,* left the paper in 1990 and reported for the *Chicago Sun-Times* and the Associated Press before joining the *Chicago Tribune* in 1998, where he remains an investigative reporter. He has covered the state Capitol, City Hall, and courts and county beats. He was twice a finalist for a Pulitzer Prize and wrote the book *The House That Madigan Built: The Record Run of Illinois' Velvet Hammer*, published by the University of Illinois Press in 2022.

*

Unlike many shopping malls in America, the Northwoods Mall still exists. The only store left from 1983 is JC Penney. Many of its other stores are created, owned, and run by local entrepreneurs.

*

Given the all-clear by the Peoria Health Department, the Skewer Inn reopened in late November 1983 with the slogan "Aren't you glad we're back?" Popular and outspoken coach of the Bradley University men's basketball team, Dick Versace, was quoted by the Associated Press as saying, "This is the safest place to eat in continental America." Co-owner Mike Kubera said, "Our standpoint on the whole incident has been, 'Hey, it happened, it's a one-in-a-million thing.'"

Despite a line outside the door on the first day of the reopening, the Skewer Inn closed permanently several months later.

*

Dianne "Happ" Hollister, who, with her daughter, decided to depart the line outside the Skewer Inn and go instead to Bob Evans, left her job as secretary to the Peoria Fire Chief in 1986 and followed her interest in children's books to become, first, youth services librarian at the Peoria Public Library and then reference librarian and children's literature instructor at Bradley University.

Dancer and botulism sufferer Monique Gruter attended graduate school in dance at the University of Iowa, where one of her solo performance pieces, titled "Stayin' High 'n' Getting' By," was a five-part exploration of the agonies and ecstasies of romantic involvements that followed one woman played by five different dancers through various relationships. The soundtrack to the performance was a collage with text narrated by Liz Davis and music by Mose Allison, Tammy Wynette, and local flamenco guitarist Tom Nothnagle.

Monique said she was trying for a tongue-in-cheek tone, evoking "absurdities, highs and lows, uncertainties, insecurities, cynicism, and confidence of developing relationships."

After Monique earned her Master of Fine Arts, she moved to Amsterdam, where she currently works at Hogeschool InHolland University.

Anna Hiter never left the hospital. She died on April 22, 1984, at age 73, of a heart attack, six months after being admitted and ten days after being taken off a ventilator.

Like Anna Hiter and others, Sande Spore and her daughter Linda Peavler were on ventilators for months. Sande died in 2020 at age 83. From the time she contracted botulism to the time of her death, Sande had difficulty moving her limbs and lifting, and was frequently heard to say when faced with physical problems, "That damn botulism."

Linda Peavler is the School Counselor at Dr. Maude A. Sanders Primary School in Peoria. In a brochure for the school, Linda is quoted as saying, "As a school counselor, I believe that all students can learn how to succeed intellectually, socially, and emotionally, and physically to become responsible members of an ever changing society." Since contracting botulism, Linda has had trouble with movement, trouble producing tears or saliva, and persistent respiratory infections.

Jan-Paul Peavler, Linda's husband, is the lead diagnostic radiographer at Saint Francis Medical Center in Peoria, Illinois. Dewey Spore, Sande's husband, died in 2006 at age 73.

John Mason was also on a ventilator for months. Later, for years, he had problems with memory and vocabulary. For the fortieth anniversary of the botulism outbreak, he designed a t-shirt that read, "The 1983 Peoria Botulism Marathon, sponsored by The Skewer Inn," with an illustration of a patty melt sandwich resting on the instrument panel of a ventilator. Let us imagine that, as a former pressman, he oversaw the printing of the shirts.

Lou Dobrydnia was unable to work at Limestone High School for a year and a half after being infected with botulism. For a time, she used a wheelchair. By 2012, she was strong enough to run two half marathons.

In January 2013, Lou was diagnosed with Guillain-Barre syndrome, a disease in which the body's immune system attacks its nervous system. Lou was paralyzed from the neck down. She spent one hundred two days in the hospital. After the paralysis started to recede, Lou again needed a wheelchair. She had to relearn what had previously been part of her muscle memory, such as using a fork.

On March 13, 2024, in a ceremony at the Peoria Civic Center, Lou was one of five individual inductees into the Greater Peoria Sports Hall of Fame for her accomplishments as a Limestone Community High School softball coach. Over her fifteen-year career, the team compiled a 309–97 record. From 1980 through 1982, the Limestone Rockets were undefeated in Mid-State 10 Conference play. Lou took four teams to the Illinois High School Association Elite Eight, including successive appearances in 1985, 1986, and 1987, when she was named Class AA Coach of the Year by the Illinois Coaches Association for Girls' and Women's Sports. Her team finished second in 1985 and fourth in 1980. Thirty-four of her players received college softball scholarships, including sixteen to play NCAA Division I.

Today, Lou works with people who are paralyzed or have otherwise lost bodily autonomy. Lou tells them, "Please let yourself get mad. Please let yourself cry, please let yourself be taken care of. But never give up the faith that God has your back."

*

Joseph Sonnabend's case opposing his eviction was the first AIDS-related civil rights litigation. An obituary in the *New York Times* on January 21, 2021, called Sonnabend "one of the most important figures in the fight against AIDS, if also one of the most unheralded."

Gregg Gonsalves, epidemiologist at the Yale School of Public Health, said, "Lots of figures in the AIDS epidemic made a contribution, often centered around one or two accomplishments, but Joe was central in so many different ways in those early years, in research, in clinical care, in policy and activism. He visited his patients when they most needed him, even on their deathbeds."

In 2000, on the occasion of receiving the first Award of Courage from amfAR for his lifetime of work as laboratory scientist, physician, and community-based clinical researcher focused on AIDS, Sonnabend said, "I've witnessed so much failure."

Coda

A bullet enters a Peoria house and strikes a can of soup.

At 3:20 a.m. on Sunday, January 14, 2024, in a house on the 1800 block of North Peoria Avenue in the East Bluff neighborhood of Peoria, Illinois, 33-year-old Jonathan Simpson heard four loud noises coming from somewhere outside his bedroom. He rose, turned on the lamp next to his bed and looked around him, but saw nothing. In his underwear, flipping on wall switches as he went, still blurry from sleep and, truth be told, a little shaken, Jonathan glanced into each room of his house. Nothing unusual in the living room. Nothing unusual in the second bedroom. In the bathroom, however, he saw a gash in the window sill he had not seen before. The window itself was intact.

Jonathan returned to the living room and sat in his television-watching chair to consider the situation. Ten minutes later, he went back to his bedroom, picked up his mobile phone from the nightstand, disconnected it from its charger, and called 911. Then he got a robe—he couldn't remember the last time he had worn it—from his closet.

Officers Mary Brach-Sunderland and Luther Jarvis arrived seven minutes later, stomping snow off their boots and removing their cold-weather gloves before crossing the sill. Jonathan explained the four loud noises he had heard, escorted them to the bathroom, and pointed toward the gash. To the officers, the gash looked to have been caused by a bullet entering the house from outside, just below the window pane and therefore not breaking the glass. Not voicing their opinions to Jonathan and not narrating their movements, the officers attempted to follow the trajectory of the bullet.

This examination led the officers to a hole in the door leading to the kitchen. Officer Brach-Sunderland opened the door and took the lead as the three entered the room. Officer Jarvis closed the door behind them. Glancing back and forth between the hole in the door and the rest of the kitchen, the two officers attempted to see where the bullet, if there had been one, might have gone next. Officer Brach-Sunderland, while being attentive to her search, was aware of the mild comic quality of the three people, two wearing bulky jackets, trying to orchestrate their movements inside the tiny kitchen without running into one another.

Soon, Officer Brach-Sunderland said, "Well, look at this," and both Officer Jarvis and Jonathan turned to see her pointing toward the left door of the two-door cabinet that hung over the kitchen counter.

The two men took a step closer, craning their necks to see a small hole in the particle board. They then pulled back their heads to make room as Officer Brach-Sunderland opened the cabinet door.

Now all three shuffled forward and stared at the same object: a can of Campbell's condensed cream of mushroom soup. A neat circular hole had been made in the red portion of the label just beside the tail of the lowercase "p" in Campbell's and above the gold circle that broached the red and white horizontal segments of the famous Campbell's label design. A spot of gray was visible in the hole, but the viscousness of the soup apparently had kept it from seeping out.

Officer Brach-Sunderland put her cold-weather gloves back on her hands and, touching only the rim, rotated the can slowly, at about the same pace as the can opener Officer Brach-Sunderland had used when, years ago, she had frequently opened cans of Campbell's cream of mushroom soup for use in tuna casserole. But she had not made that dish recently; too heavy. She also wondered, not for the first time, whether people ate Campbell's cream of mushroom soup by itself or only used it in recipes, and she wondered how Jonathan consumed the soup, or whether, as in so many kitchen cabinets, an unattended can of Campbell's cream of mushroom sat for years, as though it had been placed there by the builders immediately after completing the house.

Officer Brach-Sunderland finished rotating the can. No exit hole was revealed.

Further search of the home found no other evidence of damage. An even more thorough search found no bullet. Finally, the officers opened the soup can and emptied its contents through a sieve provided by Jonathan into the kitchen sink, but when they had finished, the sieve contained mushroom pellets and nothing else.

Outside, in the snow, which had stopped falling an hour before, the officers found no footprints near the house other than the officers' own.

As of this writing, no arrests have been made.

About the Author

Robert Fromberg wrote the memoir *How to Walk with Steve* (Latah Books, 2021), which won the Next Generation Indie Book Award for memoir; the essay and story collection *Friends and Fiends, Pulp Stars and Pop Stars* (Alien Buddha Press, 2022); and the novella *Blue Skies* (Floating Island Publications, 1991). He taught writing for many years at Northwestern University and lives in Madison, Wisconsin. More information: robertfrombergwriter.com, @robfromberg.